RABBI AND PRIEST

A STORY

MILTON GOLDSMITH

1st WORLD
LIBRARY
Literary Society

Rabbi and Priest

Milton Goldsmith

© 1st World Library, 2007
PO Box 2211
Fairfield, IA 52556
www.1stworldlibrary.com
First Edition

LCCN: 2007927848

Softcover ISBN: 978-1-4218-4562-3
Hardcover ISBN: 978-1-4218-4478-7
eBook ISBN: 978-1-4218-4646-0

Purchase *"Rabbi and Priest"*
as a traditional bound book at:
www.1stWorldLibrary.com/purchase.asp?ISBN=978-1-4218-4562-3

1st World Library is a literary, educational organization
dedicated to:

- Creating a free internet library of downloadable ebooks

- Hosting writing competitions and offering book publishing
  scholarships.

Interested in more 1st World Library books? contact:
literacy@1stworldlibrary.com
Check us out at: www.1stworldlibrary.com

1ˢᵗ World Library Literary Society

Giving Back to the World

"If you want to work on the core problem, it's early school literacy."

- James Barksdale, former CEO of Netscape

"No skill is more crucial to the future of a child, or to a democratic and prosperous society, than literacy."

- Los Angeles Times

"Literacy... means far more than learning how to read and write... The aim is to transmit... knowledge and promote social participation."

- UNESCO

"Literacy is not a luxury, it is a right and a responsibility. If our world is to meet the challenges of the twenty-first century we must harness the energy and creativity of all our citizens."

- President Bill Clinton

"Parents should be encouraged to read to their children, and teachers should be equipped with all available techniques for teaching literacy, so the varying needs and capacities of individual kids can be taken into account."

- Hugh Mackay

PREFACE

Towards the end of 1882, there arrived at the old Pennsylvania Railroad Depot in Philadelphia, several hundred Russian refugees, driven from their native land by the inhuman treatment of the Muscovite Government. Among them were many intelligent people, who had been prosperous in their native land, but who were now reduced to dire want. One couple, in particular, attracted the attention of the visitors, by their intellectual appearance and air of gentility, in marked contrast to the abject condition of many of their associates. Joseph Kierson was the name of the man, and the story of his sufferings aroused the sympathy of his hearers. The man and his wife were assisted by the Relief Committee, and in a short time were in a condition to provide for themselves.

The writer had the pleasure of meeting Mr. Kierson a few years later, and elicited from him a complete recital of his trials and an account of the causes of the terrible persecution which compelled such large numbers of his countrymen to flee from their once happy homes.

His story forms the nucleus of the novel I now present to my readers. While adhering as closely as possible to actual names, dates and events, it does not pretend to be historically accurate. In following the fortunes of Mendel Winenki, from boyhood to old age, it endeavors to present a series of pictures portraying the character, life, and sufferings of the misunderstood and much-maligned Russian Jew.

In the description of Russia's customs and characteristics, the barbarous cruelty of her criminal code and the nihilistic tendency of the times, the author has followed such eminent writers as Wallace, Foulke, Stepniak, Tolstoi and Herzberg-Fraenkel. The accounts of the riots of 1882 will be found to agree in historic details with the reports which were published at the time.

With this introduction, I respectfully submit the work to the consideration of an indulgent public.

MILTON GOLDSMITH.
PHILADELPHIA, April, 1891.

CHAPTER I

RECRUITS FOR SIBERIA

We are in Russia.

On the high road from Tscherkask to Togarog, and not far from the latter village, there stood, in the year 1850, a large and inhospitable-looking inn. Its shingled walls, whose rough surface no paint-brush had touched for long generations, seemed decaying from sheer old age. Its tiled roof was in a most dilapidated state, displaying large gaps imperfectly stuffed with straw, and serving rather to collect the rain and snow for the more thorough inundation of the rooms below than to protect them from the elements. The grounds about the house were in keeping with it in point of picturesque neglect, and were as innocent of cultivation as the building was of paint. A roughly paved path led from the highway to the tavern door. Two old and sickly poplar trees cast a poor and half-hearted shade upon the parched ground, and mournfully shook their leaves over the scene of desolation. The herbage grew in isolated patches on a black and uncultivated soil. Nature might have originally been friendly to the place, but generations of poverty and neglect had reduced it to a condition of wretched misery.

As was this particular spot, so was the entire village. Slavery had wound its chains about the inhabitants, stifling whatever energy they possessed, entailing upon them constant toil to satisfy the exorbitant demands of their task-masters. Hence, even with a genial sun and a southern climate, the fields were barren, the crops poor and the people sunk in abject poverty.

The dilapidated inn, or *kretschma*, was known in the vicinity by the ideal and appropriate name of "Paradise"—appropriate, because in it many a sinner had been tempted and had fallen from grace. It was the popular rendezvous of the village peasants. Thither the serfs living in the village of Togarog and for miles around, would repair after their labors in the fields, and forget their fatigue in a dram of rank Russian *vodka*. Upon the barren plot of ground before the tavern, the *mir*, or communal assembly, was wont to meet, and in open session elect its Elder, decide its quarrels, allot its ground to the heads of families, and frame its rude and primitive laws.

In its bare and smoke-begrimed public room, the people of Togarog assembled night after night, and discussed, as far as the autocratic government of the Czar Nicholas would allow, the political news of the day. Poor souls! They enjoyed little latitude in this direction. Items of information concerning the acts of the central government in St. Petersburg were few and vague. The newspapers, owing to an extremely severe censorship, gave but meagre accounts of the political situation in the capital, and these were of necessity favorable to the government. Now and then, however, came rambling accounts of insurrections, of acts of cruelty, of large bodies of political offenders banished to a life-long slavery in Siberia. At times came the news that the Czar had been inspired by Providence to inaugurate some new and important reform, only to be followed by the announcement that Satan had held a conference with his Imperial Majesty, and that the reform had fallen through. All such information was carried into Togarog by word of mouth, for few of the good *moujiks* could read the papers. Woe to anyone, however, who allowed his tongue too great a license! Woe to him who dared utter a suggestion that the existing laws bore heavily upon him. It was a dangerous experiment to criticise in a hostile spirit any of the abuses heaped upon the degraded people. The condition of Russia was deplorable.[1] Insurrection and rebellion nourished in all parts of the Empire. Degraded to the lowest depths, the crushed worm turned occasionally, but free itself it could not. Brave spirits arose for whom exile had no terrors. With their rude eloquence they incited their fellow-sufferers to throw off the yoke of tyranny and assert their freedom; and the morrow found them wandering toward the snow-bound confines of Siberia. Patriotism was not very much encouraged in Russia.

The proprietor of the tavern, a burly, red-faced Cossack, Peter Basilivitch by name, was in the employ and under the protection of the Governor of Alexandrovsk, in which department the village of Togarog lay. The rent paid by Basilivitch was nominal, it is true, but he sold enormous quantities of liquor, all of which he was obliged to buy from the Governor's stills; furthermore, he furnished his master with such information concerning the actions, words, and even thoughts of his patrons, as came under his observation; and as the serfs that frequented "Paradise" had no suspicion of the true relation betwixt master and man, the Governor was enabled to keep himself accurately informed as to the sayings and doings of his subjects.

Let us enter the public room, this bright Sunday afternoon in the month of April, in the year 1850. A dense crowd has assembled to-day to do honor to Basilivitch's wretched liquor. The face of the host fairly gloats in anticipation of the lucrative harvest that he will glean. He rubs his hands gleefully, as he orders his servants about.

"Here, Ivan, a pint of *vodka*, and be quick about it! Alexander, you lazy dog, here comes the village elder, Selaski Starosta—see that he is served!"

And the crowd continues to grow, until his room will scarcely seat all the guests.

There are sturdy farmers, wearing their heavy coats and fur caps, in spite of the sultry weather and still warmer alcoholic beverages, and swearing and vociferating in sonorous Russian. There are gossiping women, decked in their caps and many-colored finery. There are smartly-arrayed young girls, chatting merrily with the swains at their side. Unruly children scamper, barefooted and bareheaded, around and under the tables. Puling infants and barking dogs add their discord to the din and confusion. It is a scene one is not apt to forget.

We repeat it, this is Sunday; the one day when the arm of the laborer obtains a respite from the tasks imposed upon it during the week; and the serf of Russia knows no diversion, can find no relaxation, but in the genial climate of a tavern. But this is no ordinary occasion. Not every Sunday ushers in so bountiful a supply of customers to Peter Basilivitch's inn as this. There must be something of unusual importance, perhaps some interesting bit of rumor from the capital, that unites the inhabitants of Togarog. After the alcoholic beverages that are so freely imbibed fulfil their mission and loosen the wits and the tongues of these good *moujiks*, we may arrive at the cause. Nor have we long to wait. Already in the far corner of the dingy and smoke-obscured room, we hear voices in altercation; a hot, angry dispute forces itself upon our ears, and the people cease their revels to listen.

"Say what you will," shouted one fur-bedecked individual; "it is an outrage! We are already burdened with enough taxes. Three days of the week we must work for the master of our lands, and but three days are left us for our own support; and now they want to tax us again for a war in which we have no interest."

"But the Czar must have the money," retorted another. "The people of Poland are in a state of rebellion, and the army has already been ordered out to subdue that province."

"Let them tax the nobles, then," angrily cried a third. "Why do they constantly bleed the poor peasant? Do they want to suck the last drop of our life's blood? I tell you, we ought not submit."

"How will you help yourselves?" sneeringly asked the host, who, with napkin tucked under his chin, stood near the speakers, and lost not a word of the conversation.

How, indeed? Silence fell over the disputants. The question had been asked, alas! how often, but the answer had not yet been forthcoming.

"Let us arise and organize," at length cried the first speaker, one Podoloff by name, who was known as a man of great daring and more than average intelligence, and who had upon more than one occasion been unconsciously very near having himself transported to Siberia. "Let us organize!" he repeated. "Think ye we alone are tired of this wretched existence? Think ye that the peasants of Radtsk and Mohilev and Kief are less human than ourselves, and that they are less weary of the slavery under which they drag out a miserable existence? Let us assert our rights! With the proper organization, and a few good leaders, we could humble this proud nobility and bring it to our feet. There was a time when the Russian peasant was a free man, with the privilege to go whither he pleased, but a word from an arrogant ruler changed it all, and we are now bound and fettered like veritable slaves."

A murmur of surprise swept through the room. Such an incendiary harangue was new to the serfs of that region. Never before had such revolutionary doctrines been openly advanced. Subdued complaints, undefined expressions of discontent, were frequent, and were as frequently repressed, but such an outspoken insult to the reigning nobility, such a fearless invitation to rebellion against the authorities, were unheard of.

The village elder, a venerable and worthy man, arose and sought to check the fiery eloquence of the orator.

"Be silent, Podoloff," he commanded. "It is not for you to speak against the existing order of things. Your father and your father's father were content to live as you do, and were none the worse for it. By what right do you complain?"

"By the right that every human being ought to enjoy!" retorted Podoloff. "Our condition is growing worse every year. Last year the Czar imposed a tax on account of the disturbances in Poland. Three months later, the Governor created another tax to pay for his new palace. Now there is to be still another tax, bigger than the last. No; we ought not to stand it. It has reached the limit of endurance."

Murmurs of approval arose from various quarters, only to be quickly suppressed by the cooler heads in the assembly.

"Still we have much to be thankful for," said an old cobbler, Sobelefsky by name. "The nobles are very kind to us. They supply us with implements and find a market for our grain."

"And for that they rob us of our money and our liberty," retorted Podoloff, hotly. "Ask Simon Schefsky there, how much he owes to our gracious Governor, who last year took from him his pretty daughter, that her charms might while away his weary hours in Alexandrovsk."

"He is a tyrant!" shouted several women, their rough cheeks tingling at the recollection of recent indignities. The cry was taken up by many of the poor wretches present.

What material there was in "Paradise" for the infernal regions of Siberia!

In vain did Selaski Starosta endeavor to make himself heard. In vain did the older and more conservative among the company advise caution. The passion of an angry and enslaved people had for the moment broken its bonds, and the tumult could not be quelled by mere words.

"See!" cried Podoloff, emboldened by his success. He sprang upon a table and tore a paper from his pocket. "Yesterday I went to Kharkov to sell some cattle. I found that the people there had already organized. They have sent a petition to the Czar, asking for greater liberties. Here is a copy. Let me read it to you," and, amid a silence as profound as the occasional bark of a dog or the wail of a child would permit, Podoloff read the following:

"Russia, O Czar, confided to thee supreme power, and thou wert to her as a God upon earth. What hast thou done? Blinded by passion and ignorance, thou hast sought nothing but power! Thou hast forgotten Russia! Thou hast consumed thy time in reviewing troops, in altering uniforms, in signing the legislative papers of ignorant charlatans. Thou hast created a despicable race of censors of the press, that thou mightst sleep in peace, and never know the wants, never hear the murmurs of thy people, never listen to the voice of truth. Truth! Thou hast buried her. For her there is no resurrection. Thou hast refused liberty. At the same time thou wast enslaved by thy passions. By thy pride and thy obstinacy thou hast exhausted Russia. Thou hast armed the world against her. Humiliate thyself before thy brothers! Bow thy haughty forehead in the dust! Implore pardon! Ask counsel! Throw thyself in the arms of thy people. There is no other way of salvation for thee!"[2]

Podoloff replaced the paper in his pocket, and looked triumphantly about him. A twofold sentiment greeted the reading of this wonderful manifesto. The younger generation were disposed to applaud it, but the older men, those who preferred to bear the evils they had rather than fly to those they knew not of, shook their fur-capped heads in doubt.

"Did the writers sign their names to that article?" asked the circumspect old cobbler.

"Not they," answered Podoloff. "They valued their lives too highly. But nearly every village in the north has sent the Czar a similar petition. Nicholas must in the end perceive our misery, and lighten our burdens."

"Or make our existence doubly bitter," answered old Schefsky. "It is a dangerous experiment."

"The Government will take no notice of it, unless it be to double your taxes," said the Elder.

At the word "taxes," a new storm of wailing and imprecations broke out.

"I could not pay another kopeck," cried one cadaverous looking wretch. "I work myself to death, and as it is can hardly keep starvation from the door."

"Why don't they tax the nobles?" asked another. "They can stand it."

"Or the Jews," cried a third, whose liberal potations of alcohol had brought him to the verge of intoxication. "Let them take all they possess. A Jew don't work in the fields. He has no right to wealth!"

Here was a topic upon which all these people were cordially agreed.

"Oppress the Jews."

There was not a dissenting voice in the room.

"The Czar has need of soldiers. Why don't he take the sons of Jews for his wars?"

"We must sit and toil till our nails fall off, while the Jews do nothing but grow rich."

"We'll have no more of it! Let the Jews pay the taxes."

And so the cry went on. Glass after glass of *vodka* moistened the capacious throats that had shrieked themselves hoarse, and in the cry of "Down with the Jews!" the other more dangerous cry of "Down with the Nobles!" was for the moment forgotten.

It was with difficulty that the Elder of the commune could make himself heard above the din.

"My friends," he finally said, "I am afraid we have made bad work of it to-day. Should this get to the Governor's ears, I fear some of us will suffer. I hope, however, that what we have to-day heard and discussed will remain our secret. I trust all of you. I am sure there is no traitor among us who would betray our deliberations to the Governor. As regards our condition, let us be patient. We have nothing serious to complain of. If the Czar needs money, ours should be at his disposal. If he needs men for the army, we are his subjects and his property. Whatever he does, is for the best. Let us submit. As to the manifesto we have just heard, we will have none of it. Other *mirs* may do as they please, but we will remain loyal to our Czar and our Governor, and live our quiet, uneventful lives."

These words, delivered in a simple but forcible manner by the acknowledged head of the village, did not fail of their desired effect. The rabble, realizing the danger into which its enthusiasm had hurried it, became but too anxious to appear on the side of the Government. Those who had been loudest in their outcry, now meekly protested against disloyalty, and Podoloff suddenly found himself bereft of all friends, with the exception of three or four fearless supporters, as stanch as their leader. In vain he sought by his eloquence to regain his lost ground, but he was in a hopeless minority, and, gulping down the remaining spirits which stood before him, he prepared to leave the tavern.

"Continue to suffer," were his parting words. "No people is worse off than it deserves to be. But the day is not far distant when the serf shall be able to hold up his head, a free man, and that will be accomplished as soon as you all feel the humiliation of being slaves!"

The meeting broke up in great disorder. Sentiment appeared to be divided, but the radicals were very circumspect in their remarks, for earlier experience had taught them that, under an autocratic government like that of Czar Nicholas, silence

Milton Goldsmith

was golden. The blandly smiling host, Basilivitch, went from group to group, threw in a word here and a suggestion there, smiled at this man's eloquence and ridiculed that man's caution, all the while making a mental inventory of the facts he would lay before the Governor on the next morning.

The peasants, when they retired for the night, felt none of that pleasurable exaltation which should accompany a step towards liberty, but were oppressed by the weight of an undefined terror, as though they were on the verge of some catastrophe.

FOOTNOTES:

[Footnote 1: "Looking about, one saw venality in full feather, serfdom crushing people like a rock, informers lurking everywhere. No one could safely express himself in the presence of his dearest friend. There was no common bond, no general interest. Fear and flattery were universal."— *Tourgenieff*.]

[Footnote 2: Leroy-Boileau.]

CHAPTER II

MASTER AND MAN

A clear April morning was dawning when Basilivitch saddled his horse and rode off in the direction of Alexandrovsk, at which place he arrived at noon and at once repaired to the Governor's residence. A crowd of idle and flashily-dressed servants, all of whom were serfs, lounged about the new and stately palace, and found exhilarating amusement in setting their ferocious dogs upon the unoffending farmers who happened to pass that way. The greater the fear evinced by the victims, the greater was the delight of the humorously inclined menials, and if perchance a dog succeeded in fixing his fangs in the garments or calf of a pedestrian their mirth found vent in ecstatic shouts of laughter. Basilivitch had on more than one occasion been upon such errands as that which brought him to-day, and seemed on terms of familiarity with the liveried guardians of the palace. They obligingly called off their dogs, and at once announced the innkeeper to his excellency, General Drudkoff. The Governor had dined sumptuously and received his henchman graciously.

Stretching himself upon a sofa and lazily rolling a cigarette, he said:

"Well, Basilivitch, what news do you bring? How fare my good subjects at Togarog?"

"I have bad news, your excellency," answered Basilivitch. "My heart is sad at the information I have to impart. Insurrection is rife in our village, and not only your excellency, but also his majesty the Czar is in imminent danger."

The Governor sprang up from his couch, and his face became ashen white with fear. There was perhaps no man in all Russia more cruel, and at the same time more cowardly, than this General Drudkoff.

"Explain yourself," he cried, at length recovering from his terror. "What do you mean?"

Thereupon the loyal Basilivitch began a recital of the events of the previous evening. Nor did he spare exaggeration where it suited him to strive for effect. According to his version, Podoloff had incited his fellow-peasants to march at once to Alexandrovsk and attack his excellency in the palace. The line of march had already been formed with the arch agitator, Podoloff, at the head.

"I saw," said Basilivitch, waxing warm as his recital progressed, "I saw that it would fare ill with your excellency if the progress of the mob was not arrested. With a handful of friends, therefore, I threw myself in front of the insurgents and commanded them to disband."

"Well done," cried the Governor, upon whom every word made a profound impression. "What did Podoloff do?"

"He would have come on alone, but I overpowered him and secured him in my barn, where he spent the night in imprecations against your excellency."

"You did well, Basilivitch, and I shall not forget you. But who were Podoloff's accomplices? You say a number of men supported him in his treasonable utterances."

"Yes; there were fully a dozen of them," said Basilivitch, counting upon his fingers, and enumerating a number of poor innocents, whose only offence lay in the fact that Basilivitch owed them some private grudge. "There were quite a number of Jews in the assembly," continued the innkeeper; "and their presence seemed to cause a great deal of ill-feeling."

Now it happened that there was not a single Jew in the tavern on that memorable Sunday. The twelve Israelitish families of Togarog found sufficient relaxation and entertainment in their own circle, and did not in the least yearn after the boisterous and uncivil companionship of Russian *moujiks*. Alas! they knew but too well that taunts and insults would be their portion, if they but dared to show themselves at one of these public gatherings. Moreover, the Jews were in the midst of their Passover, a time during which the partaking of any refreshments not prepared according to their strict ritual is sternly interdicted.

Be that as it may, Basilivitch did not allow such simple facts to stand in his way. He had come with a very pretty and effective tale, and drew largely upon his imagination to make it dramatic.

"Ah, the Jews again!" hissed the Governor. "Did they take an active part in the insurrection?"

Basilivitch was forced to admit that they did not.

The Governor appeared disappointed.

"Well, what matters it?" he said. "They have been a menace to us long enough. I doubt whether they have a legal right to live in this part of Russia. We must investigate the matter. In the meantime, we will make an example of them. Give me the names of those Hebrews that were present."

Basilivitch's powers of improvisation failed him. In vain he endeavored to remember the names of the Jews who would most likely have been implicated in such an affair, but the names had slipped his memory.

"Your excellency," he stammered, "I never could tax my memory with their outlandish names."

"It is of no consequence," said the Governor. "A Jew is a Jew. We will make an example of the entire tribe. And now, good Basilivitch, of what do the people complain?"

"It is a mere bagatelle, your excellency. They would like to imitate their betters and live a life of ease and luxury; as though a serf were created for anything but labor. They complain that they cannot lie upon a bed of roses. They want their taxes remitted and would like their children to be sent to school, to be brought up to detest honest work."

"Preposterous!" exclaimed the Governor. "What else have they to complain of?"

"They say that, while they must toil from morning till night, the Jews do nothing but amass wealth; that they must provide men for the army, while the Jews remain at home."

"Stop!" cried the Governor in a fury. "Is what they say concerning the Jews true?"

"It is, your excellency. They do not work in the fields, they have no trades, they simply buy and sell and make money."

The Governor paced the room in silence, an occasional vehement gesture alone giving evidence of the agitation or fear that was raging within him. Finally, he stopped and stood before the obsequious Basilivitch.

"We will find a plan to humble the haughty race," he said. "Return to Togarog and keep your eyes open. Make out a list of the Jews in the village, and find out exactly how many boys there are in each family, and what are their ages. We will remove the brats from their parents' influence and send them to the army, where they will soon become loyal soldiers and faithful Catholics. Bring me the names of the *moujiks* who supported Podoloff in his rebellion. I shall send them to Siberia to reflect on the uncertainty of human aspirations. Now, go! Here is a rouble for you. Should any new symptoms of revolt show themselves, send me word at once."

Scarcely had the door closed upon Basilivitch, before the Governor rang for his Secretary.

"Send two officers to Togarog at once," he commanded. "It appears my good serfs are becoming unruly, and would like a taste of freedom. Let the officers disguise themselves as peasants, and carefully observe every action of Podoloff and his friends. Let our faithful Basilivitch also be watched. I have my suspicions concerning that fellow. He is too ready with his information."

The Secretary left the room to fulfil the Governor's instructions, while Basilivitch remounted his horse and returned to his *kretschma*, to serve, with smiling countenance and friendly mien, the men whom he had devoted to irretrievable ruin.

CHAPTER III

A FAMILY IN ISRAEL

In a remote portion of Togarog, and separated from the main village by a number of wretched lanes, lay the Jewish quarter. A decided improvement in the general condition of the houses which formed this suburb was plainly visible to the casual observer. The houses were, if possible, more unpretentious than those of the serfs, yet there was an air of home-like comfort about them, an impression of neatness and cleanliness prevailed, which one would seek for in vain among the semi-barbarous peasants of Southern Russia. To the inhabitants of these poor huts, home was everything. The ordinary occupations, the primitive diversions of the serfs, were forbidden them. Shunned and decried by their gentile neighbors, the Jews meekly withdrew into the seclusion of their dwellings, and allowed the wicked world to wag. Their "home" was synonymous with their happiness, with their existence.

The shadows of evening were falling upon the quiet village. Above, the stars were beginning to twinkle in the calmness of an April sky, and brighter and brighter shone the candles in the houses of the Jews, inviting the wayfarer to the cheer of a hospitable board.

It is the Jewish Sabbath eve, the divine day of rest. The hardships and worry of daily toil are succeeded by a peaceful and joyous repose. The trials and humiliations of a week of care are followed by a day of peace and security.

The poor, despised Hebrew, who, during the past week, has been hunted and persecuted, bound by the chain of intolerance and scourged by the whip of fanaticism; who, in fair weather and foul, has wandered from place to place with his pack, stinting, starving himself, that he may provide bread for his wife and little ones, has returned for the Sabbath eve, to find, in the presence and in the smiles of his dear ones, an ample compensation for the care and anxiety he has been compelled to endure.

At the end of the street, and not far from the last house in the settlement, stands the House of Prayer. Thither the population of the Jewish quarter wends its way. Men arrayed in their best attire, and followed by troops of children, who from earliest infancy have been taught to acknowledge the efficacy of prayer, enter the synagogue.

It is a poor, modest-looking enclosure.

A number of tallow candles illumine its recesses. The *oron-hakodesh*, or ark containing the holy Pentateuch, a shabbily-covered pulpit, or *almemor*, and a few rough praying-desks for the men, are all that relieve the emptiness of the room. Around one side there runs a gallery, in which the women sit during divine service. In spite of its humble plainness, the place beams with cheerfulness; it bears the impress of holiness. Gradually the benches fill. All of the men, and many of the boys who form the population of the quarter, are present.

Reb Mordecai Winenki, the reader, begins the service.

Prayers of sincere gratitude are sent on high. The worshippers greet the Sabbath as a lover greets his long-awaited bride—with joy, with smiles, with loving fervor. The service is at an end and the happy participants return to their homes.

Beautiful is the legend of the Sabbath eve.

When a man leaves the synagogue for his home, an Angel of Good and an Angel of Evil accompany him. If he finds the table spread in his house, the Sabbath lamps lighted, and his wife and children in festive attire, ready to bless the holy day of rest, then the good Angel says:

"May the next Sabbath and all thy Sabbaths be like this. Peace unto this dwelling!"

And the Angel of Evil is forced to say, "Amen."

No one, indeed, would, before entering one of these poor, unpainted huts expect to find the cheerful and brilliant interior that greets his eyes. Let us enter one of the houses, that of Reb Mordecai Winenki.

The table is covered with a snow-white cloth. The utensils are clean and bright. The board is spread with tempting viands. An antique brass lamp, polished like a mirror, hangs from the ceiling, and the flame from its six arms sheds a soft light upon the table beneath. A number of silver candlesticks among the dishes add to the illumination.

On this evening, Mordecai returned from the synagogue with his son Mendel, a lad of thirteen, and his brother-in-law, Hirsch Bensef, a resident of Kief. Mordecai was a thin, pale-faced, brown-bearded man of forty or thereabouts, with shoulders stooping as though under a weight of care;

perhaps, though, it was from the sedentary life he led, teaching unruly children the elements of Hebrew and religion. He had resided in Togarog for fourteen years, ever since he had married Leah, the daughter of Reb Bensef of Kief. His wife's brother was a man of different stamp. He was a few years younger than Mordecai. His step was firm, his head erect, his beard jet black, and his intellect, though not above the superstitious fancies of his time and race, was, for all ordinary transactions, especially those of trade, eminently clear and powerful. He was, as we shall see, one of the wealthiest Jewish merchants in Kief, and therefore quite a power in the community of that place.

Leah met the men at the door.

"Good *Shabbes*, my dear husband; good *Shabbes*, brother," said the woman, cheerfully, her matronly face all aglow with pride and pleasure. "You must be famished from your long trip, brother."

"Yes, I am very hungry. I have tasted nothing since I left Kharkov, at five o'clock this morning."

"How kind of you to come all that distance to our boy's *bar-mitzvah!* He can never be sufficiently grateful."

"He is my god-child," said the man, affectionately stroking his nephew's head. "I take great pride in him. It has pleased the Lord to deny me children, and the deprivation is hard to bear. Sister, let me take Mendel with me. I am rich and can give him all he can desire. He shall study Talmud and become a great and famous rabbi, of whom all the world will one day speak in praise. You have still another boy, while my home is dreary for want of a child's presence. What say you?"

But the mother had, long before the conclusion of this appeal, clasped the boy to her bosom, while the tears of love forced themselves through her lashes at the bare suggestion of parting from her first-born.

"God forbid," she cried, "that he should ever leave me; my precious boy." And she embraced him again and again.

Meanwhile, the husband had crossed the room to where a little fellow, scarcely six years of age, lay upon a sofa.

"Well, Jacob, my boy; how do you feel?" he asked, gently.

"A little better, father," murmured the child. "My arm and ear still pain me, but not so much as yesterday."

The boy sat up and attempted to smile, but sank back with a groan.

"Poor child, poor child," said the father, soothingly, "Have patience. In a few days you will be about again."

"Is uncle here? I want to see uncle," cried the boy.

Hirsch Bensef obeyed the call, and, going to the sufferer, kissed his burning brow.

"Why, Jacob; how is this?" he said. "I did not know that you were sick. What is the trouble, my lad?" The child turned his face to the wall and shuddered.

Reb Mordecai shook his head mournfully, while a tear he sought to repress ran down his furrowed cheek.

"It is the old story," he said. "Prejudice and fanaticism, hatred and ignorance."

And while the Sabbath meal waited, the father told his tale in a simple, unaffected manner, and the uncle listened with clenched hands and threatening glances.

The day following the events in the *kretschma*, little Jacob had wandered, in company with some Christian playmates, through the village, and seeing the door of a barn wide open, his childish curiosity got the better of his discretion, and he peeped in. A brindled cow, with a pretty calf scarcely three days old, attracted his attention, and for some minutes he gazed upon the pair in silent ecstasy. Then, knowing that he was on forbidden ground, he retraced his steps and endeavored to reach the lane where he had left his companions. The master of the farm, however, having witnessed the intrusion from a neighboring window, did not lose the opportunity to vent his anger against the whole tribe of inquisitive Jews. On the following day the cow ran dry. In vain did the calf seek nourishment at the maternal breast; there was nothing to satisfy its cravings.

The farmer, slow as he was in matters of general importance, was far from slow in tracing the melancholy occurrence to its supposed source.

"That accursed Jew has bewitched my cow," was his first thought, and his second was to find the author of the deed and mete out punishment to him.

Throughout the whole of Russia, and even in parts of civilized Germany, Jews are accused of all manner of sorcery. The *Cabala* is the principal religious authority of the lower classes among the Russian Jews, and this may perhaps inspire such a preposterous notion. The Jews, themselves, frequently believe that some one of their own number is in possession of supernatural secrets which give him wonderful and awful powers. Many were the tortures which these poor people were doomed to endure for their supposed influence over nature's laws.

It was an easy matter to find little Jacob. His hours at the *cheder* (school) were over. He was sure to be playing upon the streets, and his capture was quickly effected. Seizing the innocent little fellow by the arm, the irate peasant lifted him off his feet, and dragged him by sheer force into the barn, where he confronted the malefactor with his victim.

"So, you thought you could bewitch my cow," he hissed. "But I saw you, Jew, and, by our holy Czar, I swear that, unless you repair the damage, I shall feed your carcass to the dogs."

Poor Jacob was too terrified to understand of what crime he had been accused. He looked piteously at his tormentor, and burst into tears.

"Well?" cried the peasant, impatiently; "will you take off the spell, or shall I call my dog?"

The child, knowing that such threats were not made in vain, endeavored to plead his innocence, but the bellowing of the hungry calf outweighed the sobbing of the boy, and with an angry oath Jacob was struck to the ground, and a ferocious bull-dog, but little more brutal than his master, was set upon the helpless little fellow.

"Please, Mr. Farmer, don't kill me," he pleaded, groaning in pain.

"Will you cure my cow?" demanded the peasant.

"I'll try to; I'll do my best," sobbed the boy, whose pain made him diplomatic at last.

The dog was called off, and the child, after promising to restore the cow to her former condition, was turned out into the lane, where his mother found him an hour later, unconscious, his body lacerated, one arm broken, and a portion of his right ear torn off.

When Reb Mordecai concluded his sad narration, all about him were in tears.

"Just God!" exclaimed the uncle; "hast Thou indeed deserted Thy people, that Thou canst allow such indignities? How long, O Lord! must we endure these torments?"

"Nay, brother," sobbed the poor mother, while she caressed her ailing boy; "what God does is for the best. It is not for us to peer into his inscrutable actions. But come, Mordecai, banish your sorrows. This is *Shabbes*, a day of joy and peace. Come, the table is spread."

Father and mother placed their hands upon the heads of their children, and pronounced the solemn blessing:—"May God let you become like Ephraim and Manasseh!" and the family took their places at the table.

Then Mordecai made *kiddush*, which consisted in blessing the wine, without which no Jewish Sabbath is complete, and having pronounced *motzi*, a similar prayer over the bread, he dipped the latter in salt, and passed a small piece to each of the participants. It is a ceremony which no pious Jew ever neglects.

In spite of the recent affliction, the meal was a merry one. The poorest Israelite will deny himself even the necessaries of life during the six working-days, that he may live well on the Sabbath. Reb Mordecai was a poor man. He had a small income, derived from teaching the Talmud to the children in the vicinity, from transcribing the holy scrolls, and from sundry bits of work for which he was fitted by his intellectual attainments. He was the most influential Jew in the settlement and not even the fanatical serfs of the village could find a complaint to make against his character or person.

The theme of conversation was naturally the family festival, which would take place upon the morrow. Mendel having attained his thirteenth year and acquired due proficiency in the difficult studies of the Jewish law, would become *bar-mitzvah*; in other words, he would take upon himself the responsibility of a man before God and the world, and acknowledge his readiness to act and suffer for the maintenance of the belief in *Adonai Echod*—the only God. Mendel, under his father's tuition, had made rapid strides. He was the wonder of every male inhabitant of the community. His knowledge of the Scriptures was simply phenomenal, and his philosophical reasoning puzzled and astonished his friends.

"He will be a great rabbi some day," they prophesied.

Hirsch Bensef had journeyed all the way from Kief to take part in the family festival. There were some privileges which not even the wealthy Jews of Russia could purchase, and among them was the right to travel in a public conveyance. Hirsch was obliged to journey as best he could. A kindly disposed wagoner had permitted him to ride part of the way, but the greater portion of the distance he was compelled to walk. Still, at any cost, he had determined not to miss so important an event as his nephew's *bar-mitzvah*.

The bread having been broken, the supper was proceeded with. The fish was succulent and the cake delicious. A lofty and religious Sabbath sentiment enhanced the charm of the whole meal. Then a prayer of thanks was offered, the dishes were cleared away and the family settled themselves at ease, to discuss the topics most dear to them.

"You make a great mistake, sister," said Bensef, "if you allow Mendel to waste his time in this village. The boy is much too bright for his surroundings."

"Don't begin that subject again," said the mother, determinedly; "for I positively will not hear of his leaving. The parting would kill me."

"But," continued her brother, "have you ever asked yourself what his future will be in this wretched neighborhood? Shall he waste his precious years helping his father teach *cheder*? Shall he earn a few paltry kopecks in making *tzitzith* (fringes for the praying scarfs) for the *Jehudim* in the village? Or, shall he cobble shoes or peddle from place to place with a bundle upon his back, which are the only two occupations open to the despised race?"

"Alas!" sighed the mother, "what you say may be true. But what would you propose for the boy?"

"Let him go with me to Kief. There are nearly fifteen thousand of our co-religionists in that city; and, while their lot is not an enviable one, it is decidedly better than vegetating in a village. Our celebrated Rabbi Jeiteles is getting old and we will soon need a successor. It is an honorable position and one which our little Mendel will some day be able to fill. Would you not like living in a big city, my boy?"

Mendel hovered between filial affection and a desire to see the big world. It was difficult to decide.

"I should like to remain with father and mother—and Jacob,"

he stammered, "and yet—"

"And yet," continued his uncle, "you would love to come to Kief, where everything is grand and brilliant, where the stores and booths are fairly alive with light and beauty, where the soldiers parade every day in gorgeous uniforms. Ah, my boy, there is life for you!"

"But how much of that life may the Jews enjoy?" asked Mordecai. "Are they not restricted in their privileges and deprived of every possibility of rising in station? Is their lot any happier than ours in this village, where, at all events, we are not troubled with the envy which the sight of so much luxury must bring with it?"

"It will not always be so," said Bensef, confidently. "With each year we may expect reforms, and where will they strike first if not in the cities? Nicholas already has plans under consideration, whereby the condition of the serfs may be bettered."

"How will that benefit our race?"

"How? I will tell you. The serf persecutes the Jew because he is himself persecuted by the nobility. There is no real animosity between the peasant and his Jewish neighbors. Our wretched state is the outgrowth of a petty tyranny, in which the serf desires to imitate his superiors. Let the people once enjoy freedom and they will cease to persecute the Hebrews, without whom they cannot exist."

"Absurd ideas," interrupted the teacher. "Our degradation proceeds not from the people, but from those in authority. Our lot will not improve until the Messiah comes with sword in hand, to deliver us from our enemies. Remember the proverb: 'The heavens are far, but further the Czar.'"

"But about Mendel?" asked Bensef, suddenly reverting to his original topic, for in spite of his hopeful theories, he did not feel sanguine that he would live to see their realization.

"The matter is not pressing," said the father. "We can think it over, and decide before you return to Kief."

"No, no!" cried Leah; "Mendel must not leave us. Promise to remain, my child!"

But the boy was now delighted with the idea of accompanying his uncle. He asked a thousand questions concerning the wonderful town of Kief, which suddenly became the goal of all his hopes and ambitions.

Bensef took the boy upon his lap and told him all about the great city, which had once been the capital of Russia. Mendel listened and sighed. His eyes beamed with pleasurable anticipation. Before going to bed, he threw his arms about his mother's neck.

"Mother," he whispered; "let me go to Kief. I want to become great."

Leah held him in a convulsive embrace, but said nothing.

The morrow was Saturday—Sabbath morning. The little synagogue was crowded with an expectant throng. It was long since there had been a *bar-mitzvah* in Togarog, and Israelites came from all the villages in the vicinity to witness the happy event. Happy seemed the men, arrayed in their white *tallesim* (praying scarfs)—happy at the thought of another member being added to their ranks. Happy appeared the mothers in the reflection that their sons, too, would some day be admitted to the holy rite. When Mendel finally mounted the *almemor* (pulpit), and began his *Bar'chu eth*

Adonai, the audience scarcely breathed.

Like a finished scholar did Mendel recite his *sidrah*, that portion of the *Torah* or Law which was appropriate to the day. This was followed by the *drosha*, a well-committed speech, expressive of gratitude to his parents and teachers, and full of beautiful promises of a future that should be pleasant in the eyes of the Lord. The words fell from his lips as though inspired. It was a proud moment for the boy's parents. Their tears mingled with their smiles. Forgotten were hardships and persecutions. God still held happiness in reserve for his chosen people. When the boy concluded his exercises, kisses and congratulations were showered upon him by his admiring friends.

"Hirsch Bensef is right," said Mordecai to his wife. "Mendel ought to go to some large city. He has wonderful talents. He may become a great rabbi. Who can tell?"

"We shall see; we shall see!" replied his wife, with a look of mingled pleasure and pain. But she did not say her husband was in the wrong.

In the afternoon the entire congregation visited Reb Mordecai, so that the little house scarcely held all the people. The men came with their long *caftans*, the women with their black silk robes, their prettiest wigs, and strings of pearls; and one and all brought presents, tokens of their esteem. Naturally, Mendel was the centre of attraction. His present, past and future were discussed. A brilliant career was predicted for him, and he was held up as a model to his juniors.

Little Jacob was also the recipient of attentions from young and old. His mishap, though painful, was not an exceptional case. Similar ones occurred almost weekly in the surrounding country. What mattered it? His arm would be stiff and his ear mutilated to the end of his days; but he was only a Jew—doomed to live and suffer for his belief in the one God. It was a sad consolation they gave him, but it was the best they had to offer.

The poor children, Christian as well as Jew, came from miles around to receive alms, which were generously given. Then refreshments were served, followed by speeches and jests; and so the afternoon and evening wore merrily away, and night—a dark and dismal night—followed the happy day.

Milton Goldsmith

CHAPTER IV

A NIGHT OF TERROR

The guests had retired to their homes. The children had been blessed and sent to bed. The parents throughout the quarter, having discussed the one topic of the day, Mendel's *bar-mitzvah*, had extinguished their candles and sought their pillows, preparatory to again venturing forth into a cold and inhospitable world in search of their meagre subsistence.

In the village, too, the serfs had retired, the brawling in "Paradise" had gradually ceased, and silent night had cast her mantle of sleep over Togarog.

A dim rumbling of wagons, a clattering of horses' hoofs, a murmur of men's voices fell upon the air. Nearer and nearer came the sounds and the soldiers that produced them, until the village was reached. With as little noise as possible, the company crept through the narrow streets until they came to the inn of our friend Basilivitch, who evidently expected them, for he hastily opened the door and bade the martial band enter. There was a whispered consultation between the host and the leader of the soldiers. Basilivitch put on his cap and guided the captain through the village. Carefully the two scanned the houses, and now and then Basilivitch drew a cross upon one of the doors with a piece of red chalk. They then directed their footsteps to the Jewish quarter, where they repeated their tactics, and finally rejoined their companions in "Paradise." Here the soldiers were given their instructions, and silently and stealthily, lest they might arouse the village and invite resistance, they crept forth in twos, to the huts marked with the mystic sign of the cross. The house of Podoloff was the first they reached. Cautiously one of the soldiers knocked at the door.

"Who's there?" cried a voice, inside.

"Friends! Open at once!" was the enticing answer.

Podoloff hastily attired himself, and, cautiously opening the door, he peeped through the crevice. At the sight of the soldiers, he instinctively divined danger, and tried to bar the entrance. Too late! One of the soldiers had already thrust the muzzle of his gun into the opening, while the other forced his way into the room.

"Utter a single cry," he said, "and you are a corpse."

Resistance was useless. Podoloff, in spite of his pleading, was seized and his hands bound behind him. Then, while one man held guard over the captive's wife and children, the other ransacked the house, rummaging through filthy and worm-eaten closets, and exploring dirty coffers, into which had been thrust a wretched assortment of rags—the garb of slavery. Every scrap of paper was captured and jealously guarded. During this time, the greatest silence was preserved. Other arrests were to be made, and it was imperative upon the men to take every precaution not to arouse the intended victims prematurely.

"Forward, march!" commanded one of the soldiers; and poor Podoloff, without even daring to bid his wife farewell, was forced into the street and carried, rather than led, to Basilivitch's hostlery.

Nine others were captured in a similar manner; nine poor wretches, doomed to life-long misery in the copper mines of Siberia, many of them having not the slightest idea of the nature of their offence. Basilivitch had placed the Governor of Alexandrovsk under eternal obligations by his patriotic devotion. Of the number captured, there were three who had seconded Podoloff during the discussion at the inn, the previous Sunday afternoon. The remainder were to be exiled, because the Governor, on Basilivitch's recommendation, deemed them dangerous. A good day's work, Basilivitch! You have done the nation a signal service, and have rid yourself of six persons from whom you had at various times borrowed money, and who had of late become troublesome in their dunning. They will not trouble you from the Siberian mines.

The prisoners were thrown into two carts, which had been brought for that purpose, and a detachment of soldiers accompanied them without delay to Alexandrovsk. There they were put into prison for a month, until it pleased the Governor to take notice of them. Then followed the mere mockery of a trial, during which the prisoners were not permitted to utter a word in self-defence, and as a fitting end to this travesty of justice, the ten unfortunates were launched upon their weary foot-journey to the frozen North, destined to live and die beyond the reach, beyond the sympathy of mankind.

Let us retrace our steps and accompany the Governor's soldiers through the Jewish quarter. The refinement of cruelty demanded from the Jews a greater sacrifice than from the Catholics. The malefactors must be punished through their little ones. In pursuance of a decree of the mighty Czar, passed some years before, the Governors of the various provinces were authorized to visit the Jewish homes, and to remove from them all male children that had reached the age of five years.[3]

There was a twofold object in this course. Firstly, the humane Czar desired to accustom these babes to the rigorous soldier life of Russia, to transform the weakly scions of an oriental race into strong and hardy Russians; and, secondly, it was deemed a blessing to humanity to tear the Jewish children from their homes, parents and religion, and to bring them up in the only saving Catholic faith. Far, far from all that was dear to them, in a strange locality, among hostile people, exposed to unutterable hardships and rigorous discipline, these unfortunate beings dragged out their wretched existence. Fully half of their number died of exposure, wearing away their poor lives in a vain longing for home and friends, while the remainder survived, only to forget their kind and kin, and to furnish the raw material for future Nihilists. Many Jewish communities had already suffered from this heartless decree, and those who had been spared its terrors, anticipated them as they would some dreaded scourge, some deadly pestilence. That the Jews of Togarog and the surrounding villages had escaped its influences, was due less to the humane sentiments of the Governor than to his natural indolence. But now his ire was aroused. The Jews should feel his power.

The detachment of soldiers having seen their Russian prisoners safely on the road to oblivion, now directed their attention to the Jewish quarter.

Mordecai Winenki's house stood not far from the head of the street. No need to knock for admittance. A Jew was not allowed to lock his door, the better to give his sociable neighbors an opportunity of molesting him. Two of the soldiers entered, and groped their way through the darkness. The master of the house heard their footsteps, and timidly called out:

"Who's there?"

"Quick, Jew, give us a light!" was the sole reply.

Shaking like a leaf, poor Mordecai struck a light, and the candle cast its rays upon the fierce-looking Cossacks in the apartment. A cry escaped the man's lips, but it was quickly stifled by the rough hand of one of the soldiers.

"If you make the least noise I will strangle you. Now show me where your boys sleep!"

"Oh, God! they will take my Mendel for a recruit," cried the poor father.

"Silence, you viper! Well, why don't you move? We want to know where your boys are sleeping!"

Mordecai, convinced of the futility of resistance, shuffled across the floor in his bare feet, and opened the door of an adjoining room. There, in the innocence of youth, lay Mendel, dreaming, perhaps, of his recent triumphs. An unpitying hand landed the boy upon the floor. Paralyzed with fear, he could not speak, but gazed pleadingly from his father to the soldiers. His uncle Bensef, who had shared his bed, now endeavored to interfere, but a blow from the stalwart Cossack sent him to the opposite corner of the room. Quickly they inspected the boy, taking a mental note of his height and appearance, and, barely giving him time to put on his clothing, hurried him into the arms of the soldiers waiting without.

"You have another son! Where is he?" demanded one of the soldiers of the half-paralyzed Mordecai.

"No! no!" he sobbed; "I have no more!"

"You lie, Jew! Show us the other boy!" And without further ceremony, they broke into the third room, where Jacob lay in the arms of his terrified mother.

In vain the boy shrieked at the sight of the fierce-looking visitors. In vain the mother pleaded: "He is sick and helpless. Spare him. He is but a baby. Leave him with me!"

There was no pity in the breasts of the hardened soldiers. Neither tears nor entreaties won them over. The more the sorrowing parents implored, the louder were the oaths, the fiercer the blows of the barbarous Cossacks.

Jacob, followed by his weeping parents, was carried half-dressed into the street.

Similar scenes were enacted in every house in which there were male children. Of the twelve Jewish homes in Togarog, but two were spared. The children, in most cases scantily dressed, were hurried to Basilivitch's hostlery, where wagons were in waiting to take them to Alexandrovsk for the Governor's inspection.

Mournful was the train that followed the little band through the village. Shrieks and lamentations, prayers and imprecations resounded, until the brutal guards, wearied by the incessant clamor, finally drove the frenzied people back and set out upon their homeward journey.

The little ones sat cowering in the wagons, afraid to weep, scarcely daring to breathe. Taken from home when they most

Milton Goldsmith

needed their parents' care and love, what would become of these poor waifs? What would the future have in store for them?

General Drudkoff could now sleep in peace; the insurrection in Togarog was quelled. Its ringleaders were on the way to Siberia, and its abettors, the Jews (according to Basilivitch), had been rendered harmless.

FOOTNOTES:

[Footnote 3: This decree was repealed by Alexander II.]

CHAPTER V

THE JOURNEY TO KHARKOV

The wagons, with their helpless freight, reached Alexandrovsk shortly after daybreak. Their first stupor having passed, the children conversed with each other in whispers and tried in their own poor way to console one another. Jacob, whose mutilated ear and broken arm had not been improved by the rough treatment he had experienced, wept bitterly at first, until the savage voice of a soldier bade him be quiet. Then the child made a Spartan-like endeavor to forget his pain and fell asleep upon his brother's breast. It was nine o'clock on Sunday morning when they arrived at the Governor's palace. The devout and religious General Drudkoff usually declined to transact any business on that day; but this was an important matter of State, a question threatening perhaps the very existence of the Empire, and a departure from ordinary rules was allowable. The waifs were brought into the ante-chamber, and obliged to pass muster before his excellency, who read them a lesson upon their future career and duties. After those whose hasty abduction had made it impossible to dress, had been provided with odds and ends of clothing, the rags cast off by the children of the Governor's serfs, and which his excellency declared were much too good for Jews, the lads were again placed upon rickety carts, and, while the Governor proceeded to his religious services at the *kiosk*, they were escorted under a strong guard to the military headquarters at Kharkov.

Long and tedious was the journey. At noon a village was reached, and the travellers were furnished with a meal consisting of pork and bread. Half-famished by his long fast, one of the boys had already bitten into his portion, but stern religion interfered.

"Do not eat it," whispered Mendel; "it is *trefa!*" (unclean).

The lads gazed wistfully at the tempting morsels, but touch them they dared not.

"Why don't you eat?" roughly asked one of the soldiers, whose duty it was to walk by the side of the wagon and guard against a possible escape.

"It is forbidden," answered Mendel, who, being the oldest of the little group, took upon himself the duties of spokesman. "It is unclean."

"If it is good enough for us, it is good enough for a Jew. Here, eat this quickly!" and he endeavored to force a large piece of the dreaded meat between the teeth of one of the lads.

"If they wont eat, let them starve," said another of the guards, who was attracted by the noise. "Why do you trouble yourself about them?"

"You are right," answered the first; "let them starve."

And their fast continued.

The smiling fields through which they rode, the sunny sky

above them, the merry birds warbling in the bushes, had no attraction for the ill-fated boys. The world was but a vast desert, an unfriendly wilderness to them. But Mendel's mind, sharpened by misfortune, was not dormant. A thought of escape had already presented itself to his active brain.

"If Jacob and I could only manage to run away and reach our uncle in Kief," he mused.

Presently he plucked up courage and asked the guard: "Will you please tell me what you are going to do with us?"

"You will find out when you get to Kharkov," was the ungracious rejoinder.

To Kharkov! The information was welcome indeed. Not that Mendel had ever been in that place, but he recollected hearing his uncle say that he had come through Kharkov on his way from Kief. It must be on the direct route to the latter city. O God! if he could but escape!

A dark, stormy night found the travellers in the miserable little village of Poltarack. The weary horses were unharnessed and the soldiers looked about for comfortable quarters for the night. They found refuge in a dilapidated structure, the only inn of which the place could boast. The children were led to a barn, where a bountiful supply of straw served them as a bed. A piece of bread and a glass of rank brandy formed their evening meal, and hunger left them no desire to investigate whether the humble repast was *kosher* (clean) or not.

The footsteps of the guards had scarcely died away in the distance, before Mendel sprang to the door and endeavored to open it. It was securely locked and the boy turned disconsolate to his companions. It was the hour when, at home, their fathers would send them lovingly to bed, when their mothers would tuck them comfortably under the covers and kiss them good-night; and here they lay, clad in tatters, numb with cold, pinched with hunger; pictures of misery and woe. Heart-rending were the sighs, bitter the complaints, in which the poor lads gave utterance to their feelings.

"Come, boys!" at length cried Mendel, "it wont do to grieve. Let us bear up as bravely as possible. They will take us to Kharkov and leave us at military headquarters. Perhaps we can escape. If we are kept together it will be difficult, but if they separate us, it will perhaps be easy to give the soldiers in charge the slip. If you get away, do not at once go back home or you will be recaptured. Go on until you come to a Jewish settlement, where you will be cared for. Jacob, you must try to stay with me, whatever may happen."

Long and earnest was the conversation between the boys, all of whom, in spite of their tender years, realized their perilous position.

Then Mendel arose and recited the old and familiar Hebrew evening prayers and the little gathering made the responses; then, weary and homesick, the boys cried themselves to sleep.

At break of day, the Cossacks pounded at the barn-door, and the boys, after breakfasting on dry bread, again set out upon their tedious journey. The soldiers who had accompanied the wagons, were replaced by others; the new men were in a better humor and more graciously inclined than those of the preceding day. They even condescended to jest with the young recruits and to civilly answer their many questions. From their replies, Mendel gleaned that the commander at Kharkov would distribute them among the various military camps throughout the province, where constant hard labor, a stern discipline and a not too humane treatment would eventually toughen their physical fibre and wean them from the cherished religion of their youth.

The weather was unfriendly, the sky was overcast, and the boys, shivering with cold and apprehension, at length made their entry into Kharkov. The commander of the garrison, a grim-visaged, bearded warrior, received them, heard the story of their capture from one of the guards, amused himself by pulling the boys' ears and administering sundry blows. He then divided them into twos, to be escorted to the various barracks about the district. Mendel and Jacob were permitted to go together, not because the commander yielded to a feeling of humanity, but because they happened to be standing together, and it really did not matter to the Russian authorities how the new recruits were distributed. A soldier was placed in charge of each couple, and, like cattle to the slaughter, the boys were led through the town.

Weary and silent, yet filled with wonder and surprise, Mendel and Jacob preceded their guard through the gay and animated streets of Kharkov. It was a new life that opened to their vision. With childish curiosity they gazed at every booth, looked fondly into every gaily decorated shop and glanced timidly at the many uniformed officers who hurried to and fro.

For a moment, their desolate homes, their sorrowing parents, their unpromising future were forgotten in the excitement of the scenes about them, and it required at times the rough command and brutal push of the soldier behind them to recall them to the misery of the moment. This soldier, a fine-looking, sturdy fellow, appeared as much interested in the animated scene as were his captives. Years had passed since he had last visited Kharkov, his native town. Much had changed during that period. A conflagration had destroyed the central portion of the city and imposing stone edifices had in many streets replaced the former crazy structures. Now and then an old building or hoary landmark would recall pleasant memories of early youth. The fountain in the centre of the square was eloquent with reminders of by-gone joys, of hasty interviews, of stolen kisses; and our brave warrior strode along with a bland smile of contentment upon his bronzed countenance. Suddenly, a man brushed past him. The two looked at each other for a moment, as if in doubt, and then with a simultaneous shout of recognition, they shook each other heartily by the hand.

"Cantorwitch!" cried the soldier. "By all the saints, this is rare good luck! How have you been?"

"Very well, friend Polatschek. But you are the last man I should have looked for in Kharkov. How well your service agrees with you."

The two friends stood and talked of all that had befallen them since their separation. Not until the calendar of gossip had been exhausted did Cantorwitch finally ask: "But what brings you to Kharkov, my boy? I thought you were on the southern frontier."

"So I was; so I was," rejoined the other. "I have been sent up with two Jewish recruits. Holy Madonna! what has become of them?"

Mendel and Jacob had disappeared, without even saying, "By your leave!" In vain the friends peered into the various shops along the street, into every open door-way, behind every box and barrel. In vain they inquired of every soldier who passed. No one had seen the runaways.

Poor Polatschek, after listening to the consolations of his

friend and fortifying himself with a quart of spirits, returned to headquarters, to spend the following ninety days under arrest for gross negligence while on duty.

CHAPTER VI

TWO UNFORTUNATES

To Mendel, Cantorwitch seemed a special messenger sent by a benign Providence. He waited for a moment until he perceived the two friends in earnest conversation, and seizing his brother by the arm, he took advantage of an approaching crowd of sight-seers to get away from the gossiping soldier. The boys ran down the nearest street as fast as their feeble limbs would carry them. Not until they had reached the limits of the town did they pause for breath, and Jacob, thoroughly exhausted, sank to the ground.

"Thank God, we are free!" said Mendel, jubilantly.

But Jacob began to weep, crying, "Oh, I'm so tired and hungry!"

"Do not cry; it is of no use. We will find our way to Kief, and there uncle will take care of us."

"I do not think I can go much farther, Mendel."

"But you must. If we remain here we shall be captured and put into prison. Let us go as far as we possibly can. Perhaps we can find a village on the road where the *Jehudim* (Jews) will shelter us until you become stronger. Come, Jacob."

The child struggled to his feet and the brothers set out upon their journey through an unknown country.

The sun, the cheerful king of day, had peeped through the April rifts and sent his bright rays upon the smiling landscape. Gradually the clouds dissolved under the genial influence and a friendly sky cheered the fugitives on their way.

The merry chirping of the birds, the buzzing of the insects, the blossoming fruit trees along the route, betokened the advent of spring. Mendel gulped down a great lump in his throat and stifled a sob, as he thought of his distant home. How happy, how joyful, had this season been, when, after the termination of the Bible studies at the *cheder*, their father had taken them for a long walk through the fields and in his own crude way had spoken of the beauties of Nature and of the wisdom and beneficence of the Creator. Then, all was peace and contentment; and now, what a dreary contrast! Mendel dashed the gathering tears from his eyes—it would not do to let Jacob see him cry—and resolutely taking his little brother by the hand, walked on more rapidly.

There was a tedious journey in prospect; God only knew when and where it would end. On they walked through bramble and marsh, over stones and fallen boughs, preferring the newly-ploughed fields to the public road, for fear of detection; trembling with fear at the sight of a human being, lest it might be a soldier charged with their recapture. On they struggled until night hid the road from their view and darkness arrested further progress. A ruined and deserted shed afforded them shelter, a stone did service as a pillow, and, embracing each other, the lads lay down to sleep.

The dawn found the wanderers astir, and after a hasty ablution at a neighboring brook and a recital of their morning prayers, they bravely started out upon their cheerless journey.

The day had dawned brightly, but before long threatening clouds obscured the sun. The wind veered to the North and howled dismally.

Sadly and silently the boys trudged onward, buffeting the wind and stifling their growing hunger.

"Mendel," finally sobbed Jacob, "I am so hungry. If I only had a piece of bread I would feel much stronger."

"Let us walk faster," replied the other. "Perhaps we will reach some village."

Manfully they pushed onward for another hour, Mendel endeavoring to entertain his brother by relating stories he had heard when a child.

Jacob stopped again, exhausted.

"It is no use, Mendel," he cried. "I am too hungry to walk any further."

"Courage, brother," answered Mendel, cheerfully. "See, there are houses ahead of us. We can surely find something to eat."

The waifs dragged their way to a weather-beaten hut and knocked at the door. A mild-visaged woman responded and surveyed the travel-stained children with something like compassion.

"We are hungry," pleaded Mendel. "Please give us a bite

of food."

"Who are you and where do you come from?" queried the woman.

"We are trying to reach Kief, where we have friends," answered Mendel. "Please do not let us starve on the road."

"Jews, eh?" asked the woman, suspiciously. "Well, no matter; you don't look any too happy. Come in and warm yourselves."

The boys were soon sitting before a roaring kitchen-fire, while the woman busied herself with providing them with a meal. Tempting, indeed, did it appear to the famished lads; but could they eat it? Was it prepared according to the Jewish ritual? It was a momentous question to Mendel, and only his little brother's pinched and miserable countenance could have induced him to violate the law which to his conception was as sacred as life itself. While Mendel debated, Jacob solved the knotty problem by attacking the savory dishes before him, and his brother reluctantly followed his example.

"It may be a sin, but God will forgive us," was his mental reflection as he greedily swallowed the food.

The woman looked on in admiration at the huge appetites of the lads. She plied them with questions, to which she received vague replies, and finally contented herself with the thought that these were perhaps wayward children who had run away from home and were now penitently trying to find their way back.

After the boys were rested, they thanked their kind hostess and set out again upon their wanderings with no other compass than blind chance, but avoiding the highways for fear of being captured by the soldiers. On they went for hours, Mendel supporting his complaining brother and whispering words of hope and courage.

By noon the sky had become darker, the storm more threatening. The wind blew in furious gusts over the dismal country, and an occasional rumbling of distant thunder filled the weary lads with dread. The road they had chosen was absolutely deserted. It lay through a bleak, scarcely habitable prairie, a landscape common enough in that part of Russia; and stones and brambles did much to retard their progress. There was not a place of shelter in sight. The outlook was sufficiently unpromising to dismay the most resolute.

Jacob sat down upon a stone and began to weep.

"I can go no further," he sobbed. "I am tired and sick."

"But you must come," pleaded his brother. "See what a storm is gathering. If we remain here we shall be drenched. We must find shelter."

"Go alone, brother," said the little one. "I'll stay here."

There was a sudden flash of lightning, which illumined Jacob's bandaged face, pale with fear and fatigue. The trembling boys looked at each other and Jacob began to cry.

"Come, Jacob," murmured Mendel, helping his brother to rise. "We shall die if we stay here. May God protect us."

Again the waifs plodded on, Mendel supporting his brother and endeavoring to protect him from the cruel wind. Darker grew the sky. Large drops of rain began to fall and with a startling peal of thunder the tempest broke in its fury. The pitiless wind sweeping through the land from the bleak northern steppes brought cold and desolation in its train. The poor children were drenched to the skin. They clung to each other and painfully made their way across the miry fields to the highway, the ancient road of the Tartar Khans.

At last Jacob succumbed to the awful strain and sank to the ground.

"Let me die," moaned the child.

"Oh, dear brother; you must live! We will find our way back to Togarog to papa and mamma. How they would grieve if I came back alone."

The child shook his head mutely to this appeal, but rise he could not. Mendel was in despair.

A bright flash lit up the landscape and showed the dim outlines of huts not many rods away.

"God be thanked!" cried Mendel, fervently. "See, Jacob, there are houses. The village is near. There we can get food and shelter. Come, lean on me and we will be there in a few minutes."

"No, go alone; I am too weak."

"I will carry you," cried Mendel. "Oh, I can do it; I am strong enough."

He attempted to lift the child from the ground, but he had overrated his strength and gave up his task in despair. What was he to do? He could not leave him in the road to perish. If he could but reach the village and summon help. They would not refuse assistance to a dying child, even if he were a Jew.

"Jacob," he said, encouragingly, "I am going for help. Don't be afraid; keep up your courage and strength until I come back. The rain will soon stop. Good-by. I shall not be long."

Kissing his scarcely conscious brother, the heroic boy bounded in the direction of the village.

Though the thunder still rolled and the lightning still flashed, the rain soon ceased and the clouds began to show cheerful patches of blue. Mendel was gone some five minutes when a covered *droshka* drove up the road as rapidly as the muddy ground would allow. The driver, amply protected by furs, seemed proof against both wind and water, yet he cursed in good round Russian at the inclemency of the weather. Suddenly, a brilliant flash lighted up the road, and he saw a lad near the wheels. With an oath, the driver reined in the frightened horses and jumped to the ground.

"What is it, Ivan? Has anything happened?" asked a lady, from the carriage window.

"Please your excellency, a little boy lying in the road, half-dead."

"Bring him here," commanded the lady, and the child was lifted into the carriage and placed on the seat before them.

"What a pretty lad," said the lady, who was no less important a person than the Countess Drentell, of Lubny, to her companion. "The poor child must be badly hurt."

"Perhaps a little brandy would strengthen him," suggested the practical coachman, who knew the value of the remedy.

The cordial revived him, and, opening his eyes, he murmured: "Wait for me, Mendel; I will go along."

"Drive on, Ivan, as quickly as possible; we must get the little fellow some dry clothes," said the Countess.

Yielding to the luxury of shelter and to the effect of the brandy, Jacob sank into a sweet sleep.

Mendel had in the meantime reached the village and knocked at the first house. A *moujik* emerged and eyed him suspiciously. "What do you want?" he asked, gruffly.

"We have been caught in the storm and my brother is out on the road, dying. Please help me bring him here."

"You are a Jew, are you not?" asked the man, savagely, as he recognized by the boy's jargon that he was a member of the proscribed race.

"Yes, sir," answered Mendel, timidly.

"Then go about your business; I wont put myself out for a Jew!" saying which, he shut the door in the boy's face.

Sadly Mendel wandered on until he met a kindly disposed woman, who directed him to the Jewish quarter.

"At the house of prayer there is always someone to be found," thought Mendel, and thither he bent his steps. Half-a-dozen men at once surrounded him and listened to his harrowing story; half-a-dozen hearts beat in sympathy with his distress. One of the number soon spread the dismal tidings; the entire congregation, headed by Mendel, hastened to where the child had been left. As they came to the highway, a *droshka* passed them at full speed; they fell back to the right and left to make room for the galloping horses and in a moment the carriage had disappeared.

When they reached the spot pointed out by Mendel they saw the impress of a child's form in the yielding ground, and a tattered little cap which was Jacob's; but the child was gone.

"The soldiers have recaptured him!" gasped Mendel, with a groan of anguish. "Oh, my poor brother; God help you!" and sank unconscious into the friendly arms of his new acquaintances.

CHAPTER VII

A RUSSIAN NOBLEMAN

After an hour's sojourn in "The Imperial Crown," the best inn of Poltava, Countess Drentell continued her journey towards her country-seat at Lubny, where the carriage arrived just before nightfall. With the creaking of the wheels upon the gravel path leading to the house, Jacob awoke and gazed sleepily about him.

"See, Tekla; he is awake!" cried the Countess. "Poor child!"

The carriage stopped; Ivan opened the door and assisted the ladies to alight.

"Carry the little one into the house and take him to the kitchen to dry," commanded the Countess. "What a surprise he will be to Loris and how he will enjoy having a playmate!"

Another servant appeared at the door to assist the Countess.

"Your excellency," he whispered, "the Count arrived the day before yesterday. He was furious at finding you absent."

Louise bit her lip and her face became pale. Then she

shrugged her pretty shoulders and broke into a careless laugh.

"Oh, well, Dimitri will forgive me when I tell him how sorry I am," she thought to herself, as she tripped up the stone steps into the house.

In the brilliantly lighted hall she was met by her husband, Count Dimitri Drentell, and she clasped her arms around his neck in a transport of conjugal affection.

"So you have come back, my dear, from those horrid barracks!" she cried. "I am so glad! But why didn't you send word you were coming, that I might have been at home to meet you? But it is just like you to keep the matter a perfect secret and give me no chance to prepare for your reception."

The Count's brow contracted. Before he had an opportunity to reply, his wife continued:

"Indeed, I'm glad you've come. If I had known that I was marrying a son of Mars who would be away in the army for eight months of the year, I doubt whether I should have left my happy Tiflis."

The Countess paused for want of breath.

"The Czar places duty to country higher than domestic comfort," answered her husband, curtly. "But how could you leave your home and your child for so long a time? It is now three days since I arrived here, expecting to be lovingly received by you and little Loris; but you had gone away, no one knew whither, leaving Loris in charge of an ignorant woman, who has been sadly neglecting the child."

"Poor fellow," laughed the Countess, in mock grief. "I

suppose he will be happy to see his mamma again. But, my dear, you must not scold me for having gone away. It was so dull at home without you, so lonesome, that I could bear it no longer, and I took a trip to Valki, to visit the Abbess of the convent there."

The cloud upon the Count's face darkened.

"I have repeatedly told you that I do not approve of your excursions into the country," he answered, gloomily; "and I am especially opposed to your locking yourself up in a convent. You pay no heed to my requests, nor do you seem to realize the dangers you incur in travelling about in that manner."

"Then let us live in our town house. I am too dull here, all alone," answered the Countess, nestling closer to her husband and kissing him.

"It was at your desire that I bought this place, immediately after our marriage. You were enchanted with it and said it reminded you of your Caucasian country. Now you are already tired of it."

"I would not be if you were here to share its delights with me," she answered, coquettishly. "But, alone!—b-r-r! It is too vast, too immense! I shall never feel at home in it."

Louise gave her graceful head a mournful shake and looked dismally at her husband.

Suddenly she cried: "Where is Loris? What have they done with my boy?"

"It is time you inquired," said her husband, reproachfully. "I doubt if he remembers you."

Louise broke into a merry laugh. "Not know his mamma? Indeed! We shall see!"

Going to a table, she rang a bell, which was immediately answered by a liveried servant.

"Bring me my Loris," she cried.

"He has already been put to bed," answered the man.

"Bring him, anyhow. I have not seen him for almost nine days."

The man disappeared, and shortly after a nurse entered, bearing in her arms a bright little fellow scarcely four years of age. Loris, the tyrant of the house, who was fast being spoiled by the alternate indulgence and neglect of his capricious mother, struggled violently with his nurse, who had just aroused him from his first sleep.

Louise threw herself upon the child in an excess of maternal devotion. She fairly covered him with kisses.

"How has my Loris been? My poor boy! Will he forgive his mamma for having deserted him?"

The boy resented this outburst of love by sundry kicks and screams.

"The child is cross and sleepy," said the Count; "let Minka put him to bed."

"Wait a moment," exclaimed the Countess, in childish glee. "I have brought him a present. Loris, my pet, how would you like a little boy to play with? A real live boy?"

Loris ceased his struggles and became interested.

"I want a pony to play with! I don't want a boy," he cried, peevishly.

"What folly have you been guilty of now?" asked Dimitri, with some misgivings, for he had had frequent proofs of his wife's impulsive extravagance.

"You shall see, my dear."

Louise rang for Ivan. When he appeared, she asked:

"What have you done with the boy we found?"

"He is in the kitchen and has just eaten his supper," answered the servant.

"Bring him up at once."

While Ivan went to fetch Jacob, the Countess related, with many embellishments and exaggerations, and with frequent appeals to her maid Tekla for corroboration, how she had found the boy on the road, how she had saved his life, and, finally, how she had decided to bring him home as a little playmate for her darling Loris. Before she had finished her story Jacob himself appeared upon the scene, the personification of abject misery. His features were still besmeared with the dirt of the highway, his clothes were in a wretched condition, and his bandaged arm and lacerated face did not improve his general appearance. Louise laughed heartily when this apparition entered the door.

"Is he not a beauty?" she exclaimed.

The Count was too much surprised to speak. After a pause,

during which poor Jacob looked pleadingly from one to the other, Dimitri asked:

"In all seriousness, Louise, why did you introduce that being into our house?"

"He is not as bad as he looks," answered the Countess. "Wait till he is washed and dressed, and you will agree that he is a handsome fellow."

The Count crossed the room and looked at the boy.

"What is your name?" he asked, gruffly.

"Jacob Winenki," answered the child, timidly.

"A Jew!" ejaculated the Count. "By our Holy Madonna, that is just what I needed to make me completely happy—the companionship of an accursed Jew!"

Jacob instinctively divined that he was not welcome, and began to cry.

"Please, I want my mamma!"

"Stop your whimpering, you cur!" shouted the enraged Count.

But Jacob's tears would not be checked so abruptly.

"Please don't send me back to the soldiers," he pleaded, in his miserable jargon. "I don't want to go with the soldiers."

At this juncture Loris joined in the cry. "I don't want him. I want a pony to play with."

"Here, Ivan," commanded the excited Count, "take this brat out into the barn, and keep him secure until I ask for him. We will investigate his case after supper. Minka, take Loris to bed at once." Then turning to his wife, who actually trembled before his infuriated glance, he said:

"Louise, you have done some very silly things since I married you, but this is the most absurd. You know my aversion to Jews, and here you bring a dirty Jew out of the streets to become a playmate of our Loris!"

"I could not leave the poor child to die in the road," pouted Louise, who, in addition to being extremely frivolous, was very tender-hearted. "If I had found a sick dog, I should have aided him."

"I would rather it had been a dog than a Jew."

"How could I know it was a Jew?"

"By his looks; by his language," answered the exasperated man.

"He was insensible, and could not speak," retorted Louise; "and his appearance no worse than that of other dirty children. Tell me, Dimitri," she added, throwing her arms about her husband's waist, in a childish endeavor to appease his wrath; "tell me why you have such an animosity towards the Jews?"

The count impressively rolled up his sleeve and displayed a scar about two inches in length upon his forearm.

"See, Louise," he said, gloomily; "that is some of their accursed work. Have I not cause to detest them? They are spiteful, vengeful, implacable."

Louise lovingly kissed the scarred arm.

"Poor Dimitri," she murmured; "how it must have pained. Tell me how it happened."

"There is no need to go into details," answered the Count, abruptly. "But if ever I acquire the power, I shall make a Jew smart for every drop of blood that flowed from the wound. Come, supper must be ready. We will not spoil our appetites by speaking of the despicable race."

Count Drentell wisely refrained from telling his wife the cause of his scar. It was not for a wife's ear to hear the tale. Eight years before, he, with a number of young officers of the army stationed at Pinsk, while in search of a little pleasurable excitement, had raided the Jewish quarter and terrorized the helpless inhabitants. After having broken every window, the party, inflamed by wine and enthusiasm, entered the house of Haim Kusel, demolished the furniture, helped themselves to articles of value that chanced to be exposed, and having caught a glimpse of Haim's pretty daughter, Drentell, the leader of the band, attempted to embrace her. The Jew, who had offered no resistance while his hard-earned possessions were being destroyed, was driven to frenzy by the insult to his daughter. Seizing a knife he drove the party from the house, but not until he had wounded several of the wretches, among whom was Drentell. Kusel had saved his daughter's honor, but he well knew that he had forfeited his life if he remained in the village. Packing up the few household articles that yet remained, he and his daughter fled from Pinsk to find protection with friends in a distant town.

At midnight, the officers, now reinforced by a number of sympathizing comrades, returned, and furious at the escape of their victim, burned his dwelling to the ground. Drentell never forgot his ignominious repulse nor the wound he received at the hands of Haim Kusel. His own offence counted as naught, so blunted was his moral sense. To inflict misery upon a Jew was at all times considered meritorious, but for a Jew to so far forget himself as to assault an officer of the Czar, was a crime for which the whole race would one day be held accountable.

While the Count and Countess are at supper, we may find time to examine into their past and become better acquainted with the worthy couple, into whose company the events of this story will occasionally lead us.

Dimitri was the only son of Paul Drentell, the renowned banker of St. Petersburg, who had been raised to the nobility as a reward for having negotiated a loan for the Government. Paul had been sordid and avaricious; his vast wealth was wrung from the necessities of the unfortunates Otho were obliged to borrow from him or succumb to financial disaster. Had he been a Jew, his greed, his miserly ways, his usuries, would have been stigmatized as Jewish traits, but being a devout Catholic he was spoken of as "Drentell, the financier."

The nobility of Russia counts many such upstarts among its representatives. It boasts of a peculiar historical develop-ment. The hereditary element plays an unimportant part in matters of state. Exposed to the tyranny of the Muscovite autocrats, they hailed with joy the elevation of the Romanoff family to the throne. The condition of the nobles was thenceforth bettered, their political influence increased. Under Peter the Great, however, there came a change. To noble birth, this Czar showed a most humiliating indiff-erence, and the nobles saw with horror the accession to their ranks of the lowest order of men. The condition of the aristocracy, old and new, was not, however, one of unmixed happiness. The nobles were transformed into mere servants of the Czar, and heavily did their bondage weigh upon them. After the death of the great Prince, they experienced varied changes. Catherine converted the surroundings of her court into a ludicrous imitation of the elegant and refined French *regime*. Parisian fashions and the French language were adopted by the nobility. It was a pleasure-seeking, pomp-loving aristocracy that surrounded the powerful Empress. But her capricious and violent son overturned this order of things and again reduced the nobility to a condition of dependence and even degradation, from which it had not yet recovered in the days of Nicholas I. For these reasons the nobility of Russia is not characterized by the proud bearing and firm demeanor which are the attributes of the aristocracy of Western Europe. A *parvenu*, who has, by an act of slavish submission, won the Emperor's favor, may be ennobled, and he thenceforth holds his head as high as the greatest. No one of these is regarded as more important than his neighbor. Dumouriez, having casually spoken to Nicholas of one of the considerable personages at court, received the reply:

"You must learn, sir, that the only considerable person here is the one to whom I am speaking, and that only as long as I am speaking to him."[4]

Hence, we rarely find a Russian noble who is proud of his ancestry or of his ancient name. It is wealth and power, momentary distinction and royal favor that make him of worth. When, therefore, Paul Drentell, because of his valuable services in raising a loan which enabled Russia to engage in war with one of her less powerful neighbors, was elevated to the nobility, it caused no surprise, and the banker at once began a life of pomp and extravagance which he thought suited to his new station. His wealth was fabulous, and was for the greater part invested in large estates, comprising confiscated lands, formerly the property of less fortunate nobles, who, deprived of their rank, were now atoning for their sins in the frozen North. His possessions included about twenty thousand male serfs; consequently, more than forty thousand souls.

Dimitri, upon his father's elevation, was sent to the army, where he distinguished himself in nocturnal debauches and adventures such as we have related, and where, thanks to his father's influence, he shortly rose to the rank of lieutenant.

About five years before the beginning of this story, Paul Drentell died and his vast estates, as well as his title of Count, descended to Dimitri, who now found himself one of the richest men in the Empire. He was, moreover, a personal friend of the young Czarewitch, Alexander, in whose regiment he served. To such a man, a notable future was open: great honors as Governor of a province or exile to Siberia as a dangerous power. One of the features of public life in Russia is the comparative ease with which either of these distinctions may be obtained.

Count Drentell was haughty and arrogant, caring for naught but his own personal advantage, consulting only his own tastes and pleasures. He was a stern officer to his soldiers, a cruel taskmaster to the serfs he had inherited, and a bitter foe of the Jews whom he had offended.

Very different was his wife, Louise. A Georgian by birth, her beauty and ingenuousness had won her great popularity at the court of St. Petersburg, to which she had been introduced by the Governor of Tiflis. She was neither tall nor short, possessed a wealth of raven black hair, perfect teeth, lustrous black eyes, a smile that would inspire poets and a voice that was all music and melody. When Count Drentell carried her off in the face of a hundred admirers, he was considered lucky indeed. Dimitri never confessed, even to himself, that he regretted his hasty choice. Louise was as capricious as she was beautiful, as unlettered as she was charming, as superstitious as she was fascinating. All that she did was done on impulse. She loved her husband on impulse, she deserted her child for weeks at a time on impulse, she succored the poor or neglected them on impulse. Her army of servants set her commands at defiance, for they knew them to be the outgrowth of momentary caprice.

Fortunately for the domestic happiness of the couple, the Count was with his command at St. Petersburg during two-thirds of the year, while his wife enjoyed herself as best she might on his magnificent estate at Lubny.

Brought up among the highlands of Tiflis, Louise possessed all of the unreasoning bigotry characteristic of the people inhabiting that region. She was religious to the very depths of superstition, and she chose Lubny for a dwelling-place, less for its resemblance to the sunny hills of her native province than for its proximity to several large Catholic cloisters for both monks and nuns, whence she hoped to receive that religious nourishment which her southern and impetuous nature craved. It was while returning from an expedition to the furthest of these nunneries, in which she frequently immured herself for weeks at a time, that she found Jacob upon the road.

The Count, who, with the companions of his youth, had lost what little religious sentiment he may have once possessed, regarded this trait in his wife with great disfavor; but neither threats nor prayers effected a change, and he finally allowed her to follow her own inclinations.

While the union was not one of the happiest, there were fewer altercations than might have been reasonably expected from the thoroughly opposite natures of man and wife.

Louise, with all her faults, was a loving wife, and when her husband's temper was ruffled, her smiles and caresses, her appealing looks and tender glances, won him back to serenity.

The supper, therefore, was not as gloomy as the stormy introduction indicated. Both had much to tell each other, for a great deal had occurred during their eight months' separation, and it was late when they left the table.

FOOTNOTES:

[Footnote 4: Wallace's "Russia."]

CHAPTER VIII

AN UNWILLING CONVERT TO CHRISTIANITY

On the following morning the Count bethought himself of the Jewish lad, and the reflection that he had harbored one of the despised people on his estates for an entire night, rekindled his anger against the whole race. He rang for Ivan and strode impatiently up and down his well-furnished library until the coachman appeared.

"Tell the Countess that I await her here, and then bring me the boy you found on the road!"

Both Louise and Jacob made their appearance shortly after. Jacob had been washed and his hair combed, and not even the Count could deny that he was a lad of uncommon beauty.

"What is your name?" interrogated the Count, with the air of a grand inquisitor.

"Jacob Winenki."

"Where do you live?"

"In the Jew lane," answered the child, slowly.

"But where? In what town?"

Jacob hung his head. He did not know.

"How did you come here?" was the next query.

Then Jacob related, with childish hesitancy, how the soldiers stole him and his brother from home and took them to a big city, and how he and Mendel ran away and were caught in a storm. Further information he could not give, having no recollection of anything that happened from the time of his lying upon the highway until he found himself in the *droshka* with the ladies.

"You say that the soldiers came to your house and took you and your brother away?" asked the Count.

"Yes, sir."

"What did they want with you?"

"One of them said he would make *goyim* (gentiles) of us," answered the boy, in his native jargon.

"I see," said Count Drentell, as the truth dawned upon him; "you were taken to become recruits. So you escaped!"

"Please, sir, Mendel and I ran away. We wanted to go home to father and mother."

"Were there more boys with you?"

"Yes, sir."

"Did they run away, too?"

"I don't know."

"There is not much information to be obtained from the child," said Drentell, angrily. Then pointing to the boy's face and arm, he asked:

"Did that happen to you on the road?"

"Oh, no; that happened at home," answered Jacob, tearfully; and he related the story of the cow and the farmer, the details of which were too deeply impressed upon his memory to be soon forgotten.

Louise understood the jargon of the boy but imperfectly, still her sympathetic nature comprehended that the boy had been seriously hurt, and she asked her husband to repeat the story of his injuries.

"Poor fellow," she exclaimed, wiping away a tear. "How cruelly he has been treated!"

"I suppose it served him right," answered the Count, rudely. "Who knows what he had been guilty of. One never knows whether a Jew is lying or telling the truth."

In spite of his doubts upon the subject, Drentell examined the boy's arm. It was evident that the bone had been broken, and that the fracture had been imperfectly set. After a short inspection, he hazarded an opinion that the boy would have a stiff arm all his life.

"It was almost well," sobbed Jacob, "but the soldiers pulled me about so that it is now much worse."

"Poor boy," sighed the Countess, "how dreadful it must be! Can we do nothing for him?"

"In the name of St. Nicholas, Louise, cease this sentimental whimpering," retorted her husband, losing patience.

"But think of a stiff arm through life, and his ear almost torn off! It is terrible to carry such mutilations to the grave."

"It does not matter much," answered the Count, "he is a Jew."

"True, I had forgotten that. It does make a great difference, does it not?" And the impulsive little woman dried her eyes and smilingly forgot her compassion.

"What will you do with him?" she asked, after a pause.

"I don't know. The wisest plan would be to deliver him up to military headquarters. He was taken from home to be a recruit, and having escaped from the Czar's soldiers, I would be derelict in my duty if I did not at once send him back."

At the word "soldiers," Jacob, who had caught but a few stray words of the conversation, began to howl and shriek.

"No, don't send me back to the soldiers," he pleaded. "They will kill me! Please don't send me back!"

"Stop your crying," thundered the Count, stopping his ears with his hands to keep out the disagreeable sounds, "or I will call the soldiers at once."

This terrible threat had the desired effect, and Jacob, gulping down his grief, remained quiet save for an occasional sob that would not be repressed.

"Listen, Dimitri," said the Countess. "I found the boy insensible in the storm. He is sick and weak. Of what service can a child like that be among the soldiers? Under rough treatment he would die in a week. Even though he be a Jew, there is no use in sacrificing his life uselessly."

"But we can't keep him here," urged the Count.

"There is no need of his remaining at Lubny. The principal motive in taking Jewish children from their homes is to make Christians of them. That can certainly be better accomplished at a cloister than in camp. Send the boy to the convent at Poltava; they will baptize him and make a good Catholic of him, and we will gain our reward in heaven for having led one erring soul to the Saviour." And the religious woman crossed herself devoutly.

While his wife argued, Drentell appeared lost in thought. Suddenly his face became illumined by a fiendish light, and he rubbed his hands in evident satisfaction.

"Louise," he said, at length, "those are the first sensible words I have heard you utter since we were married. Your idea is a capital one!"

"I am glad you think so," she replied, wisely refraining from commenting upon her husband's doubtful compliment. "The Abbess at Valki told me only the day before yesterday, that for every soul brought into the holy church, a Christian's happiness would be increased tenfold in Paradise."

"Fanatical absurdities," cried the Count, who was as free from religious sentiment as his wife was devout. "If I consent to have the child brought up in a convent, I am not actuated by any considerations of future reward or punishment. I don't believe in such antiquated dogmas. But to the convent he shall go, and when they have taught him to forget his origin and his religion, when they have educated him into a fanatical, Jew-hating priest, then will I use him to wreak upon his own race that vengeance which I have sworn never to forego."

Louise shuddered at her husband's vehement gestures and passionate words. His eyes rolled wildly, his whole body seemed swayed by uncontrollable rage. Little Jacob, although he understood nothing of the Count's words, recoiled instinctively and hid his face in his hands.

Drentell gradually regained his composure, and after walking up and down the room for a few moments, in apparent meditation, he rang the bell.

A servant entered.

"Take the boy back to the barn, and keep him there until I ask for him again," he commanded. "Then harness up at once and send for *Batushka* Alexei, the Abbot of the convent at Poltava. Tell his reverence that I desire to see him as soon as possible on matters pertaining to the holy church."

The servant disappeared, taking Jacob with him, and the Count and Countess were left alone to discuss their plans.

It was almost night when the vehicle containing the Abbot rolled up to the villa, and the *batushka* (priest) was announced. He was a powerfully built man, displaying a physique of which a Roman gladiator might have been proud. His grizzled beard reached down to his waist, and his flowing black robes gave him the appearance of a dervish. Alexei enjoyed the reputation of being very devout, and the cloister of which he was the head was known as the most thoroughly religious in the Empire. To this man the future of the Jewish lad was to be entrusted.

When the holy man entered the library, both the Count and his wife crossed themselves reverently.

"Your excellency has sent for me," said Alexei, slowly.

"Yes, *batushka*," answered the Count. "We wish to place in your pious care a young Jewish boy who, having escaped from his parents' roof, and having much to fear from the anger of his people, desires to seek present safety and ultimate salvation of his soul in the bosom of our holy church. I at once thought of you, as I believe that under your tuition the lad will be instructed in all that is essential to the perfect Christian."

"Your excellency does me too much honor," said the priest, meekly. "With the grace of our Lord Christ, I shall do my utmost to bring this lamb into the fold."

"The boy is feverish and his mind wanders," continued the Count. "If you interrogate him, he will tell you that he received certain injuries—a broken arm and a mutilated ear—from the Christians. I happen to be conversant with the facts of the case and know that he was injured by members of his own family, in their impotent frenzy to keep him from seeking the solace of the only saving church. I desire you to remember three things, *batushka*: Firstly, that this boy must be taught to forget absolutely that he belongs to that accursed people; secondly, the idea must be firmly implanted in his mind that he has been mutilated by the Jews; and thirdly, he must be taught to despise and detest the Hebrew race with all the hatred of which his soul is capable. Do you understand me?"

"I do, your excellency. You desire the boy to so far forget his former associations, that he will belong heart and soul to the church of Christ; and as a further precaution that he may never harbor a desire to return to the religion of his fathers, you desire us to impress him with an implacable hatred, a thirst for revenge against his race, for wrongs they have inflicted upon him."

The Count looked at the priest significantly; they had understood one another.

"You will find the boy docile," continued Drentell, "and unless he belies the characteristics of his people, you will find him quick and intelligent. Employ that intelligence for the good of our holy faith and to the prejudice of the Jewish race. Give him every advantage, every inducement to advance, and shape his career so that in him the church will find a faithful supporter and an earnest champion."

"And the Jews an enemy before whom the stoutest of their number shall quail," continued the priest. "So shall it be, your excellency."

"I shall expect to receive occasional reports of his progress. Let him be taught to respect me as his benefactor, and once a year I desire him to spend a week or two with me, in order that by wise counsels and salutary advice, I may assist the holy church in her noble work. Remember, too," and here the Count's features assumed a threatening look, "that this act of to-day is done by the authority of his majesty the Czar, who will hold you accountable for the strict observance of all you have promised."

The priest bowed his head humbly.

"I reverence the church, your excellency," he answered, "but above all I owe allegiance to its spiritual head, the Czar."

All preliminaries having been arranged, Jacob was sent for.

The priest, who not unnaturally expected to see a young man, was greatly surprised at the appearance of this puny child. He concealed his astonishment as well as possible, merely observing:

"I presume, your excellency, this is my future pupil."

"It is, and may he prove worthy of his eminent teacher."

"Come, my boy," said the priest, taking the mystified Jacob by the hand; "say good-by to your benefactors."

But Jacob, upon whom the sombre-robed, grim-visaged stranger did not make a favorable impression, broke from his hold and took refuge in the skirts of the Countess, as the most compassionate of the company.

"Don't let them take me away," he sobbed. "Let me remain with you."

"Be a good boy and he will take you home to your papa and mamma," said the Countess, with the best intentions in the world.

"Will he take me to Mendel?" asked the boy.

"Yes, he is going there now and will take you to all your friends."

The child wiped away his tears and a smile rippled over his face. He put his hand confidingly into that of the priest, and said:

"Come, I will go with you."

The priest, in spite of his fanaticism, took the poor Jew in his arms and kissed him tenderly. Then setting him again upon his feet, he whispered:

"I shall take him to a kind and loving mother, one from whose embrace he will not care to flee—the Holy Mother of God."

Jacob entered the wagon with his new acquaintance, and in the belief that he was going direct to the home of his parents, he fell asleep. When he awoke, he found himself borne by strong arms into the convent, whose doors closed upon him, separating him forever from his home and his religion.

CHAPTER IX

A MIRACULOUS CURE

Let us return to Mendel.

The unconscious boy was carried to the village by the sympathizing Israelites of Poltava. When he recovered his senses he found himself safely sheltered in the house of Reb Sholem, the *parnas* (president of the congregation). It was a pleasure to find kind sympathy, a warm room and a substantial meal, after the hardships of the last few days; but the constant recollection of Jacob's disappearance, the reproaches which Mendel heaped upon himself for having deserted his brother, left him no peace of mind.

The Jews of Poltava displayed their practical sympathy by dividing into groups and scouring the village and the surrounding country, in hopes of finding some clue to the whereabouts of the boy. He might even now be wandering through the fields. Night, however, found them all gathered at Reb Sholem's house, sorrowful and disheartened, as not a trace of the missing lad had been discovered. Mendel retired in a state of fever and tossed restlessly about on his bed during the entire night. He was moved by but one desire—to get to his uncle at Kief as quickly as possible. In the morning he informed his host of his plans. A carrier of the village, who drove his team to within a few versts of Kief, was induced, upon the payment of an exorbitant sum, to take the boy as a passenger, and at dawn next morning they started upon their slow and tedious journey, followed by the good wishes of the Jewish community. It was an all-day trip to Kief. Over stone and stubble, through ditch and mire moved the lumbering, springless vehicle, and Mendel, who quitted Poltava with an incipient fever, arrived at his destination in a state of utter exhaustion. The carrier set him down at the outskirts of the town. It was as much as his position was worth to have harbored a Jew—a fugitive from the military at that—and slowly and painfully Mendel found his way through the strange city, to the Jewish quarter. Every soldier that crossed his path inspired him with terror; it might be some one charged with his recapture. Not until he reached his destination did he deem himself safe.

To the south-east of the city, stretched along the Dnieper, lay the Jewish settlement of almost fifteen thousand souls. The most dismal, unhealthy portion of the town had in days gone by been selected as its location. The decree of the *mir* had fixed its limits in the days of Peter the Great, and its boundaries could not be extended, no matter how rapidly the population might increase, no matter how great a lack of room, of air, of light there might be for future generations. The houses were, therefore, built as closely together as possible, without regard to comfort or sanitary needs. To each was added new rooms, as the necessities of the inhabiting family demanded, and these additions hung like excrescences from all sides of the ugly huts, like toadstools to decaying logs. Every inch of ground was precious to the ever-increasing settlement. It was a labyrinth of narrow, dirty streets, of unpainted, unattractive, dilapidated houses, a lasting monument of hatred and persecution, of bigotry and prejudice. Mendel gasped for a breath of fresh air, and, feeling himself grow faint, he hurried onward and inquired the way to Hirsch Bensef's house. A plain, unpretentious structure was pointed out and Mendel knocked at the door.

Hirsch himself opened the door. For a moment he stood undecided, scarcely recognizing in the form before him, his chubby nephew of a week ago. Then he opened his arms and drew the little fellow to his breast.

"Is it indeed you, Mendel?" he cried. "*Sholem alechem!* (Peace be with you!) God be praised that He has brought you to us!" and he led the boy into the room and closed the door.

"Miriam," he called to his wife, who was engaged in her household duties in an adjoining room; "quick, here is our boy, our Mendel. I knew he would come."

Mendel was lovingly embraced by his cheerful-looking aunt, whom he had never seen, but whom he loved from that moment.

"What ails you, my boy? You look ill; your head is burning," said Miriam, anxiously.

"Yes, aunt; I fear I shall be sick," answered Mendel, faintly.

"Nonsense; we will take care of that," replied Hirsch. "But where is Jacob?"

Mendel burst into tears, the first he had shed since his enforced departure from home. In as few words as possible he told his story, accompanied by the sobs and exclamations of his hearers. In conclusion, he added:

"Either Jacob wandered away in his delirium and is perhaps dead in some deserted place, or else the soldiers have recaptured him and have taken him back to Kharkov."

"Rather he be dead than among the inhuman Cossacks at the barracks," returned his uncle. "God in His mercy does all things for the best!"

"The poor boy must be starving," said Miriam, and she set the table with the best the house afforded, but Mendel could touch nothing.

"It looks tempting, but I cannot eat," he said. "I have no appetite."

The poor fellow stretched himself on a large sofa, where he lay so quiet, so utterly exhausted, that Hirsch and his wife looked at each other anxiously and gravely shook their heads.

A casual stranger would not have judged from the unpretentious exterior of Bensef's house, that its proprietor was in possession of considerable means, that every room was furnished in taste and even luxury, that works of oriental art were hidden in its recesses. Persecuted during generations by the jealous and covetous nations surrounding them, the Jews learned to conceal their wealth beneath the mask of poverty. Robbers, in the guise of uniformed soldiery and decorated officers of the Czar, stalked in broad daylight to relieve the despised Hebrew of his superfluous wealth, and thus it happened that the poorest hut was often the depository of gold and silver, of artistic utensils, which were worthy of the table of the Czar himself. Nor was this fact entirely unknown to the surrounding Christians. Not unfrequently were persecutions the outcome of the absurd idea that every Jewish hovel was the abode of riches, and that every hut where misery held court, where starving children cried for bread, was a mine of untold wealth. The condition of the race has changed in some of the more civilized countries, but in Russia these barbarous notions still prevail.

Hirsch Bensef, by untiring energy and perseverance as a dealer in curios and works of art, had become one of the wealthiest and most influential men in the community. He was *parnas* of the great congregation of Kief, and was respected, not only by his co-religionists, but also by the nobles with whom he transacted the greater portion of his business.

His wife, who had in her youth been styled the "Beautiful Miriam," even now, after twelve years of married life, was still a handsome woman. Her dark eyes shone with the same bewitching fire; her beautiful hair had, in accordance with the orthodox Jewish custom, fallen under the shears on the day of her marriage, but the silken band and string of pearls that henceforth decked her brow did not detract from her oriental beauty. Hirsch was proud of her and he would have been completely happy if God had vouchsafed her a son. Like Hannah, she prayed night and morning to the Heavenly throne. Such was the family in whose bosom Mendel had found a refuge.

After a while, the boy asked for a glass of water, which he swallowed eagerly. Then he asked:

"When did you leave Togarog, uncle; and how are father and mother?"

Bensef sighed at the recollection of the sad parting and tearfully related the events of that memorable night.

"After the soldiers had carried you off," he said, "the little band that followed you to the confines of the village, returned sorrowful to their homes. I need not tell you of our misery. It appeared as though God had turned his face from his chosen people. We spent the night in prayer and lamentations. In every house the inhabitants put on mourning, for whatever might befall the children, to their parents they were irretrievably lost."

"Poor papa! poor mamma!" murmured Mendel, wiping away a tear.

"On the following morning," continued Bensef; "all the male *Jehudim* went to Alexandrovsk and implored an audience of the Governor. He sent us word that he would hold no conference with Jews and threatened us all with Siberia if we did not at once return home. What could we do? I bade your parents farewell, and after promising to do all in my power to find and succor you and Jacob, I left them and returned home, where I arrived yesterday. Thank God that you, at least, are safe from harm."

Mendel nestled closer to his uncle, who affectionately stroked his fevered brow.

"Oh! why does God send us such sufferings?" moaned the boy.

"Be patient, my child. It is through suffering that we will in the end attain happiness. When afflictions bear most heavily upon us, then will the Messiah come!"

This hope was ever the anchor which preserved the chosen people when the storms of misfortune threatened to destroy them. The belief in the eventual coming of a redeemer who would lead them to independence, and for whose approach trials, misery and persecution were but a necessary prepa-ration, has been the great secret of Israel's strength and endurance.

During the evening, a number of Bensef's intimate friends visited the house and were told Mendel's history. The news of his arrival soon spread through the community, awakening everywhere the liveliest sympathy. Many parents had been bereft of their children in the self-same way and still mourned the absence of their first-born, whom the cruel decree of Nicholas had condemned to the rigors of some military outpost. Mendel became the hero of Kief, while he lay tossing in bed, a prey to high fever.

In spite of the care that was lavished upon him, he steadily grew worse. Fear, hunger, exposure and self-reproach had been too much for his youthful frame. For several days Miriam administered her humble house-remedies, but they were powerless to relieve his sufferings. The hot tea which he was made to drink, only served to augment the fever.

On the fifth day, Mendel was decidedly in a dangerous condition. He was delirious. The doctors in the Jewish community were consulted, but were powerless to effect a cure. Bensef and his wife were in despair.

"What shall we do?" said Miriam, sadly. "We cannot let the boy die."

"Die?" cried Hirsch, becoming pale at the thought. "Oh, God, do not take the boy! He has wound himself about my heart. Oh, God, let him live!"

"Come, husband, praying is of little avail," answered his practical wife; "we must have a *feldsher*" (doctor).

"A *feldsher* in the Jewish community? Why, Miriam, are you out of your mind? Have you forgotten how, when Rabbi Jeiteles was lying at the point of death, no amount of persuasion could induce a doctor to come into the quarter. 'Let the Jews die,' they answered to our entreaties; 'there will still be too many of them!'"

Miriam sighed. She remembered it well.

"What persuasion would not do, money may accomplish," she said, after a pause. "Hirsch, that boy must not die. He must live to be a credit to us and a comfort to our old age. You have money—what gentile ever resisted it?"

"I will do what I can," said the man, gloomily. "But even though I could bring one to the house, what good can he do. It is merely an experiment with the best of them. They will take our money, make a few magical incantations, prescribe a useless drug, and leave their patient to the mercy of Fate."

Hirsch Bensef was right. At the time of which we speak, medicine could scarcely be classed among the sciences in Russia, and if we accept the statement of modern travellers, the situation is not much improved at the present day. The scientific doctor of Russia was the *feldsher* or army surgeon, whose sole schooling was obtained among the soldiery and whose knowledge did not extend beyond dressing wounds and giving an occasional dose of physic. Upon being called to the bedside of a patient, he adopted an air of profound learning, asked a number of unimportant questions, prescribed an herb or drug of doubtful efficacy, and charged an exorbitant fee. The patient usually refused to take the medicine and recovered. It sometimes happened that he took the prescribed dose and perhaps recovered, too. On a level with the *feldsher* and much preferred by the peasantry, stood the *snakharka*, a woman, half witch, half quack, who was regarded by the *moujiks* with the greatest veneration. By means of herbs and charms, she could accomplish any cure short of restoring life to a corpse. "The *snakharka* and the *feldsher* represent two very different periods in the history of medical science—the magical and the scientific. The Russian peasantry have still many conceptions which belong to the former. The majority of them are now quite willing, under ordinary circumstances, to use the scientific means of healing, but as soon as a violent epidemic breaks out and scientific means prove unequal to the occasion, the old faith revives and recourse is had to magical rites and incantations."[5]

Neither of these systems was regarded favorably by the Hebrews. The *feldshers* were, by right of their superior knowledge, an arrogant class; and it was suspected that on more than one occasion they had hastened the death of a Jew under treatment, instead of relieving him. The Israelites were equally suspicious of the *snakharkas*; not because they were intellectually above the superstitions of their times, but because the incantations and spells were invariably pronounced in the name of the Virgin Mary, and no Jew could be reasonably expected to recover under such treatment.

What was to be done for poor Mendel? Hirsch, assisted by suggestions from his wife, cogitated long and earnestly. Suddenly Miriam found a solution of the difficulty.

"Why not send to Rabbi Eleazer at Tchernigof?"

Hirsch gazed at his wife in silent admiration.

"To the *bal-shem*?" he asked.

"Why not? When Chune Benefski's little boy was so sick that they thought he was already dead, a parchment blessed by the *bal-shem* brought him back to life. Is Mendel less to you than your own son would be?"

"God forbid," said Hirsch; then added, reflectively: "but to-day is Thursday. It will take a day and a half to reach Tchernigof, and the messenger will arrive there just before

Shabbes. He cannot start on his return until Saturday evening, and by the time he got back Mendel would be cold in death. No; it is too far!"

"*Shaute!*" (Nonsense!) ejaculated his wife, who was now warmed up to the subject. "Do you imagine the *bal-shem* cannot cure at a distance as well as though he were at the patient's bedside? Lose no time. God did not deliver Mendel out of the hands of the soldiers to let him die in our house."

One of the most fantastic notions of Cabalistic teaching was that certain persons, possessing a clue to the mysterious powers of nature, were enabled to control its laws, to heal the sick, to compel even the Almighty to do their behests. Such a man, such a miracle worker, was called a *bal-shem.*

That a *bal-shem* should thrive and grow fat is a matter of course, for consultations were often paid for in gold. To the wonder-working Rabbi travelled all those who had a petition to bring to the Throne of God—the old and decrepit who desired to defraud the grave of a few miserable years; the unfortunate who wished to improve his condition; the oppressed who yearned for relief from a tyrannical task-master; the father who prayed for a husband for his fast aging daughter; the sick, the halt, the maim, the malcontent, the egotist—all sought the aid, the mediation of the holy man. He refused no one his assistance, declined no one's proffered gifts.

It was finally decided to send to the *bal-shem* to effect Mendel's cure. But time was pressing, Mendel was growing visibly worse and Tchernigof was a long way off!

Hirsch rose to go in search of a messenger.

"Whom will you send?" asked his wife, accompanying him

to the door.

"The beadle, Itzig Maier, of course," rang back Hirsch's answer, as he strode rapidly down the street.

Let us accompany him to Itzig Maier's house, situated in the poorest quarter of Kief. In a narrow lane stood a low, dingy, wooden hut, whose boards were rotting with age. The little windows were covered for the most part with greased paper in lieu of the panes that had years ago been destroyed, and scarcely admitted a stray beam of sunlight into the room. The door, which was partially sunken into the earth, suggesting the entrance to a cave, opened into the one room of the house, which served at once as kitchen and dormitory. It was damp, foul and unhealthy, scarcely a fit dwelling-place for the emaciated cat, which sat lazily at the entrance. The floor was innocent of boards or tiles, and was wet after a shower and dry during a drought. The walls were bare of plaster. It was a stronghold of poverty. Misery had left her impress upon everything within that wretched enclosure. Yet here it was that Itzig Maier, his wife, and five children lived and after a fashion thrived. In one respect he was more fortunate than most of his neighbors; his hut possessed the advantage of housing but one family, whereas many places, not a whit more spacious or commodious, furnished a dwelling to three or four. The persecutions which limited the Jewish quarter to certain defined boundaries, the intolerance which prohibited the Jews from possessing or cultivating land, or from acquiring any trade or profession, were to blame for this wretchedness.

A brief review of the past career of our new acquaintance, Itzig Maier, will give us a picture of the unfortunate destiny of thousands of Russian Jews.

Itzig had studied Talmud until he had attained his eighteenth year. But lacking originality he lapsed into a mere automaton. His eighteenth year found him a sallow-visaged, slovenly lad, ignorant of all else but the Holy Law. His anxious and loving parents began to think seriously of his future. Almost nineteen years of age and not yet married! It was preposterous! A *schadchen* (match-maker) was brought into requisition and a wife obtained for the young man. What mattered it that she was a mere child, unlettered and unfit for the solemn duties of wife and mother? What mattered it that the young people had never met before and had no inclination for each other? "It is not good for man to be alone," said the parents, and the prospective bride and bridegroom were simply not consulted. The girl's straggling curls succumbed to the shears; a band of silk, the insignia of married life, was placed over her brow, and the fate of two inexperienced children was irrevocably fixed; they were henceforth man and wife.

Both parents of Itzig Maier died shortly after the nuptials and the young man inherited a small sum of money, the meagre earnings of years, and the miserable hut which had for generations served as the family homestead. For a brief period the couple lived carelessly and contentedly; but, alas! the little store of wealth gradually decreased. Itzig's fingers, unskilled in manual labor, could not add to it nor prevent its melting away. He knew nothing but Law and Talmud and his chances for advancement were meagre, indeed. After the last rouble had been spent, Itzig sought refuge in the great synagogue, where as beadle he executed any little duties for which the services of a pious man were required—sat up with the sick, prayed for the dead, trimmed the lamps and swept the floor of the House of Worship; in return for which he thankfully accepted the gifts of the charitably inclined. His wife, when she was not occupied with the care of her rapidly growing family, cheerfully assisted in swelling the family fund by peddling vegetables and fruit from door to door.

Oh, the misery of such an existence! Slowly and drearily day followed day and time itself moved with leaden soles. There were many such families, many such hovels in Kief; for although thrift and economy, prudence and good management are pre-eminently Jewish qualities, yet they are not infrequently absent and their place usurped by neglect with its attendant misery.

In spite of privations, however, life still possessed a charm for Itzig Maier. At times the wedding of a wealthy Jew, or the funeral of some eminent man, demanded his services and for a week or more money would be plentiful and happiness reign supreme.

Hirsch Bensef entered the hut and found Jentele, Maier's wife, perspiring over the hearth which occupied one corner of the room. She was preparing a meal of boiled potatoes. A sick child was tossing restlessly in an improvised cradle, which in order to save room was suspended from a hook in the smoke-begrimed ceiling. Several children were squalling in the lane before the house.

"*Sholem alechem*," said the woman, as she saw the stranger stoop and enter the door-way, and wiping her hands upon her greasy gown, she offered Hirsch a chair.

"Where is your husband?" asked Hirsch, gasping for breath, for the heat and the malodorous atmosphere were stifling.

"Where should he be but in the synagogue?" said Jentele, as she went to rock the cradle, for the child had begun to cry and fret at the sight of the stranger.

"Is the child sick?" asked Bensef, advancing to the cradle

and observing the poor half-starved creature struggling and whining for relief.

"Yes, it is sick. God knows whether it will recover. It is dying of hunger and thirst and I have no money to buy it medicines or nourishment."

"Does your husband earn nothing?"

"Very little. There have been no funerals and no weddings for several months."

"Can you not earn anything?"

"How can I? I must cook for my little ones and watch my ailing child."

"Are your children of no service to you?"

"My oldest girl, Beile, is but seven years old. She does all she can to help me, but it is not much," answered Jentele, irritably.

Hirsch sighed heavily and drawing out his purse, he placed a gold coin in the woman's hand.

"Here, take this," he said, "and provide for the child." He thought of Mendel at home and tears almost blinded him. "Carry the boy out into the air; this atmosphere is enough to kill a healthy person. Well, God be with you!" and Hirsch hurriedly left the the house.

He found the man he was seeking at the synagogue. Poverty and privation, hunger and care, had undertaken the duties of time and had converted this person into a decrepit ruin while yet in the prime of life.

Without unnecessary delay, for great was the need of haste, Hirsch unfolded his plans, and Itzig, in consideration of a sum of money, consented to undertake the journey at once. The money, destined as a gift to the *bal-shem*, was securely strapped about his waist, and arrangements were made with a *moujik*, who was going part of the way, to carry Itzig on his wagon.

"Get there as soon as possible, and by all means before *Shabbes*!" were Bensef's parting words.

In the meantime not a little sympathy was manifested for the unfortunate lad. Bensef's house was crowded during the entire day. Every visitor brought a slight token of love—a cake, a cup of jelly, a leg of a chicken; but Mendel could eat nothing and the good things remained untouched. There was no lack of advice as to the boy's treatment. Everyone had a recipe or a drug to offer, all of which Miriam wisely refused to administer. There was at one time quite a serious dispute in the room adjoining the sick-chamber. Hinka Kierson, a stout, red-faced matron, asserted that cold applications were most efficacious in fevers of this nature, while Chune Benefski, whose son had had a similar attack, and who was therefore qualified to speak upon the subject, insisted that cold applications meant instant death, and that nothing could relieve the boy but a hot bath. Miriam quieted the disputants by promising to try both remedies. To her credit be it said, she applied neither, but pinned her entire faith upon the coming remedy of the *bal-shem*.

Friday noon came but it brought no improvement. He continued delirious and his mind dwelt upon his recent trials, at one moment struggling against unseen enemies and the next calling piteously upon his brother Jacob.

Hirsch and Miriam could witness his suffering no longer, but went to their own room and gave free vent to the tears which would not be repressed.

"Oh, if the answer from the Rabbi were but here," sighed Miriam.

"Itzig will have just arrived in Tchernigof," said her husband, despondingly. "We can expect no answer until Monday morning."

"And must we sit helpless in the meantime?" sobbed Miriam, through her tears.

The door opened and a woman living in the neighborhood entered to inquire after the patient.

"See, Miriam," she said, "when I was feverish last year after my confinement, a *snakharka* gave me this bark with which to make a tea. I used a part of it and you remember how quickly I recovered. Here is all I have left. Try it on your boy; it can't hurt him and with God's help it will cure him."

Yes, Miriam remembered how ill her neighbor had been and how rapid had been her convalescence. She took the bark and examined it curiously, made the tea and administered a portion without any visible effect.

"Continue to give it to him regularly until it is all gone," said the neighbor, and she went home to prepare for the Sabbath.

Miriam, too, had her house to put in order and to prepare the table for the following day; but for the first time the gold and silver utensils, the snow-white linen—the luxurious essentials of the Sabbath table—failed to give her pleasure. What did all her wealth avail her if Mendel must die! Her husband sat apathetically at the boy's bedside, watching his flushed face and listening to his delirious raving. The end seemed near. The boy asked for drink and Miriam gave him more of the tea.

Five o'clock sounded from the tower of a near-by church and Hirsch arose to dress for the house of prayer. *Shabbes* must not be neglected, happen what may. Suddenly there was an unusual commotion in the narrow lane in which stood Bensef's house. The door was hastily thrown open and in rushed Itzig, the messenger to Tchernigof, followed by a dozen excited, gesticulating friends.

Bensef ran to meet them, but when he saw his messenger already returned his countenance fell.

"For God's sake, what is the matter? Why are you not in Tchernigof?" he said.

"I was," retorted Itzig, "but I have come back. Here," he continued, opening a bag about his neck and carefully drawing therefrom a small piece of parchment covered with hieroglyphics, "put this under the boy's tongue and he will recover!"

"But what is this paper?" asked Hirsch, suspiciously.

"It is from the *bal-shem.* Don't ask so many questions, but do as I tell you! Put it under the boy's tongue before the Sabbath or it will be of no avail!"

Hirsch looked from Itzig to the ever-increasing crowd that was peering in through the open door. Then he gazed at the parchment. It was about two inches square and covered with mystic signs which none understood, but the power of which none doubted. In the margin was written in Hebrew, "In the name of the Lord—Rabbi Eleazer."

There was no time for idle curiosity. Hirsch ran into the patient's presence with the precious talisman and placed it under the boy's tongue.

"There, my child," he whispered; "the *bal-shem* sends you this. By to-morrow you will be cured."

The boy, whose fever appeared already broken, opened his eyes and, looking gratefully at Hirsch, answered:

"Yes, dear uncle, I shall soon be well," and fell into a deep sleep.

Hirsch closed the door softly and went out to his friends. The excitement was intense and the crowd was steadily growing, for the news had spread that Itzig Maier had been to Tchernigof and back in less than two days.

"Tell us about it, Itzig," they clamored. "How is it possible that you could do it?" But Itzig waved them back and not until Hirsch Bensef came out from the sick chamber did he deign to speak. Then his tongue became loosened, and to the awe and amazement of his listeners he related his wonderful adventures. He told them that, having left the wagon half-way to Tchernigof, he had walked the rest of the distance, reaching his destination that very morning at eleven o'clock. The holy man, being advised by mysterious power of his expected arrival, awaited him at the door and said: "Itzig, thou hast come about a sick boy at Kief." The *bal-shem* then gave him a parchment already written, and told him to return home at once and apply the remedy before *Shabbes*, otherwise the spell would lose its efficacy.

"Then," continued the messenger, "I said, 'Rabbi, this is Friday noon; it takes almost a day and a half to reach Kief. How can I get there by *Shabbes*?' Then he answered,

'Thinkest thou that I possess the power to cure a dying man and not to send thee home before the Sabbath? Begin thy journey at once and on foot and thou shalt be in Kief before night.' Then I gave him the present I had brought and started out upon my homeward journey. I appeared to fly. It seemed as though I was suspended in the air, and trees, fields and villages passed me in rapid succession. This continued until about a half hour ago, when I suddenly found myself before Kief and at once hastened here with the parchment."

This incredible story produced different effects upon the auditors present.

"It is wonderful," said one. "The *bal-shem* knows the mysteries of God."

"I don't believe a word of it," shouted another; "such things are impossible."

"But we have proof of it before us," cried a third. "Itzig could not have returned by natural means."

Then a number of the men related similar occurrences for which they could vouch, or which had taken place in the experience of their parents, and the gathering broke up into little groups, each gesticulating, relating or explaining. The excitement was indescribable.

Bensef laid his hand upon Itzig's shoulder and led him aside.

"Look at me, Itzig," he commanded. "I want to know the truth. Is what you have just related exactly true."

"To be sure it is. If you doubt it, go to the *bal-shem* and ask him yourself."

"Do you swear by—" Then checking himself, Hirsch muttered: "We will see. If the boy recovers, I will believe you."

When Itzig arrived at the synagogue that evening, he was the cynosure of all eyes, and it is safe to say that there was not in Kief a Jewish household in which the wonderful story was not repeated and commented upon.

Mendel recovered with marvellous rapidity. Whether his improvement was due to the Peruvian bark which the kind-hearted neighbor had brought, or to the power of the Cabalistic writing, or to the psychological influence of faith in the *bal-shem's* power, it is not for us to decide, but certain it is that Rabbi Eleazer received full credit for the cure and his already great reputation spread through Russia.

The fact that Itzig, whose poverty had been notorious, now occasionally indulged in expenditures requiring the outlay of considerable money, caused a rumor to spread that the worthy messenger had gone no further than the village of Navrack, where he himself prepared the parchment and then returned with the wonderful story of his trip through the air and with his fortune augmented to the extent of Bensef's present to the Rabbi. Envious people were not wanting who gave ear to this unkind rumor and even helped to spread it. But the fact that Mendel had been snatched from the jaws of death was sufficient vindication for Itzig, who for a long time enjoyed great honors at Kief.

FOOTNOTES:

[Footnote 5: Wallace, p. 77.]

CHAPTER X

MENDEL THINKS FOR HIMSELF

Mendel's fondness for study determined his future career. Nowhere were there such opportunities for learning the Talmud as in Kief. Its numerous synagogues, its eminent rabbis, its large Hebrew population, made it the centre of Judaism in Southern Russia. In its schools some of the most learned rabbis of the Empire had studied.

Throughout the whole of Russia there were, at the time of which we speak, but few universities, and these scarcely deserved to rank above second-rate colleges. Education was within the reach of very few. At the present day, "the merchants do not even possess the rudiments of an education. Many of them can neither read nor write and are forced to keep their accounts in their memory, or by means of ingenious hieroglyphics, intelligible only to their inventors. Others can decipher the calendar and the lives of the saints, and can sign their name with tolerable facility. They can make the simpler arithmetical calculations with the help of a little calculating machine, called *stchety*."[6]

In the days of Nicholas it was infinitely worse. Learning of any kind was considered detrimental to the State; schools were practically unknown. "The most stringent regulations were made concerning tutors and governesses. It was forbidden to send young men to study in western colleges and every obstacle was thrown in the way of foreign travel and residence. Philosophy could not be taught in the universities."[7]

Contrast with this enforced lethargy the intellectual activity that we meet with everywhere in Jewish quarters. No settlement in which we find a *minyan* (ten men necessary for divine worship), but there we will also find a *cheder*, a school in which the Bible and the Talmud are taught. Indeed, study is the first duty of the Jew; it is the quintessence of his religion. The unravelling of God's Word has been from time immemorial regarded as the greatest need, the most ennobling occupation of man—a work commanded by God. The Talmud teems with precepts concerning this all-important subject.

"Study by day and by night, for it is written: 'Thou shalt meditate therein day and night.'"

"The study of the Law may be compared to a huge heap that is to be cleared away. The foolish man will say: 'It is impossible for me to remove this immense pile, I will not attempt it.' But the wise man says: 'I will remove a little to-day, and more to-morrow, and thus in time I shall have removed it all.' It is the same in studying the Law."[8]

It was to this incessant study of the Scriptures that Israel owed its patience, its courage, its fortitude during centuries of persecution. It was this constant delving for truth which produced that bright, acute Jewish mind, which in days of fanaticism and intolerance, protected the despised people from stupefying mental decay. It was this incessant yearning after the word of God, which moulded the moral and religious life of the Jews and preserved them from the

Milton Goldsmith

fanatical excesses of the surrounding peoples.

That this study often degenerated into a mere useless cramming of unintelligible ideas is easily understood, and its effects were in many cases the reverse of ennobling. At the age of five, the Jewish lad was sent to *cheder* and his young years devoted to the study of the Bible. Every other occupation of mind and body was interdicted, the very plays of happy childhood were abolished. The Pentateuch must henceforth form the sole mental nourishment of the boy. Later on he is led through the labyrinth of Talmudic lore, to wander through the dark and dreary catacombs of the past, analyze the mouldering corpses of a by-gone philosophy, drink into his very blood the wisdom, superstitions, morality and prejudices of preceding ages. He must digest problems which the greatest minds have failed to solve. Either the pupil is spurred on to preternatural acuteness and becomes a credit to his parents and his teachers, or he succumbs entirely to the benumbing influence of an over-wrought intellect and is rendered unfit for the great physical struggle for existence.

What is the Talmud, this sacred literature of Israel? It is a collection of discussions and comments of biblical subjects, by generations of rabbis and teachers who devoted their time and intellects to an analysis of the Scriptures. It is a curious store-house of literary gems, at times carefully, at times carelessly compiled by writers living in different lands and different ages; a museum of curiosities, into which are thrown in strange confusion beautiful legends, historical facts, metaphysical discussions, sanitary regulations and records of scientific research. In it are preserved the wise decisions, stirring sermons and religious maxims of Israel's philosophers.

Although a huge work, consisting of twelve folios, it bears no resemblance to a single literary production. On first acquaintance it appears a wilderness, a meaningless tangle of heterogeneous ideas, of scientific absurdities, of hair-splitting arguments, of profound aphorisms, of ancient traditions, of falsehood and of truth. It is a work of broadest humanity, of most fanatical bigotry.

It is not surprising, therefore, that the Talmud contains a great number of trivial subjects, which it treats with great seriousness. It contains, for example, dissertations upon sorcery and witchcraft as well as powerful religious precepts, and presents along-side of its wise and charitable maxims many utterances of an opposite nature. "For these faults the whole Talmud had often been held responsible, as a work of trifles, as a source of trickery, without taking into consideration that it is not the work of a single author. Over six centuries are crystallized in the Talmud with animated distinctness. It is, therefore, no wonder if in this work, sublime and mean, serious and ridiculous, Jewish and heathen elements, the altar and the ashes are found in motley mixture."[9]

To the *jeschiva*, or Talmud school, Mendel was immediately sent after his phenomenal recovery. The great Rabbi Jeiteles himself became the lad's instructor. Let us accompany Mendel on this beautiful autumn day to his school.

The house of Rabbi Jeiteles was hemmed in on three sides by decaying and overcrowded dwellings, facing on the fourth a narrow, neglected lane. There was nothing in its appearance to attract a passer-by. The interior, however, was neatly and tastefully, if not luxuriously, furnished. On entering, one found himself in a comfortably arranged reception-room. On the eastern wall there hung a *misrach*, a scriptural picture bearing the inscription, "From the rising of the sun to its setting shall the name of the Lord be praised." Prints of biblical subjects adorned the remaining walls, the Sabbath lamp hung from the ceiling and thrift and comfort seemed to be thoroughly at home. Rebecca, the Rabbi's wife, a pleasant-faced, mild-tempered little woman, was busy arranging the table for the evening meal. There is not much to be said about her and absolutely nothing against her. To a profound admiration for her husband's ability, she added charity and benevolence and shared with him the respect of the congregation. It had pleased the Lord to deprive her of her three sons and the mother's love and devotion was now lavished upon her sole remaining child, her daughter Recha.

"My sons would be a great comfort to me," she often sighed, and then added, with resignation: "the Lord's will be done."

To the right of the entrance lay the staircase leading to the bed-rooms on the second floor, and to the left a door opened into the school-rooms, a recent addition to the dwelling, and in which the Rabbi's fifty-odd pupils were daily instructed in their important studies.

In the first of these rooms, the elementary department, sat the younger boys, whose spiritual and mental welfare were entrusted to an assistant, a young pedagogue, who did not believe in sparing the rod at the expense of the child, but, mindful of the unmerciful whippings he had received in his youth, endeavored on his part to inculcate the precepts of the Pentateuch by means of sound thrashings. The progress of his pupils was not phenomenal, but their training was eminently useful in aiding them to bear the blows and trials which the gentile world had in store for them. The Rabbi occasionally looked in upon the class and added his instructions to those of the assistant, who in the presence of his superior concealed his rod and assumed an air of unspeakable tenderness and loving solicitude towards his charges.

The second school-room was for the more advanced pupils, who had for the most part passed their *bar-mitzvah* and now revelled in the mystic lore of the Talmud. On rough wooden desks, whose surfaces had been engraved by unskilled hands, huge folios lay open. At the upper end of the room sat the Rabbi, on whose head the frosts of sixty winters had left their traces. His snow-white beard covered his breast and his hair hung in silver locks over his temples. His pale and finely-cut features stamped him as a man of education and refinement. The venerable patriarch had for more than thirty years filled the position of Chief Rabbi of Kief, and his reputation as a Talmudist and a man of great mental acumen was not confined to his native town.

The rattan which the Rabbi held in his hand, the better to guide his pupils, was never used for corporal punishment, for a glance or a whispered admonition from the beloved teacher was more potent than were blows from another. At his side sat his little daughter Recha, scarcely nine years of age, whose features gave promise of great oriental beauty. Her dark eyes and darker hair, her rosy lips and merry smile, formed a veritable symphony of childish loveliness. Recha deemed it a great favor to be allowed in the room with her father during school-hours, and as her presence exercised a refining influence over the boys, each one of whom loved the girl in his own juvenile way, the Rabbi offered no objections.

The boys were being instructed in a difficult passage of the Talmud. Following the movements of the Rabbi's head and body they recited their appropriate lines. Like a mighty *crescendo* swelled the chorus, for the greater the pupil's zeal the louder rose his voice, and ever and anon they were inspired to quicker time, to greater enthusiasm, until the lesson came to an end.

Alas, poor boys! Taken from the cheerful sunlight to pass the days of happy boyhood in wading through heaps of useless learning, tutored in a philosophy which demands age and experience for its perfect comprehension; of what use can all this Talmud delving be to you, when once life summons you to more practical duties? And yet how much better this training, confusing and bewildering though it be, than the absolute ignorance, the unchecked illiteracy of the Russian Christians.

Rabbi Jeiteles interrupted his class to amplify upon the passage just read. He had been a great traveller in his youth, had wandered through Austria and Germany, and had picked up disconnected scraps of worldly information, to which, in a measure, his superiority in Kief was due. There were envious calumniators who did not hesitate to assert that the Rabbi was a *meshumed* (a renegade), that his mind had become polluted with ideas and thoughts at variance with Judaism, that he had in his possession—*O mirabile dictu!*—a copy of the Mendelssohnian translation of the Pentateuch, against which a ban had been hurled. These were but rumors, however, and the better class of Hebrews paid no attention to them.

The passage under consideration was the beautiful legend concerning the necessity of understanding the Law, and the Rabbi undertook to elucidate its somewhat difficult construction. According to the wise scribes of the Talmud, each soul after death enters into the presence of its maker, and is asked to give a reason for not having studied the *Torah*. If poverty is offered as an excuse, he is reminded of Hillel, who though poor deprived himself of life's comforts that he might enjoy God's word. If the burdens and cares of wealth are advanced in palliation, he is reminded of Eleazer, who abandoned his lands and possessions to seek the consolation of knowledge. If a man pleads temptations and weakness to excuse a life of evil, he is told of Joseph's constancy. In short, it is incumbent on all to understand God's command-ments and to obey them, for "the beginning of wisdom is the fear of the Lord."

Silence reigned in the class-room, while the Rabbi, in explanation of his subject, related incidents that had occurred to him during his eventful career. The interest was intense, numerous questions were asked and graciously answered, and the *mishna* was again taken up.

At length the lesson came to an end and the school was dismissed. The pupils, glad to be released from their duties, bade their teacher good-by and tripped out into the inviting sunlight. Mendel alone remained.

"Well, my boy, what is it?" asked the Rabbi, as Mendel gazed wistfully at him.

"Rabbi, are you going out for your walk?" he asked, timidly.

"Yes," answered the other, surprised at the question.

"May I accompany you? I have so much to ask of you."

The Rabbi gladly acquiesced. Although Mendel had been but six months under his tuition, he had already become his favorite pupil. His quick perception and wonderful origi-nality of thought attracted the teacher.

The teacher and pupil walked through the miserable streets of the quarter until they reached the open fields. Here the Rabbi stopped and drew a long breath.

"How different this is," he said, "from the contaminated air one breathes in the narrow lanes of our quarter."

"You have travelled much, Rabbi," said the boy. "Tell me, are the Jews treated as cruelly all over the world as they are in Russia?"

"Unfortunately they are, in some other countries. Why do you ask?"

"Because I think—Rabbi, are we not ourselves to blame for our wretched existence?"

Jeiteles looked at the boy in surprise.

"That is a very grave question for a boy of your age," he said. "What gave you such an idea?"

"I have been thinking very much of late that if we were more like other people we might be made to suffer less."

"God forbid that we should become like them," answered the Rabbi, hastily. "Israel's greatest calamities have been caused by aping the fashions of other nations. Our only salvation lies in clinging to our customs and faith. Do not attempt to judge your elders until you are more conversant with your own religion. Obey the Law and do not trouble yourself concerning the religious observances of your people."

The boy took the rebuke meekly and the two walked on in silent meditation. After a pause, Mendel again took up the conversation.

"In to-day's lesson," he said, "we learned that the fear of God is the beginning of wisdom; that study is God's special command. A wise Rabbi furthermore said upon this subject: 'He gains wisdom who is willing to receive from all sources.' Am I right?"

"You have quoted correctly. Go on!"

"Is there any passage in the Talmud which forbids the learning of a foreign language or the reading of a book not written in Hebrew?"

The Rabbi gazed thoughtfully upon the ground but could not recollect such a passage.

"Last week," continued Mendel, "while in the city, I saw a book in Russian characters. I bought it and took it home to study. My uncle tore the book from my hands and threw it into the fire, all the time bewailing that anything so impure had been brought into the house. Then I was obliged to run to the house of worship and pray until sunset for forgiveness. Was there anything so very wrong in trying to learn something beside the Talmud?"

The worthy Rabbi was sorely puzzled for a reply. His knowledge of the world had long ago opened his eyes to the narrow-minded bigotry which swayed the Russian Jewish people in their prejudices against anything foreign. He, too, deplored the fact that intellects so bright and alert should be content to linger in these musty catacombs. Full well he knew that the constant searching for hidden meanings in the Scriptures was the direct cause of many of the superstitions which had crept into Judaism. He, too, had in his youth yearned for more extended knowledge than that derived from the Talmud's folios, and had in secret studied the Russian and German languages at the risk of being discovered and branded as a heretic. He understood the boy's craving and sympathized with him; but could he conscientiously advise him to brave the opposition and prejudices of his people and pursue that knowledge to which he aspired?

"Well, Rabbi," said the boy, eagerly, "you do not answer.

Have I violated any law by asking such a question?"

Rabbi Jeiteles wiping his perspiring brow with a large red handkerchief, sat down upon a moss-grown log and bade the boy sit at his side.

"My dear Mendel," he began, "you are scarcely old or experienced enough to comprehend the gravity of your question. It is important for Israel the world over to remain unpolluted by the influence of gentile customs. The Messiah will surely come, nor can his arrival be far off, and a new kingdom, a united power will reward us for our past sufferings and present faith. Were Israel to become tainted with foreign ideas, she would in each country develop different propensities, learn different languages and her religion would become contaminated by all that is most obnoxious in other faiths. It is to preserve the unity of Israel, the similarity of thought, the purity of our religion, that we look with horror upon any foreign learning. Now, compare our mental condition with that of the Russian *moujiks*, or even nobles. What do they know? What have they studied? Very little, indeed! They know nothing of the great deeds of the past that are revealed to us through the Scriptures; they cannot enjoy the grand and majestic philosophy of our God-inspired rabbis. Brought up in utter ignorance, their life may be likened to a desert, barren of all that pleases the eye and elevates the mind."

"But," interrupted the boy, "might we not hold on to our own, even while we are learning from the gentiles? Our language, for example, is, as I have heard you say, a terrible jargon. We have forgotten much of our Hebrew and use many strange words instead. We have but to open our mouths to be recognized at once as Jews and to be treated with contempt. If we were but to learn the Russian language, it might save us from many a cruel humiliation and the

Hebrew tongue might still be preserved in our own circle."

"You mistake, my boy; our humiliations do not proceed from any one fact, such as jargon or customs, but from a variety of circumstances combined, principal among which are envy of our domestic happiness, fanaticism because of our rejection of the Christian religion, and a cruel prejudice which has been handed down through generations from father to son. No amount of learning on our side can change this. Persecutions will continue, the gentiles will never learn that the Jew is made of flesh and blood and has sentiments and feelings the same as they. Our right to humane treatment will not be recognized any more than at present, and harder, unspeakably harder, will be the sting and pain of our degradation, if by deep study we rise mentally above our sphere. The ignorant man suffers less than the person with elevated susceptibilities. Learning, therefore, while it would not improve our treatment at the hands of the gentiles, would but serve to make us the more discontented with our own unfortunate condition."

The Rabbi was right; he spoke from bitter experience, and Mendel slipped his hand into that of his teacher and gazed thoughtfully before him.

"A great head," muttered the old man, looking fondly at the boy. "If his energies are directed into the proper channels, he will become a shining light in Israel."

"Come, Mendel, let us go home," he said aloud, and they started silently for the town, both too much engrossed in thought to speak. Only once, Mendel asked:

"Rabbi, you are not offended by my questions?" and the Rabbi replied:

"No, my boy. On the contrary, I am glad that you are beginning to think for yourself. The world is but a group of thinkers and the best heads among them are usually leaders. This has been an agreeable walk to me. Let us repeat it soon."

"Nothing would give me greater pleasure," cried Mendel, with undisguised delight. "And if you will be so kind, I should like to hear all about your travels."

The Rabbi promised, and, having reached the Jewish quarter, pupil and teacher parted for their respective homes.

FOOTNOTES:

[Footnote 6: Wallace, p. 179.]

[Footnote 7: Foulke, "Slav or Saxon," p. 91.]

[Footnote 8: Rabbi Chonan.]

[Footnote 9: "Graetz's History of the Jews," vol. 4, p. 309.]

CHAPTER XI

THE RETURN OF THE RENEGADE

It was just a week since Mendel and the Rabbi had walked out together.

Hirsch Bensef rushed with gigantic strides up the street leading to his house, and long before he reached his door he shouted, at the top of his voice:

"Miriam! Miriam! I have news for you!"

Miriam had recovered her health, and was in the kitchen preparing meat for the following day. This was a most important operation, requiring the housewife's undivided attention. According to a Mosaic command blood was sacrificed upon the altar of the Temple, but was strictly forbidden as an article of diet. The animal is slaughtered in a manner which will drain off the greatest amount of the life-giving fluid, and great importance is attached to the processes for extracting every particle of blood from the meat which is brought upon the Jewish table. A thorough rubbing with salt and an hour's immersion in water are necessary to its preparation. Scientists who acknowledge that the blood is the general vehicle for conveying the parasites and germs of disease, recognize in this command of Moses a valuable sanitary measure, worthy of universal imitation.

Miriam heard her husband's distant call and, with her hands full of salt, she ran to the door.

Hirsch entered, completely out of breath.

"Who do you think has arrived?" he gasped.

"How should I know?"

"Guess."

"I might guess from now until the coming of *Meschiach* and still not be right."

"Pesach Harretzki, your cousin and old admirer."

Miriam sank into a chair and a smile rippled over her pretty features.

"Pesach Harretzki here? When did he arrive?"

"To-day. This morning. Itzig Maier, who knows all the news in town, has just told me. He has come back from America to visit his old parents and take them with him across the ocean."

"Has he changed much?" asked Miriam.

"No doubt of it! Itzig says he is without a beard and looks more like a *goy* (gentile) than like one of our own people. I suppose he has lost what religion he once possessed, which by the way was not much."

"You will invite him to call on us, of course."

Hirsch looked askance at his wife and frowned.

"I don't know," he answered, reflectively; "we shall see."

Hirsch Bensef, the *parnas* of the chief congregation, and whose reputation for piety overtopped that of any other man of the community, might well pause before inviting the new arrival to his house. Pesach Harretzki was one of those perverse lads that one meets occasionally in a Hebrew community, who, feeling the wild impulse of youth in every vein, throws over the holy traditions of his forefathers and follows rather the promptings of his own heart than that happiness which can only be found in a firm adherence to the law and its precepts. Unrestrained by his parents' anxious pleadings, bound by no will save that of momentary caprice, he overstepped the boundary which separates the pious Jew from his profane surroundings and thereby forfeited the respect and good-will of the entire community. The young man had never been guilty of actual wrong-doing, but had in a thousand petty ways displayed his utter disregard of the customs that were so dear to the hearts of his co-religionists. The Sabbath found him strolling through the city instead of attending divine service at the synagogue. Of the Talmud he knew very little, having preferred to play with his gentile friends to wasting his hours in the *cheder*. He had been known to eat *trefa* at the house of a *goy*, and with a fastidiousness that was without parallel in the annals of Kief, he had shaved off all of his beard, leaving only a jaunty little mustache. So it happened that his name became a terror to all pious Israelites. There was but one attraction in Judaism which still fascinated Pesach, and that was his charming cousin Miriam. She alone possessed the power of bringing him back when he had strayed too far from the fold and her bright eyes often recalled him to a sense of duty. He loved the girl, and had she shown him any encouragement he might still have reformed the evil of his ways. But even had

Milton Goldsmith

Miriam favored his advances, her father, one of the most pious men of Kief, would have dispelled all hope of an alliance between the two. Old Reb Kohn, after endeavoring in vain to bring the reprobate to his senses, finally forbade him the house. Shortly after, the betrothal of Miriam Kohn with the learned and wealthy Hirsch Bensef was announced. Pesach became despondent and put the finishing touch to his ungodly career by becoming intoxicated with beer on the Passover. In consequence of this and former misdeeds, he was ostracized from good Jewish society, and finding himself shunned by his former associates he departed from Kief to seek his fortune in a foreign land.

After wandering about Germany for a year or two, picking up a precarious living and a varied experience, he set sail for America, where he arrived without a penny. Fortune smiled upon the poor man at last. He drifted into an inland city, Americanized his name to Philip Harris, and succeeded, through honesty, thrift and perseverance, in building up a large business and accumulating a respectable fortune. It was only after success had been assured that he communicated with his parents in Russia, and in spite of his past record great was the rejoicing when the first letter was received. He whom his friends had mourned as dead was alive and thriving; he had moreover become rich and respected and had been the means of establishing a Jewish synagogue in the land of his adoption. The last two facts, coupled with the munificent gifts which he sent to the synagogue in Kief and to his parents, were sufficient to lift the ban which had so long rested upon his name and to re-establish him in the good graces of the community. Pesach, the *meshumed*, continued these contributions to the synagogue and to his parents, and the Jews of Kief, having forgotten his former escapades, referred to him thenceforth as "Pesach the Generous." He had now returned after an absence of twelve years, and the whole settlement was in a state of pardonable excitement.

"Is he still a Jew? Has he remained true to the old faith?" was asked on every side.

It being Friday, the Sabbath eve, the synagogue was crowded and curiosity to see the stranger was at its height. The men frequently looked up from their prayer-books, and the women from their seats in the gallery craned their necks to get a view of the sunburnt, closely-shaven American. Yes, he had changed; no one would have recognized him. Of all the pious men that filled the house of worship, he was the only one who was without a beard. It was against the Jewish custom to allow a razor to touch the beard, and had not Philip's benevolence paved the way it is doubtful whether his presence would have been tolerated within those sacred precincts. In all other respects, however, he bore himself like a devout Israelite. He stood by the side of his father, earnestly scanning the pages of his prayer-book, the greater part of whose contents were still familiar to him. His beardless face was in a measure atoned for.

What a throng of visitors there was that evening at Harretzkis house! The little room could scarcely hold them all. Among them was Rabbi Jeiteles, who shook the suave and smiling stranger by the hand, congratulated him upon his appearance and asked him a hundred questions about his travels. Indeed, it seemed as though the worthy Rabbi intended to monopolize his company for the rest of the evening. Then came Hirsch Bensef and his charming wife, the latter trembling and blushing in recollection of the days when she and her cousin Pesach loved each other in secret. Philip recognized her immediately.

"Why this is my dear cousin Miriam," he said. "How well

you look! You seem scarcely a day older than when I left you. Is this your husband? Happy man! How I used to envy you your good fortune? But that is all over now!" and he turned with a sigh to meet other friends.

He recollected every man and woman in Kief; moreover, he had a kind word and pretty compliment for each and the worthy people returned home more than ever impressed with the true excellence of Pesach Harretzki.

"What a *medina* (country) America must be to make such a finished product of the ungodly youth that Kief turned out of doors twelve years ago!" Such was Bensef's remark to his wife, as they wended their way homeward.

On the Sabbath morn the capacity of the synagogue was again tested to the utmost. Those who had not yet seen Philip hastened to avail themselves of this opportunity. The man from America had become the greatest curiosity in the province. And to him, the great traveller, every incident, however trivial, served to recall a vision of the past. The devout men about him, wearing the fringed *tallis*, the venerable Rabbi at the *almemor*, the ark with the same musty hangings, the Pentateuch scrolls with the same faded covers which they bore in the years gone by, all appealed mightily to his heart and a tear forced itself unchecked through his lashes. Philip would have been unable to explain to himself the cause of his emotion. The past had not been particularly pleasant; there was nothing to regret. Perhaps some psychologist can account for that sweet and melancholy sentiment which the recollection of a dim and half-forgotten past brings in its train.

It was delightful to Philip to find himself once more in the presence of all that had been dear to him. His mind reviewed the many vicissitudes he had undergone, the many changes he had witnessed, and he fervently thanked the God of Israel that he was permitted to revisit the scenes of his childhood, and that the people who had rejected him in his youth now received him with open arms. After prayers the *hazan* (reader), assisted by the Rabbi, opened the Holy Ark and took therefrom one of the scrolls. To Philip, as a stranger, was accorded the honor of being one of those called up to say the blessing over the *Torah* (Law). He touched the parchment with the fringes of his *tallis*, kissed them to signify his reverence for the holy words, and began with "*Bar'chu eth Adonai.*"

"He knows his *brocha* yet, he is still a good Jew!" was the mental comment of the congregation.

Then followed Rabbi Jeiteles in a short but pithy address, in which he laid great stress upon the fact that Jehovah never allows his lambs to stray far from the fold, and that charity and benevolence cover a multitude of sins. He incidentally announced the fact that Harretzki had offered the synagogue new hangings for the ark, covers for the scrolls and an entirely new metal roof for the *schul* (synagogue) in place of the present one, which was sadly out of repair.

Such generosity was unparalleled. In spite of the sanctity of the place, expressions of approval were loud and emphatic. For a time the services were interrupted and general congratulations took the place of the prayers. Philip's popularity was now assured. All opposition vanished and the American became a lion indeed. Bensef no longer hesitated as to the propriety of inviting the stranger to his house. As *parnas* he must be the first to do him honor and after the services were at an end the invitation was extended and accepted.

It was a pleasant assemblage that gathered at Bensef's house.

Philip, his father and mother, Rabbi Jeiteles, Haim Goldheim (a banker and intimate friend of the host), and several other patriarchal gentlemen, pillars of the congregation, were of the company. Miriam was an excellent provider and on this occasion she fairly outdid herself.

"Perhaps," thought Bensef, "there still lingers in her breast a spark of affection for the man who is now so greatly honored."

But, no! Miriam loved her husband dearly, and if she was attentive to her cousin it was but the courtesy due to a man who had been so far and seen so much.

Mendel, too, was at the table and could not take his eyes from the handsome stranger whose praises every mouth proclaimed. The boy regarded him as a superior being.

Tales of adventure, stories of travel, were the topics of conversation during the evening. After the dessert the talk took a more serious turn. The liberty enjoyed by the Jews in America was a fruitful theme for discussion and many were the questions asked by the interested group. That Israelites were politically and socially placed upon the same footing with their Christian neighbors was a source of gratification, but that some religious observances were in many cases neglected or totally abolished, appeared to these pious listeners as very reprehensible.

"You see," said Philip, in explanation, "where a number of Jewish families reside in one place it is still possible to obey the dietary laws, but in inland towns, where the number of Israelite families is limited, it becomes an impossibility to observe them. Nor do they deem it necessary that all the ceremonies that time has collected around the Jewish religion should be strictly observed. Those Israelites who soonest adopt the customs of their new country soonest enjoy the benefits which a free and liberty-loving nation offers."

Hirsch Bensef shook his head, doubtingly.

"Then you mean to imply that it becomes necessary to abolish those usages in which one's heart and soul are wrapped!" he said.

"Not at all," answered the American. "There are thousands of Jews in America as observant of the ordinances as the most pious in Kief. Yet it seems to me that a Jew can remain a Jew even if he neglect some of those ceremonials which have very little to do with Judaism pure and simple. Some are remnants of an oriental symbolism, others comparatively recent additions to the creed, which ought to give way before civilization. What possible harm can it do you or your religion if you shave your beard or abandon your jargon for the language of the people among whom you live?"

"It would make us undistinguishable from the *goyim*," answered Bensef.

"The sooner such a distinction falls the better," said Philip. "You may recollect reading in history that in the time of Peter the Great the Russian nobility wore beards and the Czar's efforts to make them shave their faces provoked more animosity than did all the massacres of Ivan the Terrible. Now a nobleman would sooner go to prison than wear a beard."

"We never read history," interposed the childish treble of Mendel. "If we did we should know more about the great world."

"That is indeed a misfortune," said Philip, sadly. "Every

effort to develop the Jewish mind is checked, not by the gentiles, but by the Jews themselves. Had I been allowed full liberty to study what and how I pleased, I should never have been guilty of the excesses which drove me from home. A knowledge of the history of the world, an insight into modern science, will teach us why and wherefore all our laws were given and how we can best obey, not the letter but the spirit of God's commands."

The faces of the little group fell visibly. This was rank heresy. God forbid that it should ever take root in Israel. Mendel alone appeared satisfied. He was absorbed in all the stranger had to say. This new doctrine was a revelation to him. But Philip did not observe the impression he had created. He had warmed up to his subject and pursued it mercilessly.

"The Israelites in America," he continued, "are free and respected. They enjoy equal rights with the citizens of other religious beliefs. They are at liberty to go wherever they please and to live as they desire, and are often chosen to positions of honor and responsibility. Such distinctions are only obtained, however, after one has become a citizen, and citizenship means adherence to the laws of the land and assimilation with its inhabitants. It was not long before I discovered, through constant friction with intelligent people about me, the absurdity of many of my ideas and prejudices. The more I associated with my fellow-men the more difficult I found it to retain the superstitions of by-gone days."

"But in giving up what you call superstition," said the Rabbi, "are you not giving up a portion of your religion as well?"

"By no means," said Philip, eagerly. "If Rabbi Jeiteles will pardon my speaking upon a subject concerning which he is better instructed and which he is better qualified to expound than myself, I will endeavor to tell why. You well know that until after the destruction of the second Temple the Jews had no Talmud. They then obeyed the laws of God in all their simplicity and as they understood them, and not one of you will assert that they were not good and pious Jews. Then came the writers of the Talmud with their explanations and commentaries, and the laws of Moses acquired a new meaning. Stress was laid upon words instead of upon ideas, upon conventionalities instead of upon the true spirit of God's word. After five centuries of Talmudists had exhausted all possible explanations of the Scriptures, the study of the Law eventually paved the way for the invention of the *Cabala*. A new bible was constructed. The pious were no longer content with a rational observance of the Mosaic command, but a hidden meaning must be found for every word and in many cases for the individual letters of the Pentateuch. The six hundred and thirteen precepts of Moses were so altered, so tortured to fit new constructions, that the great prophet would experience difficulty in recognizing any one of his beautiful laws from the rubbish under which it now lies buried. New laws and ceremonies, new beliefs and, worse than all, new superstitions were thrust upon the people already weakened by mental fatigue caused by their incessant delving into the mysteries of the Talmud. The free will of the people was suppressed. Instead of giving the healthy imagination and pure reason full power to act, the teachers of the *Cabala* arrogated to themselves the power to decide what to do and how to do it, and as a result the Jewish observances, as they exist to-day in pious communities, are bound up in arbitrary rules and superstitious absurdities which are as unlike the primitive and rational religion of Israel as night is to day."

This bold utterance produced a profound sensation in Bensef's little dining-room. Murmurs of disapproval and of indignation frequently interrupted the speaker, and long before he had finished, several of his listeners had sprung up and were pacing the room in great excitement. Never before had any one dared so to trample upon the time-honored beliefs of Israel. For infinitely less had the ban been hurled against hundreds of offenders and the renegades placed beyond the pale of Judaism.

The Rabbi alone preserved his composure. Mendel lost not a word of the discussion. He sat motionless, with staring eyes and wide open mouth, as though the stranger's eloquence had changed him into stone.

"No, this is too much!" at length stammered Hirsch Bensef. "Such a condemnation of our holy religion is blasphemy. Rabbi, can you sit by and remain silent?"

The Rabbi moved uneasily upon his chair, but said nothing.

Philip continued:

"That your Rabbi should be of one mind with you is natural, but that does not in any way impair the force of what I have said. You will all admit that you place more weight upon your ceremonials than upon your faith. You deem it more important to preserve a certain position of the feet, a proper intonation of the voice during prayers than to fully understand the prayer itself, and in spite of your pretended belief in the greatness and goodness of God, you belittle Him by the thought that an omission of a single ceremony, the eating of meat and milk together, the tearing of a *tzitzith* (fringe) will offend Him, or that a certain number of *mitzvoth* (good acts) will propitiate Him. Do you understand now what I mean when I say that superstition is not religion?"

"But," returned Goldheim, "the *Shulkan-aruch* commands us to do certain things in certain ways. Is it not our duty as

God-fearing Jews to obey the laws that have His sanction?"

"Undoubtedly! If you were certain that this book contained His express commands it would be incumbent upon you to observe them, only, however, after having sought to understand their meaning. But you know, or ought to know, that the book was written by a man like yourselves, who was as liable to err as you are. Many of these commands were excellent at the time in which they were given, but change of circumstances has made them absurd."

"What is godly at one time cannot become ungodly at another," said Bensef, with determined obstinacy.

"No; but what is beautiful and appropriate in one land may become the reverse in a different country, or at another period. Let us take an example: It is an oriental custom to wear one's hat or turban as a mark of respect. In Palestine such a usage is proper and the man who keeps his head covered before his fellow-men certainly should keep it covered before God. In America, however, I am considered ill-bred if I keep my hat on when I am conversing with the humblest of my associates; should I therefore keep it on when I am addressing my God? Thus, many of your religious observances take their origin outside of religion and are appropriate only to the country in which they were conceived."

"But to appear before God bareheaded is surely a sin!" stammered Hirsch Bensef, who would gladly have ended the conversation then and there.

"Not a sin, simply a novelty," answered Philip.

"But our proverb says: 'Novelty brings calamity.'"

"Proverbs do not always speak the truth," replied the American. Then after a pause he continued, reflectively: "There is another class of ceremonials which find their origin in one or the other of the commands of Moses, and which through the eagerness of the people to observe them for fear of Divine wrath, have been given an importance out of all proportion to their original significance. For instance, Moses, for reasons purely humane, prohibited the cooking of a kid in its mother's milk, wisely teaching that what nature intended for the preservation of the animal should not be employed for its destruction. This law has been so distorted that the eating of meat and milk together was prohibited, and the severity of the resulting dietary laws makes it necessary to have two sets of dishes—one for meat, the other for all food prepared with milk. And so in a thousand cases the original intention of the command is lost in the mass of foreign matter that has been added to it."

Philip paused and, toying with his massive watch-chain, tried hard not to see the indignant glances that threatened to consume him. Bensef arose from his chair in sheer desperation.

"What would you have us do?" he asked, angrily. "Desert the ceremonies of our forefathers and surrender to the ungodly?"

"Not by any means," was the quiet rejoinder. "Worship God as your conscience dictates, continue in your ancient fashion if it makes you happy, but be tolerant towards him who, feeling himself mentally and spiritually above superstition, seeks to emancipate himself from its bonds and to follow the dictates of his own good common-sense."

With these concluding words, Philip arose and prepared to leave. The remaining guests also arose from their chairs and looked at each other in blank dismay. Rabbi Jeiteles stepped to the American and placed his hand upon his shoulder.

"My dear Pesach," he began, "what you have just said sounds strange and very dangerous to these good people. To me it was nothing new, for during my early travels I heard such discussions again and again. Your arguments may or may not be correct. We will not discuss the matter. One thing you must not forget, however: the Jews in Russia and elsewhere are despised and rejected; they are degraded to the very scum of the earth. Social standing, pursuit of knowledge, means of amusement, everything is taken from them. What is left? Only the consolation which their sacred religion brings. The observance of the thousand ceremonials which you decry, is to them not only a religious necessity, a God-pleasing work; it is more, it is a source of domestic happiness, a means of genuine enjoyment, a comfort and a solace. Whether these observances are needed or are superfluous in a free country like America I shall not presume to say, but in Russia they are a moral and a physical necessity. You have spoken to-night as no man has ever spoken before in Kief. Were the congregation to hear of it, you would again find yourself an outcast from your native town, shunned and despised by all that now look upon you as a model of benevolence and piety. For your own sake, therefore, as well as for the peace of mind of those among whom your words might act as a firebrand, we hope that you will speak no more upon this subject and we on our part promise to keep our own counsel."

Philip readily consented and with his aged parents he left for his home, at the other end of the quarter.

The friends bade each other a hasty good-night, and not another word was spoken concerning the discussion.

"Uncle," said Mendel, as he was about to retire, "is not

Harretzki a very wise man?"

"My boy," replied his uncle; "our rabbis say, 'Much speech—much folly.'"

CHAPTER XII

FORBIDDEN BOOKS

Philip remained in Kief about two weeks, during which time he was hospitably entertained by the leaders of the Jewish community. There was some difficulty in obtaining a passport for his parents, for, anxious as the Russians are to expel the Jews, by a remarkable contrariety of human nature they throw every obstacle in the way of a Jew who endeavors to emigrate.

Mendel never missed an opportunity of passing Harretzki's house. It had a strange fascination for him, and if he but saw the American at the window and exchanged greetings with him, the boy returned home with a happy heart.

Once—it was the day before Philip's departure—Mendel again passed the wretched abode in which the stranger dwelt. The door was open and Philip was busied with preparations for his coming voyage. Mendel gazed wistfully for some minutes and finally mustered up courage to enter and ask:

"Can I be of any service to you, sir?"

Philip, who had taken a decided fancy to the boy, said, kindly:

"Yes; you may assist me. Here are my books. Pack them into this chest."

With a reverence amounting almost to awe, Mendel took up the books one by one and arranged them as Philip directed. Now and then he opened a volume and endeavored to peer into the wondrous mysteries it contained, but the characters were new to him; they were neither Hebrew nor Russian, and the boy sighed as he piled the books upon each other. Philip observed him with growing interest.

"Are you fond of books?" he asked, at length.

"Oh, yes. If I could but study," answered the boy, eagerly, and big tears welled up into his eyes.

"And why can't you?"

"Because I have no books but our old Hebrew folios, and if I had they would be taken from me."

"Continue to study the books you have," said Philip, "you will find much to learn from them."

"But there are so many things to know that are not in our books. How I should like to be as wise as you are."

Philip smiled, sorrowfully.

"I know very little," he answered. "I am not regarded as a particularly well-educated person in my country. What good would learning do you in Kief?"

"It would make me happy," answered the boy.

"No, child; it would make you miserable by filling your little head with ideas which would bring down upon you the anathemas of your dearest friends."

There was a pause, during which Mendel worked industriously. Suddenly he said:

"Might I ask a favor, sir?"

"Certainly, my boy; I shall be happy if I can grant it."

"Let me take one of your books to keep in remembrance of you?"

"You cannot read them; they are written in German and English."

"That does not matter. Their presence would remind me of you. Besides I might learn to read them."

"But if a strange book is found in your possession it will be taken from you."

"I will conceal it."

Philip reflected a moment; then carefully selecting two books, he presented them to the overjoyed boy.

"Remember," he said, "that ignorance is frequently bliss. A Rabbi once said: 'Beware of the conceit of learning.' It is often well to say, 'I don't know.'"

Then the American spoke of the difficulties he had experienced in acquiring an education, how he had worked at a trade by day and gone to school during the evening. Mendel had a thousand questions to ask, which Philip answered graciously; but the packing having come to an end, and Mendel having exhausted his inquiries and finding no further excuse to remain, the two bade each other an affectionate farewell. Mendel ran home with his sacred treasures carefully concealed under his blouse, and with great solicitude he locked them up in an old closet which served as his wardrobe. The following morning Philip and his parents were escorted to the limits of the city by the influential Jews of Kief, and the travellers started upon their long voyage to America.

During the next few weeks Mendel was at his Talmudic studies in the *jeschiva* as usual, but there was a decided change in his manner—a certain listlessness, a lack of interest, which were so apparent that Rabbi Jeiteles could not but observe them.

"I fear that the boy has been studying too hard," he said to his wife one day. "We must induce him to take more exercise."

After the close of the lesson, the teacher said:

"Come, Mendel; it is quite a while since we have walked together. Let us go into the fields."

Mendel, who adored his preceptor, was well pleased to have an opportunity of relieving his heart of its burden, and gladly accepted the invitation. For a while the two strolled in silence. The air was balmy and nature was in her most radiant dress.

"Tell me," at length began the Rabbi; "tell me why you appear so dejected?"

"You will reproach me if I confess the cause," answered the boy, tearfully.

"You should know me better," answered the Rabbi. "You ought to be aware that I am interested in your welfare."

"Well, then," sobbed Mendel, no longer able to repress his feelings, "I am unhappy because of my ignorance. I wish to become wise."

"And then?" asked the Rabbi.

The boy opened his eyes to their full extent. He did not comprehend the question.

"After you have acquired great wisdom, what then?" repeated the Rabbi.

"Then I shall be happy and content."

The Rabbi stopped and pointed to a dilapidated bridge which crossed the Dnieper at a place to which their walk had led them. Sadly he called his pupil's attention to a sign which hung at the entrance of the structure and which bore the following legend: "Toll—For a horse, 15 kopecks; for a hog, 3 kopecks; for a Jew, 10 kopecks."

"Read that," he said; "and see how futile must be the efforts of wisdom in a country whose rulers issue such decrees."

"Perhaps you are right," said the boy, sorrowfully; "and yet I feel that God has not given me my intellect to keep it in ignorance and superstition. It must expand. Look, Rabbi, at this river. They have dammed it to keep its waters back; but further down, the stream leaps over the obstruction and forces its way onward. Its confinement makes it but sparkle the more after it has once acquired its freedom. Is not the mind of man like this river? Can you confine it and prevent its onward course?"

The Rabbi gazed with looks of mingled astonishment and admiration upon the boy at his side.

The boy continued:

"I would become wise like you and Pesach Harretzki. I would acquire the art of reading other works besides our ancient folios. Rabbi, will you teach me?"

"Has Harretzki been putting these new ideas into your head?" asked the old man.

"No; they were there before he came. You yourself have often told me: 'Study rather to fill your mind than your coffers.' I have some of Harretzki's books, however, and at night when I cannot sleep I take them out of my closet and look at them. But they are not in Hebrew and I cannot read them. Rabbi, I beg of you to teach me."

Rabbi Jeiteles was in a quandary. He hated the bigotry and narrow-mindedness which forbade the study of any subject but the time-honored Talmud. He himself had been as anxious as was Mendel to strive after other knowledge. On the other hand, he bore in mind the prejudice which the Jews entertained against foreign learning, and he clearly foresaw the many difficulties which Mendel must encounter if his desire became known.

"Well, Rabbi, you do not answer," said the boy, inquiringly.

"Bring me your books to-morrow and I will decide."

Mendel seized the preceptor's hand and kissed it rapturously.

"Thanks," he murmured.

Teacher and pupil turned their steps homeward, the one perplexed, the other overjoyed.

The sun had not fully risen on the morrow, when Mendel, with his precious books carefully concealed, sought the Rabbi's presence, and the two withdrew into an inner room, beyond the reach of prying intruders. The teacher glanced at the titles. They were Mendelssohn's "Phaedon," and Ludwig Philippson's "The Development of the Religious Idea," both written in German. Mendel did not take his eyes from his teacher; he could scarcely master his impatience.

"Well, Rabbi," he asked, "of what do they speak?"

"Of things beyond your comprehension," replied the teacher. "The writers of both these books were good and pious Jews, who, because of their learning, were branded and ostracized by many of their co-religionists. Their only sin lay in the use of classical German. You must know that many hundreds of years ago, our ancestors lived in Germany, and, mingling with men of other creeds, learned the language of their time. By and by, persecutions arose and gradually the Jews were driven into closer quarters and narrower communities. Many emigrated to Poland and Russia, carrying with them their foreign language, which was little changed except by the addition of Hebrew—and, in this country, of a few Russian words—so that what was once a language became a semi-sacred jargon in which the translations of our holy books were read. When Mendelssohn began to write in the ordinary German, he was thought to be ashamed of his fathers' speech and to have abandoned it for that of their oppressors. Pause before you choose a path which may estrange you from all you love best."

"Did these men accomplish no good by their writings?"

"Much good, my son; but through much travail."

The more the teacher talked, the more gloomy the picture he drew, the greater became the enthusiasm of the pupil, the firmer his determination to emulate the example of the men of whom he now heard for the first time. The Rabbi at last consented to instruct the boy in the elements of the Russian and German languages.

While the old man did not for a moment close his eyes to the perils which his pupil invited by his pursuit of knowledge; while he did not conceal from himself the fact that his own position would be endangered if the nature of his teachings was suspected, he was happy in the thought of having before him a youthful mind, brave to seek truth. Rabbi Jeiteles was a learned man; his youth had been spent in travel. He had seen much and read more, and even in the bigoted community in which he lived he kept abreast of the knowledge of the times.

The first lesson was mastered then and there. It was a hard and tedious task and progress was necessarily slow, but Mendel possessed two great essentials to progress, indomitable perseverance and an active intellect, and his teacher displayed the painstaking care and patience with which love for his pupil inspired him.

Day by day, Mendel added to his store of knowledge. He was still the most industrious Talmud scholar of the college; his remarkable aptitude and zeal for the studies of his fathers was in nowise diminished; but when the hours at the *jeschiva* were at an end, instead of returning to his uncle's home, or of spending his time upon the streets with his boisterous playmates, he would walk with Rabbi Jeiteles in the fields, or remain closeted with him, pursuing his investigations in new fields of knowledge. Nor were his labors at an end when he had retired to his bed-room. In the still hours of the night, when every noise was hushed and he deemed himself safe from intrusion, he would rise, silently open his closet for his carefully concealed volume and creep back to bed. Then, by the aid of secretly purloined candle ends, he would read hour after hour, and often the dawn found him still at his books.

Milton Goldsmith

CHAPTER XIII

PERSECUTIONS IN TOGAROG

The flight of time brings us to the year 1855—the epoch of the Crimean War.

Ever since the days when Bonaparte was driven from burning Moscow, there was a popular belief that the Russian soldiery was superior to that of the western nations. The Emperor Nicholas was a thorough soldier as well as a tyrant, possessing an enormous and well-equipped army, which he deemed invincible. This boasted superiority was now to be tested. For years the Russians had been groaning under heavy taxes. During this period they had been finding fault with their central government in a mild, Siberia-fearing manner. To keep them from brooding on their oppressed condition, visions of glory and conquest were to be opened to them by a foreign war. As the patriotic enthusiasm and military fervor increased, the praises of Nicholas were sounded throughout the vast dominion. "The coming war was regarded by many as a kind of crusade, and the most exaggerated expectations were entertained of its results. The old Eastern question was at last to be solved in accordance with Russian ideals, and Nicholas was about to realize Catherine's grand scheme of driving the Turks out of Europe. That the enemy could prevent the accomplishment of these schemes was regarded as impossible. 'We have only to throw our hats at them,' became a favorite expression."[10]

The greater portion of the army was concentrated at the Southern extremity of Russia, for it was here that the fleets of the allied powers would be encountered. Like devastating swarms of locusts the semi-barbarous warriors descended upon the fertile fields, destroying all that lay in their path. Great was the misery of the peasantry in that section of the Empire; greater still the hardships endured by the Jews, who were despoiled of their possessions and driven from their homes.

In the village of Togarog the Jewish quarter was exactly as we last saw it—poverty-stricken and dilapidated. Nothing appeared to be changed in it except the miserable inhabitants. The Governor of Alexandrovsk continued to persecute the Jews with relentless ferocity, and the kidnapping of their children was followed by other acts almost as cruel. If a Jew was suspected of possessing money, he was forced by the gentle persuasion of the Governor's men to disgorge. Broken in fortune and in spirits, the Israelites were indeed in a pitiable plight.

Mordecai Winenki was reduced to dire want. Deprived of the means of livelihood by the removal of his former pupils, despoiled of his meagre savings, the reward of years of toil, there was no occupation open to him but to peddle, the meagre income from which, added to the earnings of his wife by knitting and sewing for the neighboring peasantry, gave them a scanty subsistence.

For six days of each week they toiled patiently, saving and scraping to provide for the holy Sabbath, the celebration of which alone compensated for days of misfortune and privation. On the Sabbath all work was laid aside; the dreary room blazed with the lights of many candles; white, unsullied linen adorned the table; a substantial meal was served, and joy returned to the oppressed and weary hearts. Then the father and mother spoke lovingly of the dear ones whom a cruel despotism had torn from them, and a prayer of thanks was sent to the God of Israel that one of the boys, at least, was alive and well; for Mendel since his arrival in Kief had regularly corresponded with his parents, and his progress and welfare were in a measure a compensation for the trials they had endured. Of Jacob they had never discovered a trace, and they had long since believed him dead.

It was the Sabbath eve. Mordecai and his wife were seated in their humble little room, happy for the time being, in spite of their deplorable condition. A sudden noise in the street interrupted their conversation. The narrow Jewish quarter became animated, and a company of Russian soldiers, led by the Elder of the village and followed by a group of ragged urchins, marched with martial tread through the crooked lane.

"Soldiers!" cried Mordecai and his wife, in one breath. "God help us, they will quarter them on us!"

It was the advance guard of the great army that had entered Togarog. Before Mordecai and his wife could recover from their fright, the door opened and half a dozen soldiers entered the room.

"Give us something to eat!" cried one of the men, boisterously, as he relieved himself of his gun and knapsack. His example was followed by his comrades.

"We are hungry," said another of the men. "We have had nothing to eat since five o'clock this morning. Get us our supper!"

"We have nothing to give you," replied Mordecai, trembling. "Why do you come to us?"

"Not from choice, I can tell you," said a soldier, angrily. "Lots were cast and we were unlucky enough to be sent here. As we are here, however, let us make the best of it and see what your larder contains."

"Bah!" said another, as Mordecai did not move; "you can't expect these people to wait upon us! We must help ourselves," and suiting the action to the word, he strode to the cupboard and pulled it open.

The harvest was more plentiful than they had anticipated. Cooking, like all other work, being forbidden on the Sabbath, provisions sufficient for the holy day were prepared on Friday, and stood temptingly upon the shelves. In a twinkling the succulent viands were placed upon the table and quickly devoured by the half-famished soldiers. The repast, however, failed to satisfy the hunger of these sturdy warriors.

"Come," cried one of them, "what else have you to eat?"

"Nothing," answered Mordecai, sullenly.

"You lie, Jew. Tell us where we may find something to eat."

"You have just eaten all there was in the house," said Mordecai, gulping down a rising lump in his throat, as he thought of the fast he would have to endure on the morrow.

"Then give us money that we may buy our own food!" shouted one of the soldiers.

"I have no money; it is all gone, all gone," said the poor

man, sadly.

"Ha! ha! ha! that is a good joke!" retorted the soldier, while his companions laughed immoderately. "A Jew without money! I'll wager there is gold and silver in every closet. I know you Jews; you are sly dogs."

"Look for yourselves," cried Mordecai, driven to desperation. "You are welcome to all the gold and silver you can find."

The soldiers took him at his word and began to ransack the house, while Mordecai and Leah, paralyzed with fear, great beads of perspiration starting from their foreheads, sat idly by and watched the work of destruction. Not an article of furniture was left entire in the wild search for treasure, which, according to popular belief, every Jew was supposed to possess. Finding nothing, they bestowed a few resounding curses upon the inmates of the house, and in sheer desperation wended their way to the village inn and sought the solace of Basilivitch's vodka.

Poor Mordecai! Poor Leah! For hours they sat just as the soldiers had left them, great tears streaming down their pale and haggard faces, viewing the destruction of their few earthly possessions, the loss of all they could still call their own. They knew not what course to pursue, whether to remain or to flee. The unexpected blow appeared to have robbed them of their faculties; all power of reflection seemed to have left them, and trembling and groaning they remained where they were, in fearful expectancy of what might follow.

Towards midnight the soldiers returned. The liberal potations in which they had indulged had washed away the last semblance of humanity. Food and money had been the motives of their previous excesses, but on their return, hunger and cupidity had made way for lust. Mordecai's wife became the object of their insults, and in the resistance which she and her husband offered, both were beaten unmercifully. Finally, the soldiers, overpowered by the close quarters and by the fumes of the wretched liquor they had imbibed, dropped off, one by one, into a drunken sleep.

"Let us take what we can, Leah," said the wretched man, after assuring himself that the soldiers were all fast asleep, "and let us flee."

"We dare carry nothing—we dare not even travel, for this is the Sabbath," answered Leah, sadly.

Poor Jews! In the midst of sorrow, as in the midst of joy, the behests of their holy religion are never forgotten.

"Yes, we may travel," replied Mordecai. "It is a matter of more importance than life and death, and the Talmud authorizes the desecration of the Sabbath in time of great danger."

"Then let us go at once," whispered Leah.

Hand in hand they left the miserable hut, the place they had for so many years called home, and wandered out into the world, without a prospect to cheer them on their desolate way.

FOOTNOTES:

[Footnote 10: Wallace.]

CHAPTER XIV

A HAPPY PASSOVER

It is the eve of the Passover feast, the birthday of Israel's nationality. All is bustle and excitement in the Jewish quarter of Kief. Kitchen utensils and furniture have been removed from the houses and are piled up in the streets. Dust rises in clouds, water flows in torrents through the muddy gutters. Children, banished from the vacant rooms, are romping and playing, shouting and crying in the lanes. Feather beds and blankets, clothing and linen are being aired. Within the houses scourers and scrubbers are cleaning, dusting and white-washing. The great national house-cleaning is in progress. From closet and cupboard, dishes and cooking utensils are brought out for their eight days' service.

To-morrow is *Pesach* (Passover). An entire nation await with passionate longing the arrival of this festival and accord it a hospitable welcome. The man of wealth lavishly displays on this day his gold and silver, his finely wrought utensils and crystal dishes. The poor man has labored day and night to save enough to give the guest a worthy reception. The stranger and the homeless are made welcome at every table, that they, too, may enjoy, free from care and sorrow, the advent of the *Pesach*.

What yearning, what hopes, what anticipations usher in this feast of feasts! Winter, with its manifold hardships, is past. Nature awakes from her frigid lethargy, and the balmy air gives promise of renewed life and happiness.

The preparations are at length complete. Every nook and corner is scrupulously clean; all *chometz* (leaven) has been banished from the house; even the children have carefully emptied their pockets of stray crumbs. The round and tempting *matzoth* (Passover bread) have been baked—the guest is at the door!

In the dining-room of Hirsch Bensef sat a goodly circle of friends at the *seder* (services conducted on the eve of Passover). The lamps shone brightly, and the lights in the silver candelabra threw their sheen upon the sumptuously set table, with its white embroidered cloth and its artistic dishes and goblets. At the head of the table stood a sofa covered with rich hangings and soft pillows, a veritable throne, upon which sat the king of the family, clad in snow-white attire. In the midst of richly-robed guests, surrounded by an almost oriental luxury, the master of the house had donned his shroud. It is a custom akin to that of the ancient Egyptians, who brought the mummies of their ancestors to the festive board, that in the excess of carnal enjoyment they might not forget the grim reaper, Death. Upon the table stood a plate of *mitzvoth* (a thicker kind of *matzoth* prepared specially for the *seder*), covered with a napkin, and upon this were placed a number of tiny silver dishes containing an egg, horseradish, the bone of a lamb, lettuce and a mixture of raisins and spices—all symbolical of ancient rites. Before each guest there stood a silver wine cup, to be refilled three times in the course of the evening. In the centre of the table stood the goblet of wine for *Elijahu Hanovi* (the Prophet Elijah), the hero of a thousand legends, and the fondly expected forerunner of the redemption of Israel and the coming of the

Milton Goldsmith

Messiah. By each plate was a copy of *Hagada*, the order of service for the evening. It is a book of facts and fancies, containing a recital of Israel's trials in Egypt; of its deliverance from the house of bondage; of its wanderings in the desert, and the sayings of Israel's wise men—a mixture of Bible stories, myths and prayers.

Contentment, peace and joy were plainly written upon the faces of the participants. The terrors of persecution were forgotten in the recollection of the miraculous deliverance of the Jews from their Egyptian task-masters. Reb Hirsch Bensef having pronounced a short blessing over the wine, pointed solemnly to the plate of unleavened bread before him.

"See," he said, "this is the bread your fathers ate in *Mizraim*. He that hungers let him partake of it, he that is in need let him eat and be satisfied."

As though in response to the hospitable invitation, there came a soft rap at the door. Mendel opened it and the bright light revealed a man and a woman, whose haggard faces and tattered garments presented the very picture of misery.

"Father! Mother!" Mendel cried, joyfully. "God be praised!" and he threw himself into the arms of his father.

With a single impulse the entire company arose and welcomed the unexpected guests. Mordecai and his wife had travelled on foot from Togarog to Kief, and, after terrible hardships, had arrived in time for the Passover. Great was the pleasure at their unlooked-for appearance, and as they hastened to tell the story of their sorrows and wanderings, sincere was the joy at their providential escape and the safe termination of their journey. All Israel is one family, and had the wanderers been in nowise related to Bensef, their reception would have been equally cordial and sincere.

A short time sufficed to remove the last traces of their terrible journey and to clothe them in the best that the wardrobe of their hosts afforded. Two more plates were set, two more goblets of wine were served and the ceremonies were continued.

So excited was Mendel over the arrival of his parents that he could scarcely compose himself sufficiently to follow the *seder* and ask the conventional question concerning the significance of the *Pesach* festival. In reply, the head of the house recited from his *Hagada* how the Lord punished Pharaoh for his obduracy, how the children of Israel were eventually led from captivity, how the Red Sea was divided that the chosen people might traverse its bed while the Egyptian perished miserably, and how the Lord conducted his people safely through the wilderness to the promised land. Then followed praise and thanksgiving, the *Hagadas* were pushed aside and feasting followed, continuing far into the night.

The woes and adventures of Mordecai and his wife elicited the hearty sympathy of their hearers, and the enjoyment of the evening was greatly enhanced by the knowledge that the dear ones were, for the present at least, safe from persecution.

The quiet dignity which had distinguished Mendel since he had become a student vanished. He became a child again, embracing and caressing his parents, weeping at their sorrows, laughing over their deliverance, and asking a thousand questions without waiting for replies.

It was decided that for the present the fugitives should remain with Bensef as his guests.

At the conclusion of the meal, the *Hagadas* were again taken up, and to the prayers of thanksgiving was added a prayer for the welfare of that little soul that was lost to Israel, the missing child Jacob.

CHAPTER XV

TWO LOVING HEARTS

The Crimean War had reached its disastrous conclusion. Russia had suffered ignominious defeat, the allies were successful in the Black Sea, and the despised Turks had shown a bold front along the Danube. It was evident that the military organization was as corrupt as the civil administration, that fraud and dishonesty were prevalent and neutralized the bravery of the troops.

"Another year of war and the whole of Southern Russia will be ruined," so wrote a patriot of 1855.

Under this great humiliation, the people suddenly awoke from their lethargy. The system of Nicholas had been put to the test and found wanting. The Government believed that it could accomplish everything by its own inherent wisdom and superiority, and had shown itself wofully incompetent. Dissatisfaction was deep and widespread. Philippics and satires appeared, and reforms were so boldly demanded that the Czar could not close his ears to the universal clamor. In the midst of disasters abroad and dissatisfaction at home, Nicholas died, and was succeeded by his son, a man of very different type.

The new monarch was well aware of the existing abuses, many of which had been carefully concealed from Nicholas by his obsequious counsellors. As heir-apparent he had held aloof from public affairs, and was therefore free from pledges of any kind; yet, while he allowed popular ideas and aspirations to find free utterance, he did not commit himself to any definite policy.

To Alexander, the Russians, Jew and gentile, now looked for relief. There were many abuses to correct and oppressive laws to repeal, and the public heart beat high with hope at the prospect of reforms. He repealed the laws limiting the number of students at each university; he reduced the excessive fees for passports; he moderated the rigorous censorship of the press, and, in fact, the Czar's acts justified the hopes of his subjects. Hundreds of new journals sprang into existence. He introduced reforms into the civil and military administrations, and, best of all, he created the *semstvos* or town assemblies of the people.

To the Jews, Alexander was particularly gracious. He removed many of the restrictions imposed by his predecessor. The stringent laws limiting the number of marriages in a community were moderated. In some few instances their quarters were enlarged, and an order was issued restoring to their parents all children that had been forcibly taken from them during the reign of the old Czar.

What rejoicing was there in Israel! How many families, separated by the inhuman decrees of Nicholas, were now reunited! Every home was gladdened either by the restoration of some beloved son, or in sympathy with the general rejoicing. One family in Kief waited in vain, however, for the return of a missing child. It was hoped by Mordecai that under the general amnesty Jacob, if indeed he were still living, would be allowed to return; but there were no tidings of him, and the conviction that he had met his death was strengthened.

A new and promising era opened for the oppressed and persecuted Hebrews. It appeared as if their patient resignation under adverse circumstances would eventually be rewarded by the concession of equal rights with their fellowmen. To be sure, all persecution did not cease. The badge of disgrace was still worn by every male Jew, the owning of land and the following of many trades was still forbidden. The Jew was still the object of derision throughout the Empire; he was still judged by a severer code of justice than were his gentile neighbors; the entire race was still held responsible for the crime of the individual. But active hostilities ceased and the Hebrews rejoiced thereat.

Mendel continued his studies, and in the course of a few years his fame spread from *jeschiva* to *jeschiva*, from congregation to congregation. By the time that he was twenty-one years of age, he had published a book in Hebrew, which, while it respected the religious sentiment of his people, paved the way for assimilating the modern knowledge. The work created a profound impression. The chief synagogues of Moscow and of Warsaw invited him to take up his residence with them. His reply was that as his parents resided in Kief, he preferred to remain there.

There was another attraction in Kief more powerful than that exercised by his parents, more potent to keep the young philosopher in the city of his adoption. Mendel was in love. His heart, schooled in the wisdom of many nations, had surrendered unconditionally to the charm of Recha, the beautiful dark-eyed daughter of Rabbi Jeiteles. Recha was rapidly nearing her seventeenth year and each month, nay each day, added to her charms. Like most girls of her ancient race, she was well developed for her years, and her symmetrical figure, lustrous eyes and raven tresses presented a picture of oriental beauty, whose peer did not exist among the Slavonic types that lived and loved round about her. So at least thought Mendel, and so thought a score of enamored youths beside. Recha's beauty was by no means her chief attraction. The graces of her mind and heart were in keeping with her lovely exterior. From her father she had acquired learning, wit and wisdom, and from her mother charm of manner and gentle ways.

The student's affection for the girl into whose society he was daily thrown, exercised great influence in holding him to the path of duty. To become worthy of such a treasure was his one desire. All that was best and brightest in his soul was aroused when he thought of Recha. It was she that inspired him, and his mind appeared more active when he thought of her. She was the beacon that guided his steps through the difficult paths of learning. Nor was his love unrequited. Young, handsome, intelligent beyond the generality of Jewish youth, Mendel was to Recha the embodiment of all that was good and noble.

No word of love had ever passed Mendel's lips, and yet there was a sympathetic understanding between them; they found a paradise in each other's society. Recha had not a few admirers. Go where she would, she found herself surrounded by willing slaves, who at the slightest encouragement would have thrown themselves at her feet. In vain were *schadchens* employed by many of the wealthy and influential Jewish residents in Kief to seek the hand of Jeiteles' lovely daughter in marriage. But Recha had neither eyes nor ears for any of them.

One evening Mendel entered the Rabbi's house in unusual haste, his face wearing an expression of mingled doubt and hope.

The Rabbi and his wife were absent. Recha observing his perturbation, asked eagerly:

"Has anything happened?"

"Here, Recha, read this letter."

Recha read the missive which Mendel handed to her. It was a flattering invitation from the congregation of Odessa. "Our Rabbi is old and infirm," stated the letter, "and desires a staff in his declining years. Your reputation as a scholar has reached our people and we would consider it an honor to have you with us."

As Recha read, she turned deadly pale and the paper almost fell from her hands.

"What will you do?" she faltered at length, while the great tears stood in her eyes.

Mendel's heart throbbed with wild delight as he saw her evident emotion, and her eyes fell under his ardent gaze. Seizing her hand, he asked, in a low voice:

"What would you have me do?"

Recha gazed fondly into Mendel's eyes, and said:

"I should be very unhappy if you left home. What would my father do without you? Think of the void it would create in the lives of your parents and of your uncle. What would the congregation do without you, whom they already regard as an oracle? Stay with us in Kief."

"God bless you, my dear," replied the young man, fervently. "I will remain; I shall never leave this place unless you go with me as my wife."

It was simple and unromantic.

The lovers, happy and contented, sat side by side, discussing their roseate future, and when the Rabbi and his wife returned, the young folks advanced to meet them.

"Rabbi," said the student, bravely, "Recha has promised to be my wife."

"*Mazal tov*," ejaculated both Jeiteles and his wife. "May the Lord of Israel bless you."

The messenger from Odessa was dismissed with a negative reply.

There was a merry gathering the following Saturday afternoon to congratulate the betrothed couple. Sincere were the wishes for their future happiness that were showered upon them. It is a characteristic of Israelites the world over to feel a lively interest in whatever befalls their co-religionists, high or low. "Despised and rejected" by their gentile neighbors, they sought for consolation and found it in the society of their own kin, and thus arose this sympathy, this love for one another which has so strongly cemented the hearts of the Jews.

"Clannish" has been hurled at them as a term of reproach. So are the frightened sheep clannish when they huddle together in the shelterless field, for protection against the blasts of the pitiless storm.

The interval between the betrothal and the wedding is usually short, and the happy day that made Mendel and Recha man and wife was not long in coming.

"I have a request to make," said the student to the Rabbi, a few days before the all-important event took place.

"Name it, my son," replied the Rabbi.

"I do not wish Recha to have her hair cut off. Her tresses are her crowning beauty, and it would grieve me to the heart to see her shorn of them."

The Rabbi shrugged his shoulders and uttered a short ejaculation of surprise.

"A breach of so old a custom," said he, "will be looked upon by the whole congregation as impiety."

"I know," replied Mendel, "but in this instance, I must brave their displeasure."

"But," said the Rabbi, still hesitating, "if—God forbid—your wife should meet with any misfortune, it would be attributed to the anger of God at this innovation."

"I must do what I think is right," replied Mendel, "and if the example of Recha induces others to disobey an offensive and obnoxious injunction, the people will be the gainers."

After much deliberation, the Rabbi and his wife at last consented. Not so easily, however, were the rest of the congregation reconciled.

We will anticipate a little to remark that there was no calamity in the course of Mendel's conjugal experience, which could be traced to Recha's luxuriant hair.

Great were the preparations with which the happy day was ushered in.

The closely veiled bride, supported by her mother and aunt, was conducted into the room in a shower of barley, and was led to the supremely happy groom, who, arrayed in cap and gown and wearing a praying scarf, stood ready to receive her. Seven times the maiden encircled her future husband and then took her position at his side, after which the father of the *kalle* (bride) began the important services. Holding a goblet of wine in his right hand, he invoked God's blessing with the tenderness of a loving father and the solemnity of a priest. Short and impressive was the chanted prayer. The couple sipped the wine, the ring was placed on the bride's finger, the words uttered, a glass broken into fragments under the heel of the groom, prayers were recited by the Rabbi, and the religious ceremony was at an end. Then followed the congratulations of the friends, the good-natured pushing of the assembled guests in their eagerness to kiss the bride or shake the radiant groom by the hand. A bounteous feast closed the festivities. Mendel and Recha were bound to each other by indissoluble ties.

The newly wedded pair took up their residence with Rabbi Jeiteles, whose advanced age incapacitated him at times from attending to the onerous duties of his office. Mendel was ever at his side as a helper, until he grew into the office. Despite the honors showered upon him he remained the modest, unassuming, amiable young man, whom flattery could not affect nor pleasure lure from the course of strict duty.

When at the end of a year Recha presented him with a little girl-baby, which they called Kathinka, he was the happiest man on the face of the earth.

CHAPTER XVI

THE CHOLERA AND ITS VICTIMS

A new danger threatened our friends. Scarcely had the fanatical Russian given the Jews a brief respite from persecution, when Nature seized the rod and wielded it with relentless hand, smiting Jew and gentile, the pious and the ungodly, with equal severity. The cholera had broken out in Central Russia and its devastations were terrible beyond description. The country from Kief to Odessa was as one vast charnel-house. As has always been the case during epidemics, the Jews suffered less from the ravages of the disease than did their gentile neighbors. The strict dietary laws which excluded everything not absolutely fresh and clean, the frequent ablutions which the religious rites demanded of the Jews and their freedom from all enervating excesses, bore excellent results in a diminished mortality. Nevertheless, many a victim was hurried to an untimely grave, many a family sat in sackcloth and ashes for a departed member.

Amid the general consternation caused by the rapid spread of the plague, the *feldshers* were unceremoniously relegated to the background. Their surgery was practically useless and their drugs proved powerless to stay the disease. The *snakharkas*, on the other hand, prospered greatly.

Milton Goldsmith

Superstition flourished; prayers, sacrifices, incantations, magical rites, exorcisms, were invoked to allay the evil. The *moujiks* called frantically upon the saints for assistance, and then deliberately frustrated any relief these might have afforded by committing frightful excesses. Many a saint fell into temporary disfavor by his apparent indifference to the sufferings of his devotees.

The priests invented new ceremonials and each village had its own peculiar method of appeasing divine wrath. In Kief, the disease had taken a particularly virulent form. The filthy Dnieper, contaminated by the reeking sewerage of the city, was in a great measure to blame for the rapid spread of the disorder, but to have advanced such a theory would have been useless; the ignorant inhabitants ascribed the scourge to any source but the true one. At one time the *feldshers* were accused of having propagated the plague for their own pecuniary benefit, and the excited populace threw a number of doctors out of the windows of a hospital and otherwise maltreated the poor practitioners who fell into their clutches.

In Kanief, the inhabitants, crazed with fear at the progress of the plague, adopted an original and ingenious method to check it. At midnight, according to a preconcerted plan, all the maidens of the village met on the outskirts of the place and formed in picturesque procession. At the head marched a girl bearing an icon of the Madonna, gaudily painted and bedecked with jewels. Behind her came her companions, dragging a rope to which was attached a plow. In this order they made the circuit of the village, and it was confidently believed that the cholera would disappear within the magical circle thus described.[11]

Many and equally ingenious were the devices employed in Kief by the ignorant peasants. A wonder-working icon was brought from St. Petersburg, where, according to tradition, it had performed many miracles. Yet the plague continued, fed by the ignorance and intemperance of the people.

Surrounded by such dense superstition, it is not strange that the Jews, too, should resort to absurd rites to rid themselves of the dreaded guest. The poorer classes, living in the lower portions of the quarter, were the chief sufferers. There, where a dozen half-starved wretches were crowded into one small room, the plague was at its height. A hundred souls had already succumbed and the list of victims was growing daily. Alas! the misery of the stricken families! Deprived of medical attendance, of drugs, of fresh air, there appeared little hope for the denizens of the infected district.

The busiest man during these troublous times was Itzig Maier, the beadle, whose acquaintance we have already made as the messenger sent by Bensef to the *bal-shem* at Tchernigof. The condition of Itzig and his family had not improved since we last saw him. The little fortune which, if gossip spoke truly, he had acquired by his adroit manoeuvring at that time, had been dissipated; his family had grown larger and was a constant drain upon his meagre resources, while his income appeared to diminish as his expenses increased. Besides, Itzig had a daughter who was now of a marriageable age, and he was obliged to toil and save to provide a dowry. Beile was unattractive and uninteresting, and Itzig did not conceal from himself the fact that without a dowry it might prove difficult to bring her under the *chuppe.*

Of late Itzig had had little time to think of his family. In the house and in the hovel, wherever the cholera had knocked for admittance, there was Itzig Maier, performing his duties with an unfailing regularity—preparing the shrouds, attiring the dead and comforting the mourners—all unmindful that he might be the next victim. His services were in constant demand and money was actually pouring in upon him.

The first to visit, aid and counsel the stricken community was Rabbi Jeiteles, whose unselfish devotion to duty led him from house to house, administering simple remedies to the suffering, closing the eyes of the dead and consoling the grieving survivors. He knew no fear, no hesitation. To his wife's anxious words of warning he had but one reply, "We are all in God's hands."

Earnestly he went about his work, conscious of his danger, yet putting all thought of self aside until he, too, fell a victim to the dread destroyer.

One day, while performing the last sad rites over a dead child, he was stricken, and before he could be removed to his home he had breathed his last.

Great was the grief in the Jewish community in Kief. From one end of the quarter to the other the inhabitants mourned for thirty days, bewailing the death of their beloved Rabbi, as though each household had lost a revered parent.

The plague continued its ravages, and the people in their wild terror resorted to the *bal-shem* for amulets and talismans. On every door could be read the inscription, "Not at home." But the cholera would not be put off by so flimsy a device and entered unbidden. Even the death of a grave-digger did not stay the dread disease, although it had been prophesied that such an event would end the trouble. The cabalistic books were ransacked for charms and mystic signs with which to resist the power of the conqueror, but all in vain.

One morning Itzig ran as fast as his shuffling legs would bear him, up the dirty lane that led to his abode, and fell rather than walked into the low door that led into his hut. His wife was engaged in washing a baby—the seventh—and Beile, an ill-favored, sallow-complexioned girl, sat at the window sewing.

"Jentele," cried Itzig, sinking into a chair, "God has been good to us!"

"Have you just found that out?" asked his wife, petulantly. "What is the matter? Have you come into a fortune?"

"Beile, leave the room," said Itzig.

"Why, father?"

"Leave the room! I want to talk to your mother."

Beile put away her work and walked out into the lane.

"Rejoice with me, Jentele," said the delighted husband, as he rubbed his shrivelled hands. "Beile is a *kalle*; she will marry to-morrow."

"Has anybody fallen in love with her?" asked the mother.

"No; but she will marry all the same."

"Well, speak out, man! You kill one with suspense."

"Do you know Reb Bensef, our *parnas*?"

"Yes; but what has he to do with our Beile?"

"Reb Bensef being very much distressed by the death of Rabbi Jeiteles, went to Tchernigof to ask counsel of the *bal-shem* and has just returned."

"Well, what did the wise man advise?" asked Jentele, burning with impatience, while her partially washed baby lay kicking in her arms.

"Listen, I am coming to that," answered Itzig, with provoking slowness. "He said that if a poor man would marry an equally poor girl, under a *chuppe* erected in the cemetery between two newly made graves, God's anger would be appeased and the scourge would end. To-day Bensef sought me out. 'Itzig,' he said, 'you have a daughter. I know a husband for her. I will give an outfit to both bride and groom and provide them with money to last a year, if you will consent to their marrying in the cemetery.' What do you think of it?"

"Who is the young man?" queried Jentele, her face expressing neither pleasure nor pain.

"You know the *jeschiva* student, Kahn?"

"He is poor, very poor, indeed."

"What is that to us? Reb Bensef will provide clothing and money for a whole year."

"And when that is all gone?" queried his wife, resuming operations upon the baby.

"Then God will provide. Did we have more when we married?"

"It is an opportunity of a life-time," mused Jentele, looking at her parched and yellow better-half. "Do as you think best."

Armed with the support of his wife and without consulting his daughter, whose voice in a matter of such minor importance seemed to him unnecessary, Itzig hastened to Bensef's house and expressed his consent to the arrangement. Together the worthies went to the synagogue, where the unsuspecting Kahn was engaged in prayer. A few words sufficed to explain the situation. Kahn looked timidly at Bensef, then upon the ground; finally, he shrugged his shoulders and signified his readiness to be led to the altar. It mattered not to him what disposition they made of him. He was poor and without prospects and could never hope to support a wife by his own exertions. The way was now made easy. Besides, in thus sacrificing himself for the extinction of the plague he was doing a *mitzva* (a good deed) in the sight of the Lord. To refuse was out of the question. The young man was led in triumph to Itzig's house and introduced to his future wife, who heard of the arrangement for the first time and evinced neither pleasure nor dissatisfaction.

The betrothal was duly announced and hasty preparations made for the coming ceremony, since delay meant new victims to the plague.

Mendel strove with all his eloquence to prevent the carrying out of this monstrous purpose. Every fibre within him revolted at such folly, and he hurried from house to house, entreating the most influential members of the congregation to aid him in opposing it. But the scourge spoke more eloquently than did the young Rabbi—the people listened to him but shook their heads. Many who doubted the efficacy of the plan, lacked the moral courage to oppose an act which met with the approval of the greater portion of the community.

"Every means should be employed to prevent the disease from doing further mischief," argued some. "We have vainly tried everything else, let us try this. God may at last listen to our prayers."

"The *bal-shem* has commanded it; it is sure to prove successful," said others.

After a day spent in earnest but ineffectual arguments, Mendel saw that his endeavors in this direction were futile, and concluding that further interference would be useless, he sorrowfully wended his way homeward.

The sun shone fiercely on the morrow upon a desolate landscape. All nature appeared to be under the ban of the plague. The leaves upon the trees were sere and withered, the brooks were dry and the birds had long since hushed their melody. The highways were deserted, save where at intervals a solemn funeral train carried the dead to a final resting-place.

A strange procession wended its way to the Jewish cemetery. It was not a funeral, although from the tears and lamentations of those who took part in it, it might have been mistaken for one. Young and old, men and women, all in whom superstition still dwelt, followed the cortege to the field of death and accompanied the bride and bridegroom to the improvised altar. Thanks to the generosity of Bensef, Beile was richly attired, and the groom in spite of his poverty was neatly clad. They walked hand in hand, happy in the consciousness that they were performing a service to humanity. As the grotesque train entered the burial-ground the lamentations became louder at the sight of the scores of newly-made graves. The bride and groom lost their happy look, for a stern and terrible reality confronted them. The *chuppe* had been erected between two freshly-dug graves. The people ceased their wailing and became as silent as the awful place in which they stood.

Mendel, who had been requested to tie the solemn knot, had refused to do so and had absented himself. The ceremony was, therefore, performed by the Rabbi of another congregation, who hurried through the short service with almost eager haste. Jentele kissed the weeping bride, Itzig embraced his son-in-law.

Suddenly the father tottered and with a moan fell to the ground. His face became livid, his eyes sank in their sockets, his blue lips frothed, and his whole body shook with agony.

"The cholera! the cholera!" shouted those nearest him, and while many fled for their lives, a dozen willing hands lifted up the prostrate beadle and endeavored by every means in their power to restore him to consciousness. In vain were all their ministrations, in vain their prayers and exhortations. For a short while Itzig suffered intense agony, then his shrunken form became rigid, his head fell back, his homely and shrivelled features relaxed into a hideous grin, and the unfortunate beadle travelled the way of the hundreds he had in his time borne to this very spot.[12]

FOOTNOTES:

[Footnote 11: Wallace, p. 78.]

CHAPTER XVII

COMMON-SENSE VS. SUPERSTITION

In spite of the sacrifice, in spite of the fanaticism of the gentiles and the equally great superstition of the Jews, the plague continued with unabated violence. But few families in Kief had been spared a visit from the dread reaper.

On the Sabbath following the events just narrated, the Israelites went to their places of worship as usual, and ardent prayers for deliverance ascended to the Almighty. Mendel, notwithstanding his youth, officiated in the place of the departed Rabbi Jeiteles, and on this occasion he formally entered upon the duties of his honorable office.

Sermons, as we understand them, were not in vogue among the Russian Jews, and lectures in the synagogue on topics unconnected with religion or morality had not been dreamed of. Jeiteles would at times discourse upon some knotty point in the *Torah*, and on the more important holidays expound the meaning of certain ceremonials. When Mendel ascended the pulpit, the stricken congregation, with hushed and eager expectation, awaited his words.

Mendel began by alluding to the sad demise of the beloved Rabbi. He spoke of his great heart, of his benevolence and wisdom, and as his powerful and sympathetic voice rang through the vast synagogue, few were the eyes that were not suffused with tears.

"Friends," he continued, "in an epidemic such as is at present raging in our midst, our thoughts are naturally directed to *Adonai*, and we implore His mercy. If such a misfortune tends to turn our prayers heavenward, to arouse our humanity towards our suffering fellow-men, then indeed the evil may become a blessing in disguise. But if you lay the blame of your misfortunes to God alone, and believe that He inflicts His creatures with disease because He is angry with the world, you degrade the Lord into an angry, revengeful Being of human type, instead of the grand and supreme *Adonai Echod* whom our forefathers worshipped.

"The many absurd observances of which you have been guilty, and which culminated in the marriage at the cemetery, are blasphemous. I will tell you why. If God has really sent this trouble, it is done for a wise purpose, and God will know when to remove the infliction without such barbaric ceremonies to propitiate Him. If, on the other hand, your own negligence of the laws of health is to blame, then absurd rites, even though sanctioned by a wonder-working Rabbi of some distant city, are of no avail; but the only effective way to terminate the trouble is to investigate our way of living, and to correct whatever we find prejudicial to our well-being."

That this new and hitherto unheard-of doctrine should cause a profound sensation was but natural. A murmur through the audience showed plainly that sentiment was divided upon the subject. Mendel, disregarding the interruption, continued. In clear and concise terms he pointed out the historical fact that throughout all the epidemics of the past, Israel, by the perfection of her sanitary laws, enjoyed almost an immunity from disease. He hurriedly enumerated the many excellent Mosaic laws concerning diet and cleanliness, and endeavored to show that the ablest physicians of modern times could not improve upon these commands. Then he spoke of the recent discoveries by the German doctors, and the promulgation of the new theory that contagious diseases were due to the existence of germs which could only be exterminated by certain well-defined means, prominent among which was cleanliness. While he spoke his audience hung breathlessly upon his words, and, as they gazed upon the inspired countenance of the young man, they felt that he expounded the truth, and they believed in him.

"And now, my friends," continued Mendel, "let us drop superstition and substitute common-sense. Let us show our gentile neighbors that we can combat this epidemic with intelligence. In the first place, let us determine upon some well-defined plan. Let us organize. With unity of purpose much can be accomplished. The greatest danger of the disease lies in its contagious nature. Our first duty, therefore, is to isolate those who are sick. In this way the spreading of the plague may be checked. There is nothing new in this plan. Moses commanded that all persons suffering with infectious diseases should be placed outside of the camp of Israel. That you have not already resorted to this means shows rather a kind heart than a quick wit.

"You have doubtless observed that those living upon the swampy ground near the river mourn a greater number of departed than those dwelling further inland. That locality must, therefore, exercise a prejudicial influence upon the health of the people. It is here that the poor and destitute live. Let us care for them. Let the more wealthy and more fortunate families take into their houses those to whom Providence has been less bountiful. You whose daily business takes you to the hovels of the poor, know how wretched and filthy they are, how even the healthy can scarcely bear the foulness of their atmosphere. How great must be the power of such pest-holes to extend the plague when once it finds a foothold there! Let us tear down those hovels. There are enough rich men among you to build new and better houses. You have heard that many have become ill through drinking the water from the wells. Water you must drink; but a German doctor tells us that heat will kill the germs of disease. Let us, therefore, boil all the water we drink and diminish the tendency to sickness in that way. Finally, it is necessary to avoid all excesses, to live temperately, to observe strict cleanliness. Thus you may cheat the plague of a great number of victims. God sends the good, my friends, but we bring the evil upon ourselves. This evening I shall be pleased to see at my house all those who are willing to devote their time and money to the great cause, and we will there discuss the ways and means of driving out the cholera, and thus avenging the death of our beloved and regretted Rabbi Jeiteles."

Such enthusiasm as greeted the speaker when he descended from the pulpit had never been known in the synagogue. His manner as well as his words, his beauty and imposing presence as well as his profound and magnetic intellect, had carried the hearts of his auditors. The men clasped him warmly by the hand and promised their co-operation, and the women in the gallery gave vent to their approval in a no less hearty manner. When the Sabbath service came to a close, the only sentiment among the members of the congregation was in favor of immediate action.

The news of the sermon spread rapidly through the community, and the other congregations became interested and promised their support.

The young Rabbi still lived with his mother-in-law, and a

large company assembled at the house to carry out the plans suggested by him that morning. The meeting included all the wealthy and influential men of the quarter, and they entered into the spirit of the new ideas with as much enthusiasm as they had displayed in the superstitious observances of a few days before. Those willing to take an active part in the great hygienic work were divided by Mendel into committees, one of which was to undertake the arduous work of isolation and of providing willing and capable nurses to wait upon the sick; another to superintend the disinfection or removal of the wretched hovels in the lower portion of the Jewish quarter; a third to visit the families into which the scourge had already forced an entrance, and inculcate such lessons of cleanliness as would materially lessen the chances of further contagion.

Mendel placed himself at the head of all these bodies, so that he might the better direct their actions. He then explained to them in detail the various theories that had been advanced throughout the civilized world as to the cause of the cholera and the methods employed in western countries to combat the disease. He had read much and his powerful memory had retained all that was useful and important, and he spoke with such decision that all those pious men, among whom any delving outside of the sacred limits of the Talmud was strictly prohibited, now listened, in open-mouthed wonder, to the instruction of their youthful sage without once demanding whence he had obtained his knowledge. It sufficed them to know that they now possessed a tangible weapon with which to fight their dreaded enemy, and they were ready to follow their leader wherever he chose to conduct them.

The great work was begun without delay. Before undertaking it, however, it was necessary to obtain the Governor's consent to the improvements, and to Mendel fell the task of calling upon the mighty man at his palace.

When Alexander II. ascended his father's throne, his first important act was to appoint new Governors of the various provinces, for it was a notorious fact that the heads of these departments were as a rule totally unfit to direct the affairs with which they were entrusted. He replaced the old and corrupt Governors by young and vigorous men, heartily in accord with his ideas of reform. General Pomeroff, a friend and stanch admirer of the Emperor while he was still Czarewitch, was selected to govern the influential province of Kief. Pomeroff was a strikingly handsome man, progressive in his views, humane in the treatment of his subordinates, quick to perceive merit where it existed and anxious to assist in any work which promised to redound to the credit of his province. With this man Mendel sought an interview. It was with difficulty that he gained admittance to the presence of the august ruler, into whose sanctum no Jew had yet entered, but after a long delay he succeeded in meeting the Governor face to face.

"Your excellency," said Mendel, in a quiet and dignified manner, speaking in perfect Russian, "I come to seek your assistance in a matter of great importance to a large class of your subjects."

The Governor, surprised as much by the purity of language as by the temerity of the Jew, looked at the young man, scrutinizingly, for some moments.

"What do you wish?" he asked, at length. "Make your application short, for I have much to do."

Mendel unfolded his views briefly to the astonished Governor. He expressed his desire to rid the Jewish quarter as far as practicable from the effects of the plague.

"The cholera has almost run its course," he said, "and while our efforts might have been impotent to check its ravages during its early course, they may serve to prevent its further spread and to diminish the number of its victims. We are amply provided with willing hands and with the necessary money, but we desire your excellency's sanction, and your permission to remove those hovels from our quarter which are dangerous to the general health of its inhabitants."

Governor Pomeroff had arisen and was striding up and down his apartment. When Mendel concluded, he stopped and held out his hand.

"Give me your hand," he said; "you are a man after my own heart. Go on with your work, and I will give instructions that no one shall interfere with you. If you need assistance, call upon me and I will do what I can for you."

"I thank your excellency," replied Mendel, overjoyed, "but your good-will is all we ask. The cholera is a frightful evil, and if we succeed in lessening its ravages we shall be well repaid for our trouble."

"I expect you to come and report to me from time to time," said the Governor, so far forgetting his dignity as to accompany the Jew to the door.

Mendel bowed and left the apartment. In the ante-room, a number of servants had collected, and no sooner did the young man appear than they began to banter and annoy him. It was perfectly legitimate for the serfs to derive as much amusement from the Jews as possible.

"Here comes the Jew," cried one, "and by the Holy St. Peter he is still alive."

"Well, Jew," said another, seizing Mendel by the beard; "by

what charms did you force your way into the Governor's presence? Impudence is a great characteristic of your race."

At that moment the door opened and Governor Pomeroff appeared at the threshold.

He severely rebuked the astonished servants for their rude behavior, apologized to Mendel for the indignities he had been obliged to endure, and sent a guard with him to conduct him to his home.

The Rabbi returned to his people with a light and happy heart. He had been more than successful, for he had gained a friend in the Governor, and his mind lost itself in visions of the good this powerful ally would enable him to effect.

FOOTNOTES:

[Footnote 12: Herzberg-Fraenkel's "Polnische Juden" cites a similar incident.]

CHAPTER XVIII

THE GOVERNOR'S PROJECT

Great were the energy and zeal which the Hebrew community of Kief displayed in carrying out the plans of their young Rabbi. Mendel himself led them on with an ardor that knew no abatement. He visited the most dangerous pest-holes, helped to move the sick, brought relief and consolation to the suffering and bereaved, while ever at his side was his wife, Recha. Her devotion to the cause was only second to the love she bore her husband. Undaunted by the awful fate that had befallen her father, she followed Mendel into the thickest of the danger and like a ministering angel brought comfort and relief. Their example was contagious. Young and old, male and female, vied with one another in doing good and in mitigating suffering. The superstitious dread with which they had formerly regarded the disease had disappeared and with it much of the danger which fear or an over-wrought imagination causes. A large building was secured and fitted up as a hospital. Thither the sick were conveyed and there kept in strict quarantine. It was not difficult to find nurses among those who had already had the disease, when told that they need not fear its recurrence.

Many of the miserable dwellings of the poor were demolished and the ground cleansed and fumigated, their former inhabitants in the meanwhile finding ample accommodations in the synagogues or in the houses of the wealthy. There was not a family of well-to-do Jews that did not harbor a number of those who were thus summarily deprived of shelter. Every well which might have become contaminated was filled up with earth and stone, and strict injunctions were issued to use no water that had not been thoroughly boiled. The schools were temporarily closed to avoid the danger of infection, exercise in the fields was recommended, and so well were all these regulations observed that at the end of six weeks the Jewish quarter was practically free from the disease, while the grim monster still raged among the families of the less prudent gentiles. Then the work of reconstructing what had been demolished was taken up. Thanks to the offerings of Hirsch Bensef and his friends, money was not lacking and willing hands were found to supply the necessary manual labor. Where wretched huts and unpainted hovels had offended the eye, unpretentious but clean and comfortable dwellings now were seen. The lower portion of the town had been entirely remodelled and vied in point of neatness with the more aristocratic quarter. As home after home was completed, the former inmates took possession and great was the rejoicing. It was impossible, however, to do away with all the poor hovels that abounded in the Jewish quarter: such an undertaking would have required a vast amount of money and years of labor. It was only where the need was most pressing that the work of regeneration was carried on.

The sad fact soon forced itself on Mendel that the portion of Kief allotted to the Jews was entirely inadequate for the fifteen thousand inhabitants who were condemned to dwell there. So overcrowded were some of the houses that it seemed a miracle that the death-rate had not been even greater; yet there seemed to be no remedy for the evil. The limits had been fixed by the government and against its decree who dared appeal? By *Rosh-Hashana* (New Year's) there was not a single case of cholera in the Jewish quarter. One morning, several days after the New Year festival, Mendel sat in his snug parlor with his wife and her mother, speaking hopefully of the coming time.

"How happy we would be," said Recha, "if father were alive to see all the good that has been accomplished. His only ambition was to improve the mental and physical condition of our people. He would have taken the greatest interest in your undertaking, and would have been the most zealous of your helpers."

Mendel sighed.

"I feel, Recha," he said, "that all this work was inspired by his death. Had it not been for the grief it caused me, I doubt whether I should have felt it my duty to open the eyes of our good people, but might have allowed them to continue in their accustomed way. Troubles, dear Recha, are frequently blessings in disguise, and under the rod of affliction we may recognize the loving hand of God. Our hearts groan under the heavy blows of misfortune, but in the end we will find ourselves the stronger, the better, the more perfect for the tribulations we have undergone."

Recha felt the truth of her husband's words and dried her eyes.

"I look into the year just begun with great hopes," continued Mendel. "Among our own people the greatest harmony prevails. The sorrows we have suffered in common have served to knit our souls more closely together, and the little quarrels and petty jealousies that formerly agitated our community have ceased. All is bright and beautiful without. The Emperor purposes to introduce various reforms and the

Governor is favorably disposed towards us. Let us trust that those who have suffered losses through the merciless hand of death may find some consolation in the greater happiness and prosperity of the community."

Mendel was interrupted by a knock at the door, and Recha upon opening it gave admittance to a soldier, whose uniform proclaimed him one of the Governor's body guard.

"I seek Mendel Winenki," said the man, with military precision.

Recha became pale as death; a terrible suspicion flashed through her mind. Mendel, too, was ill at ease.

"What do you want of me?" he asked.

"His excellency, the Governor, has instructed me to conduct you into his presence," answered the soldier.

"For what purpose?" asked the Rabbi, anxiously.

"I do not know. I am simply to take you with me."

The greatest consternation prevailed among the little group. For a Jew to be summoned before the Governor betokened no good.

"You would arrest my husband!" cried Recha, placing herself between the soldier and the Rabbi. "He has done no wrong. You shall not take him!"

"Calm yourself, Recha," said the Rabbi, gently. "There is no need of borrowing trouble. The soldier has not intimated that I am to be punished. The Governor was at one time very friendly to me; perhaps it is upon a friendly matter that he now wishes to see me."

Kissing his wife and mother-in-law and bidding them be of good cheer, Mendel accompanied the guide to the Governor's residence. It was a long walk through a number of densely populated streets to the animated *podol*, or business centre. Hundreds of shops lined the streets, but they were empty and deserted. The cholera had deprived them of their customers and in many cases of their proprietors. Business was practically suspended during the continuance of the plague. On leaving the *podol*, the road led up a steep incline to the Petcherskoi. This was the official portion of the town. Here stood the vast Petcherskoi convent, a mass of old buildings, formerly a fine specimen of Byzantine architecture, but now gradually yielding to the ravages of time. Here, too, were the barracks, and the martial tread of the exercising regiments rang out clearly in the September air. Beyond the barracks, and by its high position commanding a fine view of the city, stood the Governor's palace, an imposing pile of Russian architecture, which, when Kief was still the capital of the Empire, was the scene of regal festivities and despotic cruelty.

The ante-room of the Governor was filled with a motley crowd of petitioners. There were deputations from the provincial towns, haughty noblemen attired in lace coats and bedecked with badges, officers, soldiers and *gendarmes* in gorgeous uniforms. Mendel's courage sank when he saw the formidable group before him.

"Remain here," commanded the guard who had accompanied him, "and I will announce your presence to his excellency."

A moment later he returned and, to the surprise of the waiting petitioners, beckoned Mendel to follow him into the private cabinet. That a Jew should be shown such favor was scarcely calculated to put the rest in a good humor, and loud murmurs of discontent arose from all parts of the room.

If Mendel had any fears of the reception which awaited him, they were at once dispelled by the Governor's cordial greeting:

"Well, Rabbi," he exclaimed, smilingly, extending his hand, "I have waited in vain for you to bring me the promised tidings and have sent for you in sheer despair. Why did you not come to see me?"

"Your excellency," replied Mendel, "I have been busy day and night, but had I thought that you took an interest in our work I would have hastened to inform you of our progress. Thank God, the result has exceeded our fondest expectations."

"I have heard of it," replied Pomeroff. "It has been the subject of a hundred discussions at court and at the exchanges, and there is nought but praise for the man who was the first to fight the cholera here in Russia with the weapons science has furnished mankind."

Mendel blushed and said, modestly:

"That man is a Jew, your excellency. It is not usual for one of our race to be the recipient of compliments at the hands of the gentiles."

The Governor's brow darkened and he remained silent for a moment. Finally he replied:

"Such praise would be more plentiful if all Jews were like you."

"They are, your excellency," answered Mendel, warmly. "Oh, if you but knew how brave, how noble a heart beats beneath the rough exterior of the Jew; if you but knew how passionately he yearns for an opportunity to show himself in his true character, you would pity him more and judge him less harshly."

"It is upon that very topic that I wish to converse with you," said the Governor, motioning Mendel to a seat, while he threw himself upon a comfortable lounge. Lighting a cigarette, he settled himself for a long conversation, apparently unmindful of the dignitaries who awaited an audience without. "I would give the Jew an opportunity to become not only a useful but a respected citizen."

"Your excellency is too good," said Mendel, joyously, as bright visions of emancipation flashed through his brain.

"I am told that you have great influence with your people," continued the Governor. "Am I correctly informed?"

"I am too young to influence them, but I believe I have their esteem and respect."

"They, at all events, place confidence in you," answered Pomeroff. "Now listen to me patiently. I have always been a friend of the Hebrews. As a boy, I associated with Jews of my own age and found them congenial companions. When I had arrived at the age of manhood I awoke one day to find myself in grave financial difficulties. There is no need of going into details. Suffice it to say that in my dilemma I went to one of the companions of my youth, a Jew, who had in the meantime acquired a fortune, and appealed to his generosity. My confidence was not misplaced and his timely aid saved my reputation and my honor. I am therefore favorably disposed toward your people and would help them if it were in my power to do so."

"Your excellency can do much," exclaimed Mendel.

"Let me finish what I have to say before you indulge in vain hopes," answered the Governor. "Let us discuss the situation fearlessly and without prejudice and try to find the root of the difficulty. Why are your people despised? Firstly, because they are not Christians and the gentile can never forget that it was your race that was directly responsible for the death of our Saviour; secondly, were the gentile to forget it, the religious and social observances of your race are so thoroughly at variance with his own that he does not understand you and therefore looks down upon you. Under usual conditions, however, the Jew and the non-Jew live side by side in peace and harmony. It is only in time of unusual religious or political excitement that race prejudice comes into play and then the Hebrews suffer. Were your people to adopt the Christian religion and change their oriental customs for our own, race prejudice and persecution would cease, they would be placed socially upon a footing of equality with the gentiles and the entire human race would be benefited thereby. Do I make my meaning clear?"

"I do not quite grasp it," answered Mendel.

"Briefly, then, my idea is this: You have great influence over your co-religionists. Use that influence to their lasting advantage. Persuade them to accept the Christian faith. Induce them to be baptized and with that solemn rite will end the unnumbered persecutions, the untold misery which has unfortunately been the lot of Israel. His majesty Alexander is most graciously disposed towards reform. Now, at the beginning of his career, he is eager to accept any innovation which will reflect renown upon his rule. He has already considered plans for freeing the serfs and would gladly include in that emancipation the three million Jews that reside in the Empire. I speak with his august authority when I say that as soon as the Jews embrace the holy Catholic faith not only will their troubles end, but they will find themselves raised to an enviable condition and the fittest among them will fill positions of rank and honor."

Mendel had arisen and with a pitying smile waited for the Governor to conclude his remarks.

"Your excellency does me too much honor," he said, quietly. "The man was never born, nor will he ever be, who can wean the Jews from their faith. Your excellency would find it easier to turn the waters of the Dnieper into the Arctic Ocean than to change the handful of Jews in Kief into Christians."

"But there are many who have already deserted the ranks of Israel," said the Governor.

"There are some renegades, it is true, but they do not in reality desert the faith of their people. They merely seek to escape some of the observances with which they are not in accord. Such people do not become Christians—they remain Jews to the end of their days."

"But, consider," said the Governor, earnestly, for he had set his heart upon this project. "At present you are despised and hated. You are forced to vegetate, rather than live, within the narrow confines of an uninviting and unhealthy quarter. Your natural capabilities are dwarfed. Your property and even your lives are at the mercy of the ignorant people that surround you. An acknowledgment of the faith that already counts many millions of adherents, a mere profession of belief in the great Saviour who came from heaven to save mankind, will change all this and you will at once enter into a life of peace and honor and social equality with the noblest of the land. Is it not worth considering?"

"No, your excellency," answered Mendel, boldly. "As I have already told you, it is impossible."

"Your reasons, Rabbi," said the Governor, with a shade of irritation in his voice. "Will not the new avenues for pleasure and happiness compensate for your ancient ceremonials and superstitions? The theatre, the lecture, the school will be opened to you. We will bid you enter and partake of all those delights which are in store for the best of us. Is that no inducement?"

Mendel sighed deeply, as he answered:

"Your excellency invites me to speak and I will do so frankly, even at the risk of incurring your displeasure. Think you that the prejudice which the Christian has felt against the Jew for over eighteen centuries can be eradicated in a moment by the apostasy of our race? The Russian nobility, accustomed to regard the Hebrews as accursed in the sight of God, as a nation of usurers and ungodly fanatics, is not in a fit condition of mind to forego its prejudices and welcome these same Jews as equals. The lower classes of Russians who have at the the mother's breast imbibed hatred and contempt for the despised and helpless Jew, who have from time immemorial considered the Jews as their just and legitimate prey, will scarcely condescend to offer the rejected race the hand of brotherly love simply because the Governor or even the Emperor commands it. It has been tried, your excellency, at various times; notably in Spain. Terrified by threats of torture on the one hand or seduced by promises of great reward on the other, many an Israelite accepted the Catholic faith. Alas! how bitterly was the error regretted. Instead of being admitted to that fellowship with which the gentiles had tempted them, greater humiliations, greater persecutions followed, until the horrors of the inquisition chamber and death at the stake were welcomed by the poor wretches as a relief from mental torment still more terrible."

So they talked, the mighty ruler and the humble Rabbi, while those in the ante-room waited impatiently for an audience.

Finally the Governor arose.

"I will not exact a definite answer at present," he said. "Discuss the matter with your friends and come to see me again in the course of a week or two. Perhaps you will then think better of it."

Mendel shook his head.

"In a few days we shall have *Yom-Kipur*, our Day of Atonement," he said. "If you would know how tenaciously the Israelites cling to their faith and to their God, visit the synagogue on that day; behold them in fasting and prayer, renewing their covenant with the Lord and relying upon his divine protection and assistance. You will find it an impressive sight, one that will speak more eloquently than my weak words."

"I may come," answered the Governor, half in jest and half in earnest, while Mendel bowed himself out through the crowd of angry people in the waiting-room.

We shall not attempt to analyze the thoughts of the young Rabbi, as he retraced his steps towards his dwelling. On his arrival there, he found his wife and her mother greatly alarmed as to his safety. The strange and sudden summons and his long absence had aroused terrible fears in Recha's breast that he had been thrown into prison by the Governor, and her eyes were red with weeping. It was with a bounding heart, therefore, that she heard her husband's step on the threshold, and with a joyous cry she rushed to embrace him.

"God be praised, my Mendel has returned," she exclaimed, and smiling through her tears she led him into the house.

CHAPTER XIX

YOM-KIPUR

It is *Yom-Kipur*, the Day of Atonement.

Long before nightfall the shops and booths of the Israelites are closed. The merchant has silenced his cravings for gain, the pedler and the wanderer have returned to their families, travelling leagues upon leagues to reach home in time for the holy day. The beggar has cast aside his rags and attired himself in a manner more befitting the solemn occasion. The God-fearing man has closed his heart to all but pious thoughts, and, yielding to the holy influence, even the impious cannot but think of God and of a future beyond the grave.

The holy night is approaching. A river of light streams through the arched windows of the houses of prayer, flooding the streets and penetrating into the hearts of the inhabitants. Young and old slowly wend their way to the synagogues, there to bow down before the Lord who delivered their ancestors from Egyptian bondage and who on this day will sit in judgment upon their actions; will grant them mercy or pronounce their doom; will inscribe them in the book of life or in that of eternal death. The women are robed in white, the men wear shrouds over their black *caftans* and carry huge prayer-books. At the door of the Lord's House, and before entering its sacred precincts, they ask pardon of each other for any sins or shortcomings, for the envy, the malice, the calumny of which they may have been guilty.

"Forgive me whatever wrong I may have done thee!"

The phrase is repeated from man to man, for none may enter the holy temple unless he be at peace with mankind.

Let us enter the synagogue. Hundreds of candles fill the sacred hall with their light and the whitened walls and ceiling appear to glow with glory. Rows of men in ghastly attire, constant reminder of the inevitable end of mundane greatness, stand with covered heads and with their faces turned towards the orient, fervently praying. Screened by the lattice-work of the galleries are the women, who, with their treble voices, augment the solemn chant that vibrates on the air.

Repentance, fear, self-reproach have blanched the cheeks and dimmed the eyes of the devotees. Fervent and sincere are the prayers that rise to the throne of God; contrite and remorseful are the blows with which the men beat their breasts and with which they seek to chasten their sin-encrusted hearts.

Fearfully and tearfully they make the sorrowful avowal: "We have sinned!" Down into the depths of his soul does each one search to render to himself and to God a truthful account of the deeds and thoughts that lie hidden there. And above the din, the voice of the reader is heard, beseeching forgiveness for the repentant congregation, pleading for the grace of the Lord and asking to be enrolled in the book of life and happiness. It is a solemn, heart-stirring spectacle, moving the soul of the sinner with a mighty force. An observer, who for the first time attends the *Yom-Kipur* services, can arrive at but one verdict concerning the beauty of the religion which has instituted this holy day.

The heathen is impressed with the fact that in doing wrong he has offended a god whom, by means of sacrifice, he seeks to propitiate. The Christian proclaims that he sins by compulsion in consequence of the original fall of Adam, and, as he is not a free agent in the matter of right or wrong, he can expect grace only through the mediation of his Saviour. The Jew recognizes the fact that he is entirely free to sin or to remain pure, and that, having erred, he can only hope for forgiveness by acknowledging his error, by purifying himself from all that is vile and by a sincere resolution to do better. Mere faith has never played the important part in the Jewish religion that is assigned it in that of the gentiles. The Israelite believes that if he has done wrong and sincerely repents and by his subsequent actions seeks to repair the injury, divine forgiveness will not be withheld; but the dogma that belief independent of good deeds purifies the heart has never found favor in his eyes.

The worshippers stayed until a late hour, and many of them remained in the synagogue all night. Early dawn found the congregation again at its post, as devout, as fervent as before. The candles were burning low in their sockets, casting a fitful glare upon the pale faces of the worshippers, reminding them of the flight of time, of the brevity of life, of the inevitable moment when repentance will come too late, when the account of one's good and evil deeds will be closed.

The synagogue was filled to overflowing with fasting men and women. Not a morsel of food, not a drop of water was permitted to pass their lips for twenty-four hours. "As the body can abstain from food," said the wise rabbis, "so shall the soul abstain from sin."

The terrible plague that had left its sad impress upon the community greatly increased the solemnity of the occasion. To the expressions of repentance were added the prayers of gratitude of those who had escaped its fatal breath and the lamentations of those whose hearts still smarted under recent bereavement. It was Rabbi Mendel's custom to combine instruction with devotion whenever an occasion presented itself, and to do this in such homely logic as his congregation could easily comprehend, taking especial pains to impress them with the spirit of the rites they observed. Being a great favorite with them, they listened attentively to his melodious voice and persuasive arguments, and found themselves the better for his teaching. On the Day of Atonement he had hardly begun to speak when his attention was attracted by a stranger who had entered and quietly taken a seat in the rear of the synagogue. With the exception of Mendel not one of the assembled worshippers recognized the unpretentious looking man.

It was Governor Pomeroff who had come in response to his invitation. Mendel's face flushed with emotion when he saw the Governor enter the synagogue. After that he paid no further attention to his distinguished guest, but took up the thread of his discourse.

He spoke of the effect of sin upon our earthly life and upon our possible existence after death, expounded the doctrine of punishment in the hereafter as given in the *Midrash*, and spoke of the infinite mercy of the Father in Heaven.

"Not in idle protestations," he said, "lies the road to forgiveness, but in a thorough avowal of sins committed and in a sincere determination to avoid the iniquities of the past."

Mendel's inspired words fell upon eager ears and contrite hearts. After the sermon the *hazan* again intoned the prayers, assisted by the fervent responses of the congregation.

The Governor remained a long time an interested observer of the impressive scene, until the lateness of the hour admonished him of other duties, and he left as unceremoniously as he had come.

"The Rabbi is right," he murmured, as he wended his way out of the deserted quarter; "it will be a herculean task to alienate the Jews from their faith and bring them into the fold of the Russian church; but I shall not yet abandon my project!"

The people prayed and fasted until the stars shone out in Heaven and the *shofar* (ram's horn) blast announced the death of the solemn day. Then, with cheerful hearts and smiling faces they returned to their dwellings, purified in spirit, cleansed and purged of the dross that had defiled their souls, more thoroughly in unison with the Lord, who, though the sins of His people be as scarlet, will make them white as snow.

Rabbi Mendel was not surprised next morning when a message came from the Governor, requesting his immediate presence at the palace. The summons did not create the consternation which had been caused by the unceremonious call of a few days before. On the contrary, Recha felt proud of the distinction accorded her husband in being thus made the confidant of the mighty ruler of Kief. She had implicit faith in her husband's ability to hold his ground even in the Governor's august presence.

"Have you thought over our recent conversation?" asked Pomeroff, as soon as Mendel entered.

"Yes, your excellency."

"And to what conclusion have you come?"

"Simply to thank your excellency for your kind interest in our behalf and to express the conviction that the Israelites of Kief would rather endure a thousand persecutions than abandon a jot of their holy faith."

"Have you laid the matter before the people?" queried the Governor.

"I have not, your excellency. It would have been worse than useless. You have doubtless observed how thoroughly sincere the Jews were in their devotions on *Yom-Kipur* day: such men die for their religion, they do not abandon it. If your excellency can assist us in obtaining greater liberty of action, if you can gain for our children admittance into the schools of the Empire and open for us the various avenues of trade from which we have hitherto been shut out, we will hail you as our benefactor; but if we can only buy freedom and honors at the cost of our ancient and revered religion, we will be content to follow the example of our ancestors and suffer."

A long discussion followed, in which Mendel proved that the Jews, in spite of persecution, were really happier than the unlettered and uncultured Russians and morally far superior to them.

Finally the Governor arose.

"Your hand, Rabbi," he said, heartily, "you have carried the day. I shall not revert to the subject of baptism again."

"I hope your excellency will not renounce the desire to

befriend us," answered Mendel. "There is such a large field for improvement in our community. I wish you could see the crowded condition of our streets, the wretched abodes of our poor. If you knew the secret persecutions which the petty officers of the crown visit upon us, outrages which never reach the ears of the higher authorities, your excellency would be surprised that our moral and physical condition is no worse."

"Poor Jews," said the Governor, sadly.

"O, sir," continued Mendel, earnestly; "visit the Jewish quarter! Investigate the official abuses on every hand. Extend the limits of our homes. Remove the antiquated restrictions that enslave our daily actions. Give the Jew an opportunity to develop his great capabilities and he will become a desirable citizen and a stanch patriot."

The kind-hearted Governor was visibly affected by Mendel's words.

"I will reflect upon what you have said," he replied. "You are a brave champion and your people should feel proud of you."

Governor Pomeroff, who recognized the young Rabbi's cleverness and learning, was loath to let him depart. Long after they had exhausted the topic that first engaged them, he detained him, conversing upon every conceivable subject, and listening with pleasure to the original thoughts and eloquent words of the young man. At length Mendel arose and prepared to leave.

"Your excellency must pardon me," he said, "but my poor wife will be in despair at my late return and I must hasten to reassure her."

"Go," answered the Governor; "but come again to-morrow or the day after. I have much to talk over with you."

As Mendel bowed himself out, Pomeroff muttered to himself:

"Strange man! He thinks more of allaying the anxiety of his wife than of currying favor with his ruler. He is right; such a people as he represents cannot be forced into baptism. They place their moral law and their ancient faith above temporal advantage."

As Mendel had anticipated, Recha was a prey to the liveliest fears at the protracted absence of her husband. It seemed incredible to her that the busy Governor should have kept him so long. With Mendel, however, smiles and contentment returned.

That evening the Rabbi called Hirsch Bensef and the elders of the congregation into his house and told them all about the Governor and his schemes. Great was the surprise of these worthy men and unanimous their approval of Mendel's course in the matter.

"I believe," said the Rabbi, in conclusion, "that we have gained a friend in the Governor, and I see rising above the horizon a new era of security and prosperity for Israel."

"God grant it," cried the listeners, fervently.

Milton Goldsmith

CHAPTER XX

NEEDED REFORMS

If Governor Pomeroff abandoned his original plan of Christianizing the Jews, he did not relinquish his friendship for Mendel. The Rabbi was frequently summoned to appear before him, professedly for the purpose of giving an account of this or that good work which he had undertaken, but in reality to entertain the Governor by his brilliant conversation. So frequent had these visits become that the guards about the palace were no longer surprised at the strange companionship and the term "Jew," with which they were wont to designate Mendel, gave place to the more respectful appellation of "The Rabbi."

As Mendel became better acquainted with his powerful friend, his appreciation of his noble qualities steadily increased and they became warmly attached to each other.

"Would that all the Jews were like you," Pomeroff occasionally remarked, to which Mendel would reply: "How fortunate would be our lot if all Christians possessed your nobility of character."

Then came the glorious year 1861, the year in which Russia freed millions of serfs and removed the shackles of slavery from a debased people.

While much praise should be accorded to the liberality and humanity of Alexander, the main cause of the emancipation act was the unprofitableness of serf labor. Public opinion, too, had demanded the change. What "Uncle Tom's Cabin" accomplished in this country Gogol's "Dead Souls" and Tourgenieff's "Recollections of a Sportsman" did for the Russian slaves. The disasters of the Crimean War were attributed to the corrupt condition of all classes, caused, it was claimed, by this pernicious institution of serfdom. By the edict of 1861, in the same year in which our own struggle for the emancipation of our Southern slaves began, the peasants were made free and were granted the right to purchase the lands occupied by them at the time. "Enfranchisement was effected in Russia in a manner far more skilful than in our own country, where it was accomplished through the terrible agency of a civil war. Yet the Russian people have been, perhaps, less satisfied with its results. Since then the serfs have been compelled to work harder than ever to pay for the land they had always cultivated and regarded as their own. The complete ignorance of the *moujiks* has laid them open to greater vices than serfdom possessed and drunkenness has greatly increased since the emancipation."[13]

At the time of which we speak, however, there was nought but rejoicing in Russia. Freedom had unfurled her banner, and the sanguine prophets foresaw in the near future a complete cessation of despotism and a constitutional government such as the people had demanded since the beginning of Nicholas' reign in 1825. Amidst the general joy, the Governor of Kief found an opportunity for materially improving the condition of the Jews of his province.

Mendel would have been less than human had he not

endeavored to turn this condition of affairs and Pomeroff's friendship to practical account. For himself he desired nothing. When the Governor, in order to have him constantly at his side, tendered him an honorable office in the palace, Mendel gently but firmly declined the proffered honor. All his energies were directed towards ameliorating the lot of his co-religionists.

He one day induced the Governor to stroll with him through the Jewish quarter, and with tact and eloquence called his attention to the crowded condition of the houses and streets, explaining how difficult it was to preserve health where the hygienic laws were of necessity utterly disregarded. He showed how the streets, at first ample for all requirements, had in the course of years become overcrowded; how hut had been built against hut and story erected upon story, until the lack of room deprived many a dwelling of light and air. He led the surprised Governor through the squalid lanes near the river and demonstrated how difficult it would be to master an epidemic when once it had taken root there, and how the welfare of the entire town of Kief depended upon the sanitary condition of each of its parts.

With the financial acumen of his race, he appealed to the economic aspect of the case, demonstrated how many houses, large and small, were standing idle in the city proper, bringing neither rent to their owners nor taxes to the province, and depicted the benefits that would be gained by granting the Jews the privilege of occupying such dwellings.

The Governor, who had never before visited the haunts of poverty, felt a positive repugnance to the system, or rather lack of system, that could countenance such a condition of affairs. He hurried away from the uninviting neighborhood, and, having again reached a spot where the air was fit to breathe, he promised to exert his influence with the Czar to have the boundaries of the Jewish quarter extended.

Nobly did he keep his word. He journeyed to St. Petersburg and sought an audience with Alexander. What happened at the interview the Jews of Kief never discovered, but the result was extremely gratifying. At the end of a fortnight there came a ukase extending indefinitely the limits of the Jewish quarters of all large cities, granting permission to all Jewish merchants who had been established in some branch of trade for twenty-five years or over, and to all rabbis and teachers, to reside in the city proper, in such streets as they might select, and permitting merchants of ten years' standing to dwell on certain streets carefully specified in the proclamation. It also made it lawful for Jews and Christians to live in the same building, a privilege hitherto withheld.

Many were the Jews who availed themselves of their new privileges. Bensef was among the first. His house, since the arrival of Mendel's parents, had been too small for comfort and the wealthy man desired a dwelling befitting his means. Haim Goldheim, the banker, found that there was not enough room in his house for the works of art it contained. He took a house in the fashionable Vladimir quarter, where, to the intense disgust of the aristocrats, he established himself in princely magnificence. A hundred families, at least, followed the example thus set, leaving the crowded streets, in order to breathe the purer air of the more select quarters of Kief. To their credit be it said, however, few went far from their old homes; the synagogue still formed the rallying centre of their community. About it revolved their daily thoughts and actions and the greatest recommendation a new home could have was that it was near the *schul*.

Upon Mendel, who had brought about this change, the greatest honors were showered. His congregation almost worshipped him. There were envious detractors, however, who contended that it did not behoove a Jew to become so intimate with a *goy*, and a Governor at that. They claimed that the Rabbi labored only to promote his own private ends; but, as these malcontents were among the first to seize the opportunity of bettering their condition, Mendel could afford to shrug his shoulders and smile at their insinuations.

The principal class to benefit by the new order of things were the poor, who now found abundant room and greedily availed themselves of it. To them Mendel was a saviour in the practical sense of the word, and many a grateful woman whose hovel had been exchanged for a more commodious dwelling would kiss the Rabbi's hand as he passed through the quarter on his errands of mercy.

But the young Rabbi's zeal did not end here. He convinced the Governor that the taxes exacted from the Jews were not only excessive, but disproportionate, and, as a result, they were lowered to a level with those paid by the gentiles.

Hitherto the Jews had been forbidden to cultivate land on their own account. Mendel, in presenting this subject to the Governor, laid stress upon the fact that vast tracts were lying fallow for want of agriculturists, and that the crown was thereby losing much revenue which could easily be raised by a judicious distribution of these fields among the thrifty and industrious Hebrews. Pomeroff saw the justice of the argument and a proclamation resulted, removing the restrictions placed upon the cultivation of land by the Jews.

The Jews of Kief and the surrounding provinces felt that a day of prosperity and happiness had dawned for them. In a measure they enjoyed the same liberty and privileges as did the lower classes of Russians. They were free to come and go, to live where they pleased and to engage in a score of occupations which had hitherto been forbidden, and Mendel was justly honored as the author of these changes. His fame spread at home and was heralded abroad. During his frequent visits to the Governor he came in contact with many of the great and brilliant men of the Empire. Dignitaries who at first met the Jew with a feeling of repugnance gradually yielded to the charm of his personal influence and vied with each other in honoring him, and through him Judaism was honored and respected. His character, his benevolence, his patriotism and his great mental gifts did more to convince those gentiles of what the Jew could be than the keenest arguments could have done.

A great general one day asked him:

"Why are you so different from the Jews one usually meets?"

"Your excellency is in error," Mendel replied. "I am not unlike my fellow-men. In disposition and feeling I am the same, but I have had an opportunity for mental improvement of which most of my brethren have been deprived. Give them the privilege of attending your universities, open to them the avenues of knowledge and you will create for Russia an intellectual element which will eventually place her in the front ranks of the nations."

The general shrugged his shoulders and smiled. The idea seemed preposterous.

"You have certainly an exalted opinion of your co-religionists," he said.

"I have, your excellency, and it is borne out by history. Your excellency has doubtless read of the intellectual supremacy of Spain when the Jews were in the ascendant."

His excellency had not read of it. In fighting but not in reading lay his strength and, not wishing to display his ignorance, he wisely changed the subject.

As might have been expected, violent objections were raised by the gentiles to the enlarged privileges granted the Jews. The priests were particularly virulent in their denunciation of the new liberties conferred, in which they saw but the beginning of the gradual emancipation of the Hebrews. Attacks were made against them from press and from pulpit, and all of these Mendel answered calmly and convincingly. His logic finally silenced the ravings of the unlettered and fanatical Jew-haters and the privileges once accorded were not repealed.

Had Mendel's zeal ended here he would have avoided much subsequent difficulty, but he was well aware that the Jews had not attained to the ideal he had formed, that much ignorance, fanaticism and superstition still prevailed. He desired to imitate the example of his great prototype, Moses Mendelssohn, and spread the light of learning throughout the Jewish world. He did not lose sight of the vastness of the undertaking, of the dangers he was incurring, or of the animosity he was inviting, for the Jews of Russia still regarded all learning not found in the folios of the Talmud as sacrilegious and unholy. To overcome this antagonism to secular knowledge now became Mendel's self-imposed task.

Consulting no one but his friend the Governor, and armed with a letter of introduction from this powerful ally, Mendel set out for St. Petersburg, to visit the Czar in person. It was an unheard-of experiment on the part of a Jew, but Mendel felt the inspiration of right and undertook his new mission fearlessly. What nothing else could accomplish was done by the Governor's letter of recommendation. After a little delay he was admitted into the august presence of the Czar Alexander and presented his petition.

Alexander was not a little surprised at the temerity of a Jew in thus appearing before him, but the very strangeness of the proceeding enlisted the ruler's interest in the demands of the Rabbi. After a long conference, during which Mendel eloquently pleaded his cause, he was dismissed with the assurance that the educational disabilities of the Hebrews would be in a measure removed, and shortly after his return to Kief a proclamation was issued admitting Jewish youth into the Russian schools upon terms of equality with the gentiles.

Then arose a storm of indignation among the pious Israelites. Those who had antagonized Mendel from the first, now were furious at his attempt to force intelligence upon them. They prophesied that these were but the stepping-stones to more radical changes and stubbornly refused to yield an inch, lest the proverbial ell might be seized.

"Never," they cried, "shall our children be taught the wisdom of the *goyim*. The Law and the Talmud are sufficient for our needs. Instruction in the public schools will force rabbinical studies into the background and will gradually estrange our children from the religion of their fathers. We want no new-fangled education. We are Jews and we will remain Jews."

So hostile was the greater part of the community to the idea of extending educational facilities, that the friends of Mendel, and there were many of them, advised him to make an effort to have the obnoxious privileges repealed.

This Mendel positively refused to do.

"It is but a privilege," he answered, "and not at all obligatory. You can do as you like about sending your children to the public schools. As for myself, however, I shall never cease to uphold the necessity of education in order to obtain the rights that belong to our race."

The battle thus commenced raged fiercely. Hirsch Bensef was one of the ablest supporters of the young Rabbi. Haim Goldheim was another; his wealth had procured him the friendship of several aristocratic but impoverished families in the neighborhood of his new home, and he never forgot that the blessings he now enjoyed were due to Mendel's past labors.

The young men were all on Mendel's side. They chafed under the restraint that had been put upon them and yearned for instruction in keeping with the enlarged sphere of activity now opened to them.

Thus a schism arose in Kief. The progressive Israelites siding with Mendel founded a congregation of their own, leaving the more conservative to work out their salvation in their old accustomed way. It must not be supposed that Mendel observed this break in the ranks of Judaism without a pang. He spent many a sleepless night in planning how to avert further differences and to appease existing animosities. Balzac truly says: "Every great man has paid heavily for his greatness. Genius waters all its work with its own tears. He who would raise himself above the average level of humanity, must prepare himself for long struggles, for trying difficulties. A great thinker is a self-devoted martyr to immortality."

In spite of the anathemas of the narrow-minded, in spite of the cry that the Messiah could never come as long as such sacrilege was tolerated in the household of Israel, the good work went steadily forward, to the manifest advantage of the entire body of Jews.

FOOTNOTES:

[Footnote 13: Foulke.]

CHAPTER XXI

A DEN OF NIHILISTS

Let us open the records of Kief for the year 1879.

Fifteen years have elapsed since the events last narrated; fifteen years of peace and plenty, of security and prosperity for Jew and gentile.

What sudden change do we behold! Is this the country whose future looked so hopeful in the early days of Alexander's reign? Is this the people who saw the golden promise of a constitutional government? Alas, for the instability of human purpose! The reforms then instituted have been revoked, the men who were the leaders in these reforms have been exiled to Siberia. A period of reaction has set in: Despotism and Nihilism meet face to face. The entire nation is in chains.

Russia during these troublous times presents a dreary picture. At a period when the intellectual activity of Europe is at its height, she still groans under the unrestricted despotism of an autocrat. Here the effects of progress that obtain elsewhere seem inverted. Such advance as is made in civilization and knowledge is used to buttress imperial tyranny and the knout is wielded more cruelly than ever before. We behold liberal institutions overthrown and a whole people held in bondage worse than slavery. We hear of families torn asunder, of innocent men condemned to life-long exile in Siberia, simply because they have aroused the suspicion or incurred the ill-will of those in authority. Force in its most brutal form holds sway throughout the Empire.

What wonder then that the discontented masses writhe in their despair and seek redress! What wonder that Nihilism should flourish and the service of dynamite be enlisted to accomplish what moral suasion failed to achieve! The years beginning with 1879 were disastrous for Russia. They marked the decadence of those reforms which ten years before had given promise of such glorious results.

In one of the most populous portions of Kief, in the shadow of the Petcherskoi convent, stood a large, modern house. As is the case with the generality of Russian dwellings, it was tenanted by a number of families who came and went, beat their children, ill-treated their servants and transacted their daily affairs, rarely becoming acquainted with each other.

It was a many-storied building, of plain exterior. The lower floor was occupied by the worthy family of Pavel Kodasky, a clerk in the employ of the government. His wife filled the responsible position of *concierge* to the immense house. The third and fourth floors were the abode of families equally worthy but unimportant to our story, while the upper floors were inhabited by a vast number of students and officers who, in consideration of cheap rent and convenient proximity to the university and the barracks, had here furnished themselves with comfortable bachelors' quarters.

The second floor still remains to be spoken of. It was occupied by a young officer of prepossessing appearance, who was widely known in the aristocratic circles of Kief. The dark-eyed Russian beauties adored him for his handsome bearing, his flashing eyes, his gallant and fearless demeanor; the gay young officers and dandies that hovered about the Governor's court admired him for his reckless habits, his daring escapades and his lavish expenditure of a fortune which seemed inexhaustible.

Loris Drentell, the young lieutenant of the Seventh Cossack Regiment, might well be thankful to Fortuna for the gifts she had lavished upon him. The reader will remember having met the young man before, when he was but a baby in his nurse's arms at the Drentell villa at Lubny. The promise he then gave of becoming a spoiled child was fully realized. Indulged by his father and neglected by his mother, his every wish gratified as soon as expressed, enjoying unlimited freedom in the use of a vast fortune, Loris developed a disposition in which indolence, recklessness and unprincipled ambition contended for the mastery. The young man was unscrupulous and vindictive and he obeyed no law save that of his own unbridled will. He was a type of a class of Russian aristocrats whose social position and wealth enable them to tyrannize over their associates and dependants.

Reckless and fearless as Loris was known to be, none suspected that this gay and pampered youth, this officer of the Imperial troops, was the acknowledged head of a Nihilist club. None but a chosen few knew that this apparently peaceful dwelling, with its many stories and multitudinous inhabitants, was the meeting-place of a powerful band of would-be patriots, whose mission it was to inaugurate a constitutional government by the aid of dynamite. Here was the unsuspected centre from which thousands of Nihilist documents were scattered to the ends of Russia. Here were concealed papers which if discovered would have consigned many of the greatest in Russia to Siberia or the scaffold, and here it was that the frightful engine of destruction—Nihilism—had its cradle. So great was the caution observed by the members of the secret organization that the wary and vigilant police did not dream of its existence.

Loris was walking impatiently up and down his parlor, now looking at the clock, now gazing expectantly through his window up and down the street.

"He is late," exclaimed the young man, anxiously. "I wonder what detains him."

He began nervously to roll a cigarette, without however leaving his watch at the window. Finally he smiled with satisfaction.

"At last," he cried, as he perceived his belated friend turn a corner and hurry towards the house. "We shall soon have news from the Governor."

There was a hasty knock at the door and a tall young fellow entered, carefully locking the door behind him.

"Well, Paulowitch, I began to feel uneasy," said Loris. "What kept you so late?"

"I have just arrived from Pomeroff's," whispered Paulowitch. "He had a very large audience and it was some time before I could gain his ear."

"What was the result?" asked Loris, eagerly.

"He will come to-night. I told him that there would be a meeting of officers in honor of your birthday and that we would like to have him with us."

"Does he suspect anything?"

"How should he?"

"He will find out soon enough."

"You are mistaken, Loris, if you think he will join us. I know Pomeroff too well. Although he has had much to suffer from the arbitrary rulings of the Czar, the recollection of former favors will not permit him to desert his Emperor."

"Mere sentimentality," answered Loris. "Do you forget how the Czar, in a proclamation, publicly reprimanded him for allowing the Jews too many liberties, and of harboring treasonable sympathy with them? I know that Pomeroff has been smarting under the insult ever since. He will be glad to have an opportunity of avenging himself."

Paulowitch shook his head, in doubt.

"And if, after having learned our secrets, he should refuse to join us?" he asked.

"If he does not affiliate with us, we must render him harmless. We dare not give him an opportunity to betray us."

"But what is to prevent him from informing the police of our plans and having us all sent to Siberia?"

"We have foreseen such a possibility. Moleska, his secretary, who has access to his desks and closets, and who is one of us, has full instructions how to act in such an emergency."

"Poor Pomeroff," murmured Paulowitch. "I am sorry for him."

"Nonsense!" exclaimed Loris; "we need him to insure our success. While his police are prying about to discover something new, we are in constant danger of detection and can accomplish little. If, however, he declines to join us, we dare run no risk. He must be removed."

"In that event, who do you suppose will take his place?"

"I cannot say. But the arrest and execution or exile of the Governor will cause such a disturbance in the affairs of the province that several months must elapse before order is again restored. In the meantime our association will flourish unimpeded. We will be able to scatter our pamphlets and manifestoes broadcast, and to prepare everything necessary for the final stroke, which shall rid us of the imperial tyrant and pave the way for liberty."

There was a peculiar knock at the door and a man, in the garb of a student and possessing a countenance that displayed rare intellect, was admitted. The new-comer was about twenty-three years of age. In fact, Martinski was one of the leaders of the order and most of its master moves were conceived by him.

"Well," asked Loris, addressing him, "have the papers been forwarded?"

"Yes; both Myra Sergeitch and Paulovna Tschorgini left for St. Petersburg at noon. The documents were concealed in secret compartments of their trunks. There is no danger of detection."

"But if they should be found in spite of all precautions?" asked Paulowitch.

"Bah! Who will suspect two inoffensive-looking women? Besides, the messages were written in cipher which no one can read. Should the worst happen, however, both ladies are devoted to the cause and would rather die than betray us."

"Noble hearts," said Paulowitch, reflectively. "A cause like ours makes heroes."

"Come," said Loris; "it is growing late. Let us take a stroll while our landlady prepares the feast for to-night."

It was a large and heterogeneous assembly that partook of the cheer of Loris' table that evening. There were a few army officers, some students, two or three political writers and half-a-dozen young noblemen, who, as a rule, possessed more money than brains. Supper was already begun, and the expected guest, Governor Pomeroff, had not yet made his appearance. The suspense was great, for it was felt that much depended upon securing Pomeroff as an ally. Few doubted that he would join them, for he, if any one, had just cause to detest the Czar, and the arrangements made to prevent disclosures would not be needed.

After a long wait, during which the conspirators conversed in an undertone, the door was opened and the Governor entered in company with Paulowitch. He appeared surprised to find himself in so large a company, when he had expected to meet but a few intimate friends, but he greeted all cordially and sat down in the place of honor accorded him.

The conversation was comparatively uninteresting during the progress of the repast. There was none of that conviviality which one is accustomed to find at a friendly banquet; each member of the circle appeared constrained and nervous in the presence of his comrades and an undefined suspicion that he had been decoyed into a trap of some kind flashed through Pomeroff's brain. Drinking, rather than eating, formed the chief part of the entertainment and the spirits of the party rose as the bottles were emptied.

Suddenly Loris sprang to his feet and lifting his glass proposed the toast:

"To his excellency, the Governor of Kief, the champion of liberty, the enemy of the autocrat at St. Petersburg!"

"Long may he live!" shouted his associates.

Pomeroff sat in his chair as if thunderstruck. The suspicion which up to this moment had but faintly suggested itself had become a terrible certainty. As soon as he could master his excitement he arose.

"Gentlemen," he began, endeavoring to smile, "what jest is this? You are certainly in error. Allow me to correct it. I drink to the health and long life of his majesty the Czar!"

A storm of hisses greeted this toast and Pomeroff, after trying in vain to make himself heard above the din, sat down. His face was pale and his frame shook with suppressed anger.

Quiet was finally restored and Martinski rose and addressed the meeting, speaking more directly to the Governor. He rehearsed the outrages committed upon submissive Russians by the Czar Nicholas, whose despotic government had finally driven the country into the disastrous Crimean War. He spoke in terms of praise of the noble aims and ambitions of Alexander during the early years of his reign, only to denounce in unmeasured terms the reaction which had destroyed the little good that had been accomplished. He depicted the cruelty and the tyranny practised by the Czar upon those who had incurred his displeasure, the utter lack of educational facilities and the consequent ignorance of the masses, the rigorous censorship of the press and the arbitrary rule of the men in power. He pictured in vivid colors the cruelties of Siberian exile and the sufferings of the prisoners in those distant mines, from which there was no escape but through the valley of death.

"But," continued he, warming up to a genuine outburst of eloquence, "there is still a lower depth; a dungeon, a human slaughter-house rather, has recently been contrived, the horrors of which surpass anything hitherto conceived by man. It is the Troubetzkoi Ravelin, where convicts condemned upon the most trivial charges are confined for life; a hell for those for whom the mines of Siberia are not considered severe enough. Compared to this prison, the Bastile of France was a palace of luxury. Woe to him who is obliged to enter this frightful place: hardships, hunger, disease and insanity await him.

"The convicts of Siberia cry to us for help. The scurvy-stricken prisoners of the Troubetzkoi Ravelin appeal to us to avenge their wrongs upon the author of their misfortunes. The French destroyed their Bastile. Why should we not also demolish our dungeons before we ourselves are called upon to fill them. O, Russia, how pitiable is your condition! 'Despotism has blasted the high hopes to which the splendid awakening of the first half of the century gave birth. The living forces of later generations have been buried by the Government in the Siberian snows or Esquimaux villages. It is worse than the plague, for that comes and goes, but the Government has oppressed the country for years and will continue to do so. The plague strikes blindly but the present regime chooses its victims from the flower of the nation, taking all upon whom depend the fortune and glory of Russia. It is not a political party that they crush, it is a nation of a hundred millions that they stifle. That is what the Czar has done.'[14] Down with such despotism! Down with its instigator, the Czar!"

At these concluding words, the whole party arose and, holding out their right hands in token of allegiance to their cause, they repeated the cry:

"Down with the Czar!"

For a few moments absolute silence reigned. Then Governor Pomeroff struggled to his feet.

"I fear I am out of place here," he began. "You will do me the favor to remember that I came here ignorant of your purposes. Whatever cause you may have for complaint, you have taken the wrong means for correcting your grievances. Rest assured, gentlemen, that I sympathize with your troubles, even though I cannot agree with your method of changing the condition of things. I promise, moreover, to forget what I have heard and beg of you to excuse me from further attendance." And bowing politely, the Governor moved towards the door.

"Stop!" cried Loris, excitedly, barring the passage and leading the Governor back to his seat. "Do you for a moment imagine that after having heard our deliberations and learned our secrets you will be allowed to leave here and denounce us? It is too late for you to retreat. You have cast your fortunes with us and must share our dangers and our glory."

"You mistake," answered the Governor, proudly. "I came to a feast, not to a conspiracy. Your motive for bringing me here is not known to me, but if it is to make me a traitor to my country and my Czar you do not know me. A Pomeroff has never yet stooped to treason. Again I say, let me go!"

"Governor, hear me," now said Martinski, in a tone of persuasion. "We need your assistance. Without your sympathy we are in constant fear of detection from your officers; with you on our side we can continue our noble work without fear of molestation. The work will go on, the glorious end will be achieved in spite of all difficulties, and our labors will only end when the Czar lies buried with his ancestors. Ours is not a society for wilful destruction of life or property. Our aims are just. We demand a general amnesty for political offenders and a convocation of the people for the framing of a liberal constitution, and meanwhile we demand as provisional concessions freedom of the press, freedom of speech and freedom of public meetings. These are the only means by which Russia can enter upon the path of peaceful and regular development. We will be content with nothing less. We will turn to dynamite, only when all else fails. Governor Pomeroff, will you join us in the attainment of these rights, which every civilized nation already possesses?"

"No!" thundered the Governor, his eyes flashing.

"Then I beg to call your excellency's attention to the fact that a trip to Siberia or to the gallows as a condemned Nihilist awaits you."

The Governor turned pale, but remained silent.

"Think not that we have rushed blindly into this danger," continued Martinski. "It was necessary to have you on our side or out of the way. Therefore, we brought you here this evening. We have carefully weighed our chances. Having made you our confidant we dare not jeopardize our lives by allowing you your liberty. By to-morrow you would have us all in chains. We therefore offer you the alternative of joining our fraternity or of being denounced to-morrow as an enemy of the Czar."

"I refuse to identify myself with a band of assassins,"

answered Pomeroff, boldly. "Throughout my life I have ever striven to be on the side of right and justice, have ever protected the oppressed and assisted those who came to me for help. I have been loyal to my Czar and to my country. I will not now be frightened into doing that which my nature loathes and against which every fibre of my body revolts. I defy your power and laugh at your threats. You leave me no alternative but to inform his majesty of this diabolical plot upon his life."

"And you leave us no alternative but to render you harmless," replied Martinski. At these words, all arose and silently surrounded the Governor.

Pomeroff had by this time forced his way to the door which he tried to open. It was locked. Pale with anger, he turned upon the Nihilists.

"Cowards!" he hissed, "you would force me to join your fraternity. Then I give you my brotherly greeting," and, drawing his pistol, he fired into the group.

Loris was wounded in the side, but the ball striking a rib glanced off. A dozen men threw themselves upon the Governor, who defended himself with the strength of despair; but superior numbers quickly gained the mastery, and after a short struggle Pomeroff lay helpless upon the floor.

Then one of the students took a vial of chloroform from his pocket. Seizing a napkin he saturated it with the liquid and applied it to the nostrils of the prostrated man. In a few minutes the victim was insensible.

"Flee for your lives!" ordered Martinski, "we have not a moment to lose. It is fortunate that the shot has not already brought the police down upon us. We must carry the Governor at once to his palace. Drentell, you will pass the night with me."

Under cover of a dark and cloudy night Pomeroff was carried to his home, and with the assistance of his secretary, Moleska, was carefully placed upon the couch in his private cabinet.

FOOTNOTES:

[Footnote 14: Stepniak.]

CHAPTER XXII

A MODERN BRUTUS

When Pomeroff awoke next morning, he rubbed his eyes sleepily and looked about him.

"By St. Nicholas, I have had a horrible dream," he muttered. "I must have slept on this couch all night."

On attempting to rise, however, he felt a soreness in every limb and the events of the preceding night flashed through his mind. Instantly his face became grave.

"Can it be that I have not been dreaming after all; that I was really in the lair of the Nihilists? Bah, it must be a mistake!"

He arose with difficulty and opened the window. It was a glorious day. The birds were chirping merrily in the trees that shaded the courtyard, but though the sun was high there were no signs of the usual activity below.

"It must be early," mused the Governor; "no one is stirring. What!" he cried, looking at his watch, "ten o'clock! There is something wrong."

He crossed the room and tried to open the door leading to the

Milton Goldsmith

ante-chamber. It was locked. He tried a smaller door leading to the rear of the palace. It, too, was locked and resisted his efforts to open it.

With a cry of anger and surprise, Pomeroff exclaimed:

"This is carrying the farce to extremes. So I am a prisoner in my own house! Can it be that they will carry out their diabolical threats and have me tried as a suspect? Nonsense! I will subvert their plans and turn the tables on them."

He rang the bell violently, but there was no response. As a last resort he hurled his whole weight against the oaken door, but it remained immovable.

It appeared probable to him that his enemies would carry out their threat of accusing him, and he carefully mapped out his line of defence. He would prove that he had innocently walked into a trap, set for him by a band of conspirators, who had planned to assassinate the Czar, and that he used every argument to dissuade them from their murderous project. He would prove that he had firmly refused to join their ranks, and that he had been obliged to use his pistol in his effort to escape from their midst.

Prove it? How? A little reflection showed him that he had no proofs whatever and that he was absolutely powerless to defend himself against any charges that they might bring. Wearied with his vain exertions and furious at his helplessness, he threw himself upon the sofa. As he became calmer he began to reflect upon his situation.

Slowly the hours passed without affording relief. About noon Pomeroff heard the key turn in the lock and an instant later the apartment was filled with officers of the *gendarmerie*.

The Chief of Police, Polatschek, was the first to break the silence.

"I regret, your excellency," he said, sadly, "that I am obliged to take this step against one who has been my friend and benefactor, but the Czar's orders are imperative. You will consider yourself my prisoner."

"Of what am I accused?" asked the Governor.

"You are accused of associating with Nihilists and of being at the present time involved in a plot to take the Czar's life."

"It is false," cried Pomeroff.

"We will hear your defence in due time," answered Polatschek. "In the meantime it becomes my unpleasant duty to search your desk and closets for Nihilistic papers, which the deposition accuses you of having in your possession."

Pomeroff smiled bitterly.

"Search, gentlemen. The absence of such documents will, I hope, convince you that I am innocent of this outrageous charge."

"Nothing will give me greater pleasure than to see you vindicated," said the Chief, politely, as he gave orders to ransack the drawers and receptacles of the Governor's writing-desk.

Alas, poor Pomeroff! Almost the first roll of papers examined proved of a most damaging nature, being the rules of an association of Nihilists in St. Petersburg. A further search revealed plans of a dynamite mine to be laid beneath the imperial palace at the capital.

In vain were all the Governor's denials. Never was proof of guilt more complete and convincing, and Polatschek, who was almost as much unnerved by the discovery as the prisoner, reluctantly gave orders to seize and secure the unfortunate man, and Pomeroff was hurried away to the house of detention, to await his trial.

Since the beginning of the so-called terrorist period, and the first attack upon the life of the Czar, a short time before the occurrence of the above events, the trial of political offenders had been taken from the civil tribunals and transferred to the military. Even counsel for the prisoner must be an army officer. The court to try Governor Pomeroff was hastily convened next morning. Instructions concerning the judgment to be rendered were telegraphed from St. Petersburg and the military judges had but to obey their imperial mandate. Under such conditions the trial was a mere form. The evidence against the prisoner was positive. Within an hour Pomeroff, who had no opportunity of saying a word in his defence, was sentenced to death.

"The secret 'council of ten' that once terrorized Venice, and which, without process of law, condemned men to punishment upon secret charges, preferred by unknown accusers, often where no crime had been committed, has long been regarded as the most odious form of injustice. Yet the Russian system of to-day is quite as repugnant to every idea of justice. Men who have never been tried, nor perhaps even accused, but who are simply suspected by the police, are often without the slightest investigation hurried into exile or death."[15]

On the following morning, Governor Pomeroff, the just and merciful, the friend and protector of the Jews, was secretly executed in the fortress of Kief.

Excitement was at fever heat. The Governor was beloved by all. Never had the province been so well governed as during his administration.

Among the Jews whom Pomeroff had especially befriended the grief was deep and sincere. Rabbi Mendel Winenki, in an address to his congregation, fearlessly denounced a system by which an innocent man could be put to death. In the synagogues the *kaddish* (prayer for the dead) was recited as for a beloved parent. In consequence of these demonstrations the authorities warned the Jews that any further expressions of disapproval of the Government's course would be severely punished.

Well might the Jews mourn their friend and protector. With his death their bright hopes and dreams, their prospects of emancipation, were rudely dispelled.

Within a week of Pomeroff's execution Count Dimitri Drentell, our old acquaintance whom we left at Lubny and whom the Crimean War had made a General, arrived in Kief as its future Governor.

While the majority of the inhabitants of the province were indifferent as to which creature of the imperial autocrat oppressed them, there were two classes who viewed the change with great misgivings: the Jews and the band of agitators to which Loris Drentell, the new Governor's son, belonged. The Jews had learned from their co-religionists in Poltava of the implacable hatred Dimitri bore their race. They had for fifteen years basked in the sunshine of Pomeroff's favor, but now trembled at the dismal prospect before them.

The Nihilists had equal cause for fear. Their safety required a Governor who could be controlled or hoodwinked by them.

But they well knew that this man was unapproachable, that neither bribes nor threats would avail to win him over. Besides, Loris felt that by remaining the leader of the Nihilist Club he would come in conflict with his father. The elder Drentell was not merely the civil Governor of Kief—he was also one of the Generals appointed by the Czar with unlimited power to punish the guilty; with the right to exile all persons whose stay he might consider prejudicial to public welfare; to imprison at discretion; to suppress or suspend any journal, and to take all measures that he might deem necessary for public safety. With a man of such vast powers, it was dangerous for even a beloved son to trifle. For the time being, therefore, the Nihilists were doomed to inactivity.

General Drentell began his administration with a careful examination of the evidence which had caused the condemnation of his predecessor. He had a strong conviction that Pomeroff was innocent, but if guilty he felt it his duty to ferret out the conspiracy and discover Pomeroff's accomplices. He owed it to his own safety to purge the palace of such as might be there.

With the skill of a trained detective, and with the utmost secrecy, he began the work. His first investigations were made in the palace which he was henceforth to occupy. Drentell soon discovered that Moleska, Pomeroff's secretary, had duplicate keys to the desk and closets in the private cabinet. If Pomeroff was innocent, this would explain the presence of the incriminating papers in the Governor's desk. Acting entirely upon this suspicion, he ordered the arrest of Moleska, who, overcome by terror, confessed the entire plot.

On the following day, Loris was hastily summoned into the Governor's presence. He found his father striding up and down the apartment, a prey to the most violent agitation.

"You have sent for me, father?" said the young man.

"Yes; sit down," answered Drentell, curtly. "Have you ever read the history of Rome?"

Loris opened his eyes wide at the unexpected question.

"Why do you ask?"

"Answer my question. Have you ever read the history of Rome?"

"Yes."

"Do you remember the story of Brutus, whose son was engaged in a conspiracy against the republic?"

Loris became very pale and stammered an indistinct reply.

"You do; I see it in your face! Tell me how did Brutus act towards his son?"

"He condemned him to death," faltered Loris.

"Right! He condemned him to death. The malefactor paid the penalty with his life."

The General arose and again paced up and down the room, in a vain attempt to control his agitation.

"What have these questions to do with me?" asked Loris, nervously.

"Simply this," answered the Governor, coming to a sudden stop before his son, while his eyes flashed and big blue veins stood out upon his forehead: "I have proofs that my predecessor died an innocent man. I have also the names of those Nihilists who should have suffered in his stead. Shall I tell you whose name is at the head? My duty is clear. I should follow the example of Brutus and deliver my son into the hands of the law."

Loris, a thorough coward at heart, sank into a chair.

"Father," he stammered; "you would not condemn me to death; me, your only child?"

"Coward!" cried the General, looking scornfully at his son, whom terror had robbed of strength to stand. "You have the courage to plan cold-blooded murder, but when the time comes to face your own death you show yourself a miserable poltroon. Fear nothing: you shall not die. I have passed a sleepless night, struggling between duty and parental affection. But were it known in St. Petersburg that I had shown you mercy, I would answer for it with my life."

"Father!" exclaimed the young man, remorsefully, hiding his face in his hands.

"Don't interrupt me," said the General, savagely. "I have already requested the immediate removal of your regiment to the frontier. The Turks are aggressive, and our forces in that neighborhood should be increased. By to-morrow you will receive your order to march. It is absolutely necessary that you should leave Kief. Of your misguided companions, Moleska, who revealed the conspiracy, is already in the fortress, and the others will soon follow. For your own safety, you must leave Kief before the arrests are made, or I will not answer for the consequences."

"But, father, you will be lenient towards them," cried the young man. "You will not condemn them to death.

Remember that whatever may have been their guilt, had it not been for the death of Pomeroff, you would not now be Governor of Kief."

"For shame, Loris!" cried the General, red with anger. "Are you so lost to all sense of honor that you must remind me that I stepped into office over the corpse of my predecessor and my friend, murdered by my own son? Do not provoke me too far! Your associates have been guilty of the most grievous of crimes. They must die. Besides, were they to live they would denounce you as their leader and even I could not save your life. Go! Arrange your affairs, avoid further intercourse with your companions. By this time to-morrow you must be on the way to the frontier while they will mount the scaffold."

Loris shuddered and for the first time a sentiment of humanity moved within him.

"I will not go," he said, resolutely. "I have lived and plotted with them and I shall die with them."

"No, Loris, no," replied his father, softened. "You must depart. There is no other course. A Drentell must not die a traitor's death. It would break my heart and kill your mother, who dotes upon you. It will be better not to see her before your departure. Questionings and explanations are dangerous. After all this is forgotten, you may return and work out the career I had hoped for you."

Loris, sorrowful and conscience-stricken, kissed his father's hand and slowly left the room.

On the morrow, the Seventh Cossack Regiment received orders from St. Petersburg to proceed to Kothim without delay, and long before nightfall it was on the march. Next morning twelve conspirators were arrested at their homes and dragged before the tribunal of judicial inquiry. Their trial, like that of Pomeroff, was a mockery, for their fate had already been decided. Defence was useless. The incriminating papers found in the places designated by the informer Moleska sealed their doom. Governor Drentell himself pronounced their sentence. Two days afterward they were secretly executed.

FOOTNOTES:

[Footnote 15: Foulke.]

CHAPTER XXIII

LOUISE'S PRACTICAL ADVICE

Tyranny, which for a brief period had slept, was now wide-awake and aggressively active. Throughout the entire Empire despotism stalked unimpeded. The recent attempt upon the Czar's life had increased the vigilance of the police, and the most frightful atrocities were committed in the holy name of Justice. The blood curdles with horror when reading of the indignities and the injustice visited upon the people.

"When the police deem it best," says one writer,[16] in portraying the condition of that period, "they steal noiselessly through the streets and alleys, surround a private dwelling in the dead of the night, and under some false pretense, invade every room in the house, waking the sleeping occupants. Each member of the household is given in charge of a policeman, everything is turned topsy-turvy, books, papers, private letters are carefully inspected—nothing is secret. It is not necessary that the police should have any evidence for these searches. An anonymous charge, a mere suspicion is enough. Houses have sometimes been inspected seven times in a single day. If anything is discovered to excite the suspicions of the police an arrest follows and the supposed culprit is sent to the house of Preventive Detention. There he awaits his trial for weeks and months and sometimes for years. He is brought out occasionally for examination. If he confesses nothing he is sent back to reflect. Sometimes the wrong man is arrested and confined a year or two before the mistake is discovered."

The solitary confinement to which prisoners were doomed in this house of detention was often fatal. The hardships to which they were subjected frequently led to consumption, insanity or suicide. The examination of prisoners and witnesses was dragged out to an interminable length. In one celebrated case it lasted four years and over seven hundred witnesses were kept in jail during that time. The prosecutor admitted that only twenty persons deserved punishment, yet there were seventy-three who died from suicide or the effects of confinement.

Louder and louder grew the clamor of the masses and the threats against the imperial autocrat. Wholesale arrests could not quell the popular voice. A prisoner wrote from his living tomb in the Troubetzkoi Ravelin: "Fight on till the victory is won! The more they torment me in prison, the better it is for the struggle!"

Governor Drentell entered upon his new duties at a trying time. His existence was embittered by political strife and tumult, and by complications with which he found it difficult to cope.

Let us seek him in his palace, by the side of his wife, Louise.

When we first met Louise, she was young and frivolous; now she is old and frivolous. The years have dealt gently with her, however, for she is still quite handsome and as vivacious, as capricious, as kind-hearted and as religious as when we last parted from her, twenty-seven years ago.

"Poor Dimitri," she said, dolefully, after her husband had recounted the events of the day. "Eighteen persons exiled to Siberia and two sentenced to death. How hard you toil! You will kill yourself with overwork!"

The General sighed.

"I should think," continued Louise, "that Loris could be of service to you in these difficult affairs of State. Why don't you recall our boy?"

The General's brow clouded.

"He must remain at his post for the present," he answered. "After he has achieved military glory, it will be time enough to initiate him in civil affairs."

"But you need an adviser, an assistant who can take some of your work off your hands."

"You are right! But who shall it be? There are so many Nihilists about, that I cannot be too careful whom I take into my confidence."

Louise rocked herself awhile in silence. Suddenly she said, impetuously:

"I wish we were back in St. Petersburg, or even at Lubny. Do you know, Dimitri, our days at Lubny were pleasant, after all?"

"Perhaps," answered Drentell, sarcastically, "that accounts for your incessant desire to leave the place."

"I never know when I am happy," said Louise, truthfully.

For some minutes she again rocked herself vigorously. It was her way of stimulating her mental faculties. Suddenly she cried:

"Ah, if you had only brought Mikail along. He might assist you."

"You appear too fond of Mikail's society," answered the Governor, sharply; "and that is just why I left him in St. Petersburg."

"Fool," replied Louise, half in jest, half in earnest. "Why, he is only my father confessor. You surely would not be jealous of a priest?"

"Yes, even of a priest, especially when he is as handsome and fascinating as our Mikail."

Louise broke into a merry laugh.

"Then that is why you were so solicitous about placing him with the Minister of War in St. Petersburg. You were afraid to bring him along on my account?"

"Candidly, yes. In spite of his priestly robes, I fancied he was too fond of your society and you of his, and I deemed it best for my peace of mind to leave him at the capital while we came here."

For a time Louise's mirth appeared uncontrollable.

"Why, you goose!" she said, after her laughter had subsided. "Mikail has never approached me but with the greatest respect. He knows that I have been his benefactress, and I am sure that, while he thinks me awfully ignorant, he respects me as he would an aged relative."

"And what are your feelings towards him?"

"I know what he was in the past; and, while I have unbounded admiration for his wisdom, I can never forget how he first came into our house."

"Then there is no danger of your falling in love with him?"

"None, whatever. I am old enough to be his mother."

"But his beauty—his charms?"

"They do not compare with those of my dear husband," replied Louise, as she twined her arms about Dimitri's neck, with all the coquetry of twenty-seven years ago.

There was no reason to doubt Louise's sincerity, and the General felt a little ashamed of his unfounded suspicions.

"Have you heard from the Minister since our departure from St. Petersburg?" asked Louise.

"Yes; he has written several times. He cannot sufficiently praise the keen intellect of our young priest."

"He is the very man you want. Have him come to Kief at once. You need an assistant and Mikail is bound to you by ties of gratitude and affection."

The General looked sharply at his wife. He still felt doubtful as to her feeling for Mikail. But Louise rocked away, unconscious of her husband's penetrating glance.

"Perhaps it will be best to have him come," he reflected. "Yes, it must be so. After having had him educated, after having given him the opportunity of becoming what he now

is, it would be folly not to employ him to my own advantage.
I shall write for him to-morrow."

"I shall see," he said, at length.

FOOTNOTES:

[Footnote 16: Foulke.]

CHAPTER XXIV

A DANIEL COME TO JUDGMENT

A week later Mikail arrived in Kief. He appeared to be about thirty years of age, was tall of stature, well built and sturdy. His complexion was dark, his features oriental, his face oval, framed by a coal black flowing beard, which gave him an appearance at once imposing and attractive. His large black eyes shone with the lustre of intelligence. A deep and melancholy calm seemed fixed in their commanding gaze. His quiet countenance and stately form, his black clerical garments, his sedate step and thoughtful mien added to the impressive effect of his appearance. His beauty, however, was marred by two serious defects. The lower half of his right ear had been torn away and his left arm was stiff at the elbow and almost useless.

We find him in earnest conversation with Governor Drentell and a few of the counsellors of his court.

"It is to be deplored," said the Governor, "that there seem to be no efficient means of quelling the popular discontent. Arrest and exile do not have the desired effect. Our prisons are filled to overflowing and there is scarcely a day that does not send its quota of criminals to Siberia. Here, in the southern part of Russia, the state of affairs is particularly threatening. It is becoming alarming."

"Your excellency," remarked Mikail, in a deep, musical voice, "the object of exile is, or ought to be, corrective rather than vindictive. But, in my opinion, it exasperates the community and increases the discontent."

"But," objected one of the counsellors, "to allow discontented persons to remain unmolested will make them dangerous to the State."

"Undoubtedly," replied Mikail, "unless we remove the cause of their discontent."

"Remove the cause?" interrupted Drentell, surprised. "To remove the cause would mean to grant them liberty of action, to grant them a constitutional government, to acquiesce in the thousand reforms they demand."

"Let us not disguise from ourselves the fact that the people are entitled to all they ask," said Mikail, quietly; "that the inhabitants of other countries enjoy these rights and more, too, and that they only ask for what is the prerogative of every human being—liberty and happiness. But," continued he, emphasizing the little word; "while other nations may prosper under such a rule, Russia would not. Her people are not ready to enjoy the rights they demand. They would look into the full glare of the mid-day sun before having accustomed their eyes to candle-light. When I spoke of removing the cause, I did not mean to abolish the cause of their discontent, but to obviate the necessity of sending people into exile."

The assembly, which had at first been appalled by the priest's unpatriotic sentiments, now breathed more freely.

"How would you accomplish your purpose?" asked the Governor.

"By directing the attention of the masses to something which will for the time divert their minds from their present projects."

"It has been tried," replied the Governor. "We have begun quarrels with all the countries surrounding us without accomplishing our object."

"Naturally enough. A war with Turkey or with Bulgaria is of very little interest to those living far from the scene of conflict. Beyond taking a few soldiers out of the country such quarrels are productive of no good. There must be some strong excitement in which every one can take a part and feel a personal interest, and then Nihilism will decline."

"What do you propose?" asked the Governor, whose curiosity was now thoroughly aroused.

"Nothing new," answered the priest, deliberately. "I have already had the honor of suggesting it to his excellency, the Minister of War, who graciously commended it. *We must attack the Jews.* They have enjoyed immunity long enough. For over twenty years they have lived in security, feeding upon the fat of the land, engaging in trades that are unlawful and amassing wealth which rightfully belongs to the faithful of the Holy Catholic Church." And Mikail crossed himself devoutly.

The Governor and his counsellors looked at each other, significantly.

The priest continued: "The Jews have entered every branch of trade and, worse still, have acquired lands. This is clearly against the laws of the Empire which forbid a Hebrew's owning land. They have crowded into our cities to the exclusion of our own people. Kief now contains over twenty thousand Jews, whereas I am confident that the ancient laws limit the population to less than one-half that number. They have systematically robbed and plundered the gentiles and by their wiles defrauded the poorer classes. They control the trade in intoxicants and the vast quantities drunk by the *moujiks* pass through the hands of the Jews. Their wives are arrayed in satins and laces and wear the most elaborate jewelry, while our lower classes suffer poverty and misery. Is it right, gentlemen, that the Jews should have such advantages over the faithful? Something must be done to check their dangerous progress."

"Your reverence evidently bears the race no great love," suggested one of the counsellors.

"I have cause to hate them," answered Mikail, with darkening brow and heaving bosom.

"You are right, Mikail," answered the Governor, eagerly; "they are a despicable, blood-thirsty race."

"But how will a crusade against the Hebrews relieve the troubled condition of Russia?" inquired another of the gentlemen.

"It will divert the attention of the masses from their present sinister projects. Once let them taste the blood of the Jews, give pillage and carnage unrestrained license, and they will forget their chimerical schemes, and, paradoxical as it may seem, domestic order will be re-established."

"You are right," said Drentell, rising. "It is eminently proper that the Government should give its attention to the Jews and their relations with the rest of Russia's inhabitants. I do not believe, however, that this agitation can be brought about in a month or even in a year. Unfortunately, too many of our peasants live upon terms of friendship with them, absolutely blind to the fact that they are being preyed upon. We must open the eyes of these poor victims. We must point out to them that the Jew saves money and amasses wealth, while they toil in penury; that Jews fill our schools and colleges, while our people remain ignorant; that the Jew, base, deceitful, and avaricious, fattens on their misery."

"The *moujiks* once aroused," resumed the priest, "and the race struggle begun, the Czar may sleep in peace."

"Will his majesty approve our plans?" inquired one of the counsellors.

"There will be no interference from St. Petersburg," answered the priest. "I have already prepared the Minister of War for such a course and he is thoroughly in accord with us. We have but to notify him of our intentions, and he will order a similar movement in all parts of the Empire simultaneously."

This course being decided on, the Council broke up, the Jews little dreaming of the sword that hung suspended over their heads.

CHAPTER XXV

MIKAIL THE PRIEST

In Russia, the ecclesiastical administration is entirely in the hands of the monks belonging to the "Black Clergy," in contradistinction to the village priests, called "White Clergy." A black priest must be brought up in one of the five hundred rigorous monastic establishments of the Empire. The order is under the supervision of bishops, of whom there are a great number. The black priest looks upon the parish priest as a sort of ecclesiastical half-caste, who should obey blindly, sharing all the onerous duties but none of the honors of the calling.

The history of monastic life in Russia does not differ materially from that in Western Europe. The early monks were mostly ascetics, living in colonies in a simple and primitive manner, subsisting on alms and charity. Their only aims in life were the glorification of God and to live as Christ commanded, in poverty, humility and self-denial. With the flight of time, this comfortless existence gave way to more luxurious customs. Money, lands and serfs were given to these simple monasteries, which gradually grew into a mighty power in the land, engaging in commerce, exercising jurisdiction over large domains, and moulding the religious sentiment of the Church and State. During this century, however, they grew less powerful. Secularization of church lands and the liberation of the serfs reduced many of them to poverty.

The monks, nevertheless, hold a position in the church vastly superior to that of the village priest, or *batushka*, as he is called. These *batushkas* belong to a hereditary caste, the members of which have been priests for generations. They are subject to the rulings of the district bishop; their livings, their distinctive names, even their wives—for they are allowed to marry—are provided for them by their religious superior. Their condition is not enviable. They are for the most part poor and ignorant, with no higher ambition than to perform the rites and ceremonies prescribed by their church. The parishioners are satisfied with very little, and the *batushkas* have but little to give. They preach but rarely, and only after having submitted the sermon to the provincial *consistorium*. The moral influence they exercise over the people is necessarily small.

It was to the "Black Clergy" that Mikail belonged. As far back as he could remember, his home had been in a monastery and his daily associates austere monks. He was taught that the Catholic faith is the only path to salvation. In so far, his education was similar to that of his brother priests, but while the Jew Jesus inculcated love of all men, Mikail was taught to hate the Jews. No occasion was permitted to pass, no opportunity neglected to instil the subtle poison into his young mind. The monks would point to his torn ear and palsied arm, and so vividly portray the tortures he had suffered, that Mikail clenched his little fists, his face became flushed and his bosom heaved at the recital of his wrongs. They took delight in repeating the tale, that they might witness his childish outbursts of passion and fury. This treatment had its desired effect; the boy developed into a rabid Jew-hater.

As a child, Mikail was but a servant in the monastery, ill-treated and ill-fed. The only joyful episodes of this period of his existence were the occasional visits to the Count and Countess Drentell, at Lubny, to whom he believed himself distantly related. They received him with every appearance of cordiality, made inquiries about his progress, allowed him to revel in the companionship of Loris for a day or two, and finally sent him back to his dreary prison.

As he grew up, his treatment at the hands of the Poltava monks improved. The Superior, Alexei, discovered a keen intellect in this reserved and sullen lad. It was astonishing with what avidity he read the limited number of books which the convent bookcase contained. His desire for learning appeared insatiable, and the few kopecks which he earned in showing strangers through the chapel and running errands for the monks, were invariably spent at the book shops for some bit of precious literature. By the time he was eighteen he had mastered all the learning that Alexei could impart, and the superior was by no means an illiterate or ignorant man. Mikail read Latin and German fluently, developed a talent for theology, and his shrewd arguments won the admiration of his fellow-priests.

"He has a brilliant mind," said Alexei to himself one day. "Who knows, he may yet become a bishop."

The Russian Catholic Church occupies a unique position as compared with the churches of Southern and Western Europe. She is now, as she was centuries ago, apparently oblivious of the world's advancement and impenetrable to new ideas. Her ancient traditions are still cherished. The theological discussions and quarrels, the reformations and schisms, which at various times shook the Roman Catholic Church to its centre, had no terrors for the church of Russia. Intellectual advancement, scientific research, inventive progress left her untouched and uninfluenced. Her theology remained precisely as it was in the days of Constantine and, like the self-sufficient snail, she withdrew into her shell, her convents, and allowed the world to wag as it saw fit.

This apathy is easily explained. The Czar, the autocratic temporal ruler, is also the spiritual head of the church. Hence, she has had all her thinking done for her and has remained stationary. This trait has had its influence over the intellectual character of her priests, who are for the most part indolent and ignorant, content to believe whatever their religion requires, without question or debate. Theological discussions, such as we find in Protestant countries, are hardly known in Russia.

To the monks of his convent, Mikail formed a noteworthy contrast. His mind, remarkably active for one so young, refused to accept the intricate mass of dogmas without endeavoring to analyze them and trace them back to their original sources. For years he had accepted the stories of miracles and revelations unquestioningly, but after he had begun a course of independent reading and reflection he discovered discrepancies and contradictions, which sowed the seed of grave doubts in his restive brain.

He confided his doubts to Alexei, his superior. This worthy gave the matter very little consideration; he shrugged his shoulders, stroked his beard, now a venerable white, and answered:

"I, too, had my doubts at your age, but I got bravely over them. The miracles of which the Bible speaks are undoubtedly true, for the people living in those times beheld them. That such things do not occur nowadays is no proof that they could not have happened then. Our duty is to believe what our ancient writings tell us, to see that the lamps are kept burning before the icons, and that our ceremonials are observed to the letter. A priest has no right to question what is sanctioned by tradition and belief."

For a time, Mikail was content to accept this explanation and to keep his peace. But doubt was not so easily quieted. Ever and again he would seek the solitude of his cell and ponder over the grave and perplexing questions that disturbed him. He found no solution. He had been educated in an atmosphere of bigotry and superstition, had been brought up rigorously in the belief that God himself had descended from Heaven and adopted the form of man; had been daily taught that blind faith, independent of deed, would lead to salvation. These dogmas now appeared at variance with his conception of truth. Harassed by doubts, tormented by superstitious fears for the safety of his soul, Mikail led a wretched existence.

Gradually, the monotonous, inactive life of the monastery began to pall upon him. He soon found, too, that many of his brethren believed as little as he did; that others were too indolent to reflect and believed as a matter of course. The thousand ceremonials, the carelessly recited prayers, the perfunctory invocations, the prescribed signs, crosses and genuflections before the rudely painted icons, appeared to him as hollow mockeries, and soon the place seemed redolent with deceit.

It was a severe struggle for the young man, and the Superior, who observed the storm which was surging within the doubter's breast, did not hesitate to attribute it to the wiles of Satan.

"Cast yourself at the feet of the Saviour, O thou of little faith!" exhorted Alexei. "He will help thee drive out the evil spirit! Fast, pray, torture thy body if necessary, but cleanse thy soul of its doubts, purge thy heart of the unholy thoughts which the Devil has planted there."

Mikail fasted and prayed and scourged himself until his flesh was a mass of sores. In vain the torture! The doubts would not be driven out, Satan would not be exorcised.

At the age of twenty-three, Mikail could endure it no longer.

"I must go out into the world, father," he said one day to Alexei. "The convent is too small, too limited for me. I must work and toil with and for humanity. Let me go into the parish for a short time. The Bishop, who thinks well of me, may be able to procure me the position of *blagotchinny*.[17] I will have an opportunity of learning the world, of succoring the needy, of aiding the sick. Perhaps a life of activity will dispel the shadows which have darkened my soul."

Alexei was quite willing to grant this request. He was anxious, in fact, to send Mikail from the cloister, for his doubts, which he took no pains to conceal, were beginning to affect the torpid intellects of the monks. A short conference was held with the Bishop, and Mikail obtained the coveted position.

A new life of work and constant activity now opened for the young priest, but he still found what he had sought to escape, hypocrisy and deceit.

The village priests with whom he came in daily contact were a pitiable set. He found among them many honest, respectable, well-meaning men, conscientiously fulfilling their humble tasks, striving hard to serve the religious needs of the community. There were, on the other hand, however, fanatics and rogues, men representing the worse elements of society. The people shunned the clergy, and held them up to ridicule. They formed a class apart, not in sympathy with the parishioners. They committed serious transgressions, were irreligious and transformed the service of God into a profitable trade.

Could the people respect the clergy when they learned that one priest stole money from under the pillow of a dying man at the moment he was administering the sacrament, that another was publicly dragged out of a house of ill-fame, that a third christened a dog, that a fourth while officiating at the Easter service was dragged by the hair from the altar by the deacon? Was it possible for the people to venerate priests who spent their time in gin shops, wrote fraudulent petitions, fought with crosses as weapons and abused each other at the altar? Was it possible for them to have an exalted opinion of a God-inspired religion, when they saw everywhere about them simony, carelessness in performing religious rites, and disorder in administering the sacrament?[18]

Mikail's heart turned sick. Nowhere could he find that truth which he sought. Even the better educated priests appeared to have given their creed no thought, no reflection.

Still the young priest did valuable service in the field assigned to him. Through his indomitable will be corrected many of the abuses which existed in his district, and raised the parish clergy to a higher standard of efficiency and morality.

So the years passed. The friendship between Mikail and General Drentell grew stronger as the nobleman learned to value the brilliant intellect of his *protege*. His occasional visits to Lubny continued, and the General usually profited by the clear, good sense of the young man, who displayed as thorough a knowledge of agriculture as he did of theology. Mikail and Loris, on the other hand, could never agree. The priest had no patience with the hare-brained, pampered young aristocrat, and occasional differences were the result. For the sake of the General's friendship, however, as well as for the preservation of his own dignity, Mikail restrained his feelings. At the age of twenty, Loris entered the army, and for a while the growing animosity of the two was happily checked.

The Bishop, greatly admiring his assistant's ability, offered him an important position in his consistorium. This Mikail firmly refused. He assigned as his reason that he found congenial work among the parishioners; but in reality the priest felt in his heart that his veneration for the Catholic creed was growing daily less, and that vexing doubts and difficulties had gradually crowded out the faith he had once possessed. It was at this time that General Drentell's influence obtained for him a desirable position with General Melikoff, the Minister of War. The priest gladly accepted the honor, happy to escape from the continual hypocrisy of his clerical duties.

FOOTNOTES:

[Footnote 17: A *blagotchinny* is a parish priest who is in direct relations with the consistorium of the province, and who is supposed to exercise a strict supervision over all the parish priests of his district.]

[Footnote 18: Mr. Melnikof, in a secret report to Grand Duke Constantine. Wallace's "Russia," p. 58.]

CHAPTER XXVI

A DAUGHTER OF ISRAEL

Rabbi Mendel Winenki sat in his study, reading. Before him and within easy reach stood a massive table covered with books and papers. There were strewn upon it in motley confusion ancient folios and modern volumes. It was a comprehensive library which the Rabbi had collected. There were works on comparative theology, on medicine, on jurisprudence and philosophy. The *Shulkan-aruch* and a treatise on Buddhistic Occultism stood side by side. The Talmud and Kant's "Kritik der reinen Vernunft" were placed upon the same shelf, and Josephus and Renan's "Life of Jesus" were near neighbors.

Time was when the Jew who would have exposed a single work printed in any characters but the ancient Hebrew letters would have been ostracized by his co-religionists. The Rabbi remembered with a smile how carefully he had concealed the precious volumes which Pesach Harretzki had given him, how furtively he had carried them into his bed that he might read them undetected.

How different now was the condition of things! True, the greater portion of the Jews of Kief still held tenaciously to their prejudices, absolutely refusing to learn anything not taught at the *cheder*. In the eyes of these people Mendel was a renegade and a heretic. The only thing which prevented them from hurling the ban of excommunication against him was their recollection of the good he had accomplished.

Mendel's greatest achievement was the introduction of secular education. Many years elapsed before his ideas took root, but with the spread of better instruction in the public schools, which were now open to Jewish youth, there came a desire for greater knowledge and the difficult problem worked out its own solution. At the time of which we speak many Jewish lads were pupils of the gymnasium and quite a number of them students at the University of Kief.

Seated by the side of the Rabbi, and sewing, sat his wife and his daughter, Kathinka, now a girl of eighteen. Many changes had occurred in the interval since we last saw our friends. Mendel was now a man of about forty-five and in the full vigor of contented manhood. A wealth of coal-black hair shaded his massive forehead and a long but neatly trimmed beard set off his handsome face. Recha had become stouter and more matronly, but one would scarcely take her for the mother of the blooming girl by her side.

Kathinka was a perfect specimen of Hebrew beauty. She had inherited the commanding form of her father and the regular features of her mother. To this perfection of body she united a sweetness of disposition which made her beloved by all who knew her.

Women among the Eastern Jews, as indeed among all oriental nations, being considered intellectually inferior to their lords and masters, rarely aspire to learning. Occasionally one might find an example of a well-directed and thoroughly developed mind among the daughters of Israel, even though surrounded by the retarding influences of the *ghetto.* We have seen how well Recha had been educated and her daughter Kathinka was being brought up in the same way. She was independent in thought as well as in action, but never at the cost of maidenly sentiment. Piety and purity shone in her lustrous eyes. Superior to her position, she possessed the faculty of adapting herself to her surroundings. There was no pride in her breast save that which might arise from the consciousness of doing right. The poor had a commiserating friend in her and the sick a tender nurse. The children that played in the squalid lanes of the old quarter ceased their romping when she passed and lovingly kissed her hand. She desired no better lot than to do good in her own sphere, and to deserve the approbation of her own conscience. Such was Kathinka, a girl of many graces and sterling worth—in heart and soul a Jewess.

Rabbi Mendel looked up from his books and gazed fondly at his daughter, who, seated with the full light of the window falling upon her face, appeared the embodiment of loveliness. Then turning to his wife, he asked:

"Recha, have you spoken to Kathinka about young Goldheim?"

"No," replied Recha; "I left it for you to tell."

"Briefly then, my dear," said the Rabbi, addressing his daughter, who looked up from her work in surprise; "Reb Wolf, the *schadchen,* has been here for the third time, to induce us to give him a favorable reply for Samuel Goldheim. I told him that I feared my intervention would be useless."

Kathinka blushed deeply.

"You did right, father," she answered.

"But, my dear child," said the Rabbi, thoughtfully; "tell me why you refuse Goldheim? He is a fine-looking young man, of a rich and respected family, and will make you a good husband."

Kathinka arose and, crossing to her father, put her arms lovingly about his neck.

"Dear papa," she said, softly and caressingly, "I know you love me too well to insist upon my doing a thing which will make me unhappy for life. You have often told me how you and mamma first found one another, how heart went out to heart, so that there was scarcely any need to tell each other that you loved. That is an ideal affection, and the only one that my heart could recognize. I abhor the notion of a marriage brought about by the efforts of a third party, who has no other interest in the matter than the fee he receives for his labors. There is to me something repugnant in the idea of uniting two beings to each other for life, without consulting their inclinations or their tastes."

"I agree with you, Kathinka," answered the Rabbi, stroking his daughter's long curls, "and it is far from my thoughts to see you united to any man you do not truly love. In former days the system of marrying through the agency of a match-maker undoubtedly possessed great advantages. It is incumbent upon every good Israelite to marry, but originally the villages were sparsely settled, in many places there was a lack of marriageable men, in others the maidens were in the minority, and as facilities for travelling were limited, and often entirely absent, a *schadchen*, who made it a business to bring eligible couples together, was a great convenience. The necessity for such a mediator is constantly growing less."

"But there can be no romance, no pleasant anticipation in such a union."

"My dear child, Israel has never had time for romance. Your youth has fortunately been spared the dreadful persecutions which have from time to time been visited upon our people; but, if you can picture the constant dread of outrage and the incessant fear of persecution, which have been our portion; if you can conceive the miserable existence in wretched hovels and the weary struggle for the barest necessities of life, you will understand why the Jews have had little of that spirit of chivalry and romance of which modern books give us so fascinating a picture. But tell me, Kathinka," continued the Rabbi, looking intently at his daughter, "is there not another reason for your refusal of Samuel's hand?"

Kathinka became very red, and looked pleadingly at her mother.

"My dear," said Recha, "you had better confess all to your father. He has a right to know."

Still the girl remained silent.

"Well, my child; who has stolen your heart?" asked the Rabbi, kindly.

"Father, I love Joseph Kierson," said Kathinka, faintly, hiding her blushing face upon the Rabbi's shoulder.

"What, my former pupil?" asked the Rabbi, astonished. "I must have been blind not to have observed it. And does he love you?"

"I think he does," she archly answered.

"But Joseph is poor," returned her father. "He has nothing and has as yet no profession. He is merely a student at the University."

"But he has a brilliant intellect," retorted Kathinka, proudly. "I have heard you say a dozen times that he will achieve renown. It is one of your favorite maxims that a man must rise by his own exertions. Joseph is destined to rise."

"How long has this understanding existed?" asked Mendel.

"We were fond of each other as children, when he first began his lessons at *cheder*," replied the girl, earnestly; "but it was only recently that he declared his love."

"He found that you were surrounded by admiring youths and feared that you might be taken from him," added her mother.

"And did you promise to be his wife?" asked the Rabbi.

"Oh, no, father. I could not do that without your consent. He did not even ask me. He simply told me that he deplored his ignorance and poverty and that it was his intention to study medicine and become a learned doctor that he might be worthy of obtaining my hand. That was all."

"He could not have made it plainer. And what did you answer?"

"I encouraged him in his determination and told him I would wait."

"And that is why he requested me to speak to his parents and obtain their consent to his pursuing a course of study, and that is why you took such an interest in his welfare and were so pleased when I told you that he had been admitted to the University."

"Yes," answered Kathinka, with radiant face.

"Do you know how long it will take before he has finished his course? He cannot expect to obtain his diploma in less than six years."

"I know it," replied Kathinka.

"And then it will be some time before his profession will enable him to support a wife."

"I know it. I will wait."

"Brave girl," said Mendel, fondly. "You are doing right and may he prove worthy of you."

"Will it take so long?" asked the mother. "You will then be twenty-four years old, Kathinka, and will be obliged to marry a poor man. Had you not better consider before refusing Goldheim? He is wealthy and quite learned."

"I do not care for him," replied the girl, quietly but with decision. "You married father for love, did you not?"

"Yes," said Mendel, replying for his wife. "She took me although I was but a poor Talmud scholar without a kopeck that I could call my own. Joseph will succeed. He has ambition and talent."

Kathinka kissed her father, affectionately.

"Then you are satisfied with my choice?" she asked.

"Yes, my dear, I am content. When Reb Wolf, the *schadchen*, comes for his answer we will know just what to tell him."

CHAPTER XXVII

AT THE RABBI'S AND AT THE GOVERNOR'S

Joseph Kierson was a fine manly fellow of twenty-two, not particularly handsome, but possessing what in Kathinka's eyes outweighed mere personal appearance, a fine mind, great courage and indomitable zeal. His youth had been uneventful. His father was a hard-working butcher, who in spite of his industry found it difficult to provide food for his family of half-a-dozen. Until recently Joseph had assisted his father in his business, but felt an irresistible desire to achieve something higher than was possible in that humble calling. Recognizing the need of skilled physicians in the Jewish community, he conceived the idea of taking up the profession of medicine. We have seen that his ambition was strengthened by his desire to obtain the hand of Kathinka, in whom all his hopes were centred.

Old Jacob Kierson was bitterly opposed to his son's project. His objections were in a measure selfish, for he could not reconcile himself to the thought of hiring an assistant while Joseph spent his time in idleness. Moreover, he belonged to the old school and sincerely abhorred all learning that savored of the gentiles. He therefore peremptorily forbade his son's entertaining such an impious purpose. In this emergency Rabbi Winenki's eloquence was brought into

requisition. He skilfully argued away the old man's prejudices and painted in such glowing colors the possibilities of
Joseph's future as a physician, that Kierson's scruples were
gradually quieted and he gave a reluctant consent. Joseph,
having passed a brilliant examination and being recommended by Rabbi Winenki—a name that still carried great
weight with it in Kief—was admitted into the University.

It was Friday evening. Without, the snow was falling hard
and fast; a fierce wind, from the northern steppes, howled
through the streets, and dismal was the sound of the storm. In
the houses of the Jews, however, there was peace and
comfort. The pious Hebrews, who had toiled industriously
during six days of the week to provide for the seventh, had
ceased from their labors, had cast aside their cares and
sorrows, and rejoiced in the presence of their God.

Around Rabbi Mendel's hospitable board there was
assembled a goodly company. The table was unusually
attractive on this Sabbath eve and the company uncommonly
joyous, for it was the first family gathering since the announcement of Kathinka's betrothal with the young student.
There was much surprise that this bright maiden should have
bestowed her affections upon the poorest of her suitors, but
Kathinka gazed in happy contentment at the man by her side,
to whom in her heart she had erected a holy altar of love.

The goblets with their sparkling contents, the snow-white
linen and the dainty dishes spoke a cheery welcome to the
merry guests, and the seven-armed lamp hanging from the
ceiling and the silver candlesticks upon the table threw their
friendly glow over the scene. Happiness and pleasure,
contentment and gratitude, beamed in every countenance.

There were present Mendel's father and mother, old and
venerable but still active, Hirsch Bensef and his wife

Miriam, Rabbi Winenki and his wife and daughter, (Recha's mother had died some time before,) and finally the happy Joseph Kierson with his delighted father and mother.

Their conversation was animated and cheerful. Out in the streets the wind might blow and the snow descend; here there was naught but good cheer and comfort. The storm served, however, to recall many a dark and dreary day in the past, and, like soldiers sitting about a campfire, the men related the chief incidents of their eventful lives. There was a melancholy pleasure in recalling the trials they had experienced, contrasted with which their present security was all the more comforting.

Mordecai Winenki related with tears in his eyes how he saved his wife's honor by a hasty flight from home, and how he arrived in Kief just in time for the *Pesach* festival. "Yes, it was a marvellous escape from the soldiers; *Adonai* be praised for it!" Old Kierson had a story of privation and suffering to relate, events which carried his hearers back to the days of Nicholas, the Iron Czar, and they smiled to think that those days were gone, never to return. The Rabbi told, for the hundredth time, of his memorable trip from Togarog to Kharkov; related how he and Jacob had been torn from their mother's fond embrace, how they had suffered, how they finally escaped from the guard that accompanied them, and how, after enduring the misery of hunger and thirst, Jacob disappeared to be seen no more.

"Poor Jacob," sighed the bereaved mother; "nothing has been heard of him since. The poor lad must have perished under the rough treatment of the soldiers."

"Peace to his soul!" said the Rabbi, reverently, and the company responded "Amen."

These bitter-sweet memories were compensated for by the great improvement which had taken place in the condition of the Jews during the past twenty years. Mendel related how, on arriving in Kief, he found his uncle in a weather-beaten hovel, through the neglected roof of which the snow leaked in little rivulets. Hirsch Bensef now resided in a commodious dwelling in one of the best streets of the city.

Would this state of affairs continue? Would Governor Drentell show the same leniency and magnanimity towards the Hebrews as did his predecessor? The new ruler had now been in power for nearly a year, during which time there had been no hostility, no curtailing of their liberties.

"God grant that our condition will not grow worse," said the Rabbi. "The mental improvement of our people during these twenty years has been marvellous. If it continues at the same pace, there is no telling whither our progress will eventually lead us."

Thus passed the Sabbath meal in pleasant conversation, during which plans were laid for future improvement. After supper, friends and relatives trooped in to congratulate the newly-betrothed couple.

While this homely feast was going on at the Rabbi's house, an entertainment of a different nature was in progress in the Petcherskoi quarter.

The Governor's palace was ablaze with light. The glare of a thousand lamps shone through the windows upon the falling snow, converting icy crystals into scintillating gems. Long lines of sleighs and covered carriages were drawn up before the entrance, and from them emerged richly uniformed officers and handsomely attired ladies. Within, liveried lackeys relieved the guests of their furs, and ushered them into the presence of the Governor and his wife, who, with smiling countenance, greeted each new arrival.

It was a court ball, such as the Governors of the various provinces give; miniature reproductions of the magnificent entertainments in which the Imperial Court at St. Petersburg delights.

Here all was beauty and refinement. The court circle of Kief was composed of officers attached to the provincial government, men who remained in the city only so long as their official duties demanded. They were accompanied by their wives and daughters, ladies who for the most part possessed every advantage of education, who had studied abroad and brought into Russia the choicest of French and German fashions. There were also many young army officers, always welcome guests at these affairs, in which young ladies were apt to predominate. It is not strange, therefore, that these balls should present the most fascinating aspects of Russian life, and form a charming contrast to the dark scenes of ignorance and misery which it has been our duty to depict.

The ball at the Governor's was given to introduce into polite Russian society Loris Drentell, the Governor's son. Loris had returned after a short absence from Kief. There was no need of his remaining away any longer. No one suspected that a Drentell had been even remotely connected with the Nihilist plot, and there were none of the conspirators left to tell of his connection with it. The trouble in Turkey had subsided and there was no longer any necessity for keeping Loris' regiment on the frontier. The lieutenant was, therefore, recalled and a grand ball was given in his honor.

Court balls in Russia do not differ materially from those of other countries, and we will leave the gay cavaliers and pretty women whirling through one of Strauss' waltzes, while we enter the Governor's private room.

General Dimitri Drentell and his intimate advisers had withdrawn from the festivities and had sought the seclusion of the cabinet. Mikail the priest had just entered.

"Ah! Mikail," said the Governor; "you are a late caller."

"The train brought me from St. Petersburg but a few minutes ago, and I hastened to present myself to your excellency at once. Had I known that there was a ball this evening, I should have deferred my visit until to-morrow."

"Make no apologies," answered Drentell. "We would have been disappointed had you not come to-night. What news do you bring us from the capital?"

"The best, your excellency. I spoke to his imperial majesty in person. He desires to be commended to you, and approves of your energetic measures in bringing the suspected Nihilists to judgment. He counts your excellency among his stanchest supporters."

The Governor flushed with pleasure. Bright visions of future advancement passed through his mind.

"And our policy as regards the Jews?" he asked.

"Has his sanction! In fact, any project which will divert the minds of the populace from political questions, meets with imperial favor. But the animosity towards the Jews must not appear too sudden and unwarranted. Convinced that they have in many cases assumed privileges not allowed them by law, and rendered themselves punishable by the statutes, the Minister of War has decided to appoint a commission of inquiry, which shall investigate the following questions."

The priest took an official paper from his pocket and read:

"*First*—In what trades do the Jews engage which are injurious to the well-being of the faithful inhabitants?

"*Second*—Is it impracticable to put into force the ancient laws limiting the rights of the Jews in the matter of buying and farming land, and in the trade in intoxicants.

"*Third*—How can these laws be strengthened so that they can no longer be evaded?

"*Fourth*—To what extent is usury practised by the Jews in their dealings with the Christians.

"*Fifth*—What is the number of public houses kept by the Jews, and what is the injury resulting to Christians by reason of the sale of intoxicants.

"The commission is to report to the Minister of War as soon as practicable," continued Mikail, replacing the paper in his pocket. "I have the honor to be one of the commissioners, and as soon as we have obtained definite information upon these points—information which is sure to be damaging—we will be ready to proceed against the accursed race."

"But if the reports are not damaging to the Jews?" asked one of the officials.

"They will be," answered the priest; "the commission has been appointed for that purpose."

"Then woe to the Jews!" answered the official.

"Yes, woe to the Jews!" responded the priest, and the malignant expression of his countenance boded ill to his kindred.

"Come! let us return to the ball room," said Drentell, taking the priest by the arm.

"Your excellency must pardon me," answered Mikail, "My clothes are travel-stained, and I am neither in a condition nor in the humor to enjoy the festivities."

"But Loris is here," continued the Governor.

Mikail suppressed a grimace of displeasure.

"There is no haste. I shall see him to-morrow," he answered, and bowed himself out of the room.

"Strange man," muttered the Governor, when the door had closed upon the priest's retreating form. "I almost fear him when he is attacked by his fits of gloomy anger. Poor Jews! You will find Drentell a different man from your soft-hearted Pomeroff. Ah, if Mikail but knew; if he but knew!"

CHAPTER XXVIII

THE PRIEST IN THE SYNAGOGUE

Mikail did not allow the grass to grow beneath his feet. Stimulated by the approval of the Czar as well as by his own undying hatred, he lost no time in collecting the statistics that were required for his purpose.

Hitherto he had been content to accept hearsay evidence in his estimate of Jewish life and character; he had never knowingly come in contact with one of the race. Convinced, however, that public opinion was not half severe enough, he determined to personally investigate their manner of life. For some days, therefore, he made periodical trips through the old Jewish quarter, sounded the Christians with whom the Jews occasionally associated, and with an acute but not impartial eye, made his observations.

It was Saturday of the week following the events narrated in the last chapter. The snow that mantled the earth was frozen solid, and the bells tinkled merrily as the sleighs skimmed over the glistening road. A cold bracing air sent the blood surging through the veins of the pedestrians and brought the ruddy glow of health to their cheeks.

The priest, bent upon new discoveries, walked rapidly in the

Milton Goldsmith

direction of the Jewish quarter. Suddenly he stopped. He had almost run against a man who was hurriedly walking in the opposite direction.

"What, Loris! is it you?" he cried, upon recognizing his protector's son. "What are you doing in this part of the town?"

"I might repeat the question," answered Loris. "Why is a priest roaming about these streets, when he should be counting his beads up in the Petcherskoi convent?"

Mikail frowned. Loris' sneering tone grated harshly upon him.

"I owe you no explanation," he said, curtly; "but if it will give you any satisfaction to know, I am following up a subject of importance to the State."

"And I," said Loris, confidingly, "am following up a far more interesting subject. You should see her, Mikail! Such a head, such eyes, such a form! To think that I have wasted so many months abroad while Kief held such a treasure!"

"What do you mean?" asked the priest, dryly.

"A young girl, of course. She must live about here some-where. I saw her come up this street, but when I turned the corner she had mysteriously disappeared. I tell you, Mikail, she is a beauty. I shall not rest until I find her!"

"You are seeking perdition," exclaimed the priest, wrath-fully. "A pretty face is Satan's trap to lure a weak soul into his toils."

"Convent talk!" answered Loris, disdainfully. "Why do I

stand here and speak to a priest about a woman? When you take your vows of celibacy you pretend to dislike anything that wears petticoats. But I doubt whether even you could resist the temptation of a handsome face and voluptuous form."

Mikail's eyes flashed. He was about to reply to Loris' sneer, but, by a severe effort, he checked his rising anger, and without another word turned on his heel and walked away.

"Ill-natured cur!" muttered Loris. "They are all alike— hypocritical fools! With all their pretended virtue, I would not like to expose the best of them to even a moderate temptation."

Mikail walked through a maze of lanes until he came to the street which had formed one of the boundaries of the "Jews' town." He now observed, for the first time, groups of Jewish men, women and children, dressed in their holiday attire, pass him and enter a large building not far away.

"It is their Sabbath, and they are going to their barbarous worship," thought the priest, as he crossed himself.

He went further into the quarter, carefully avoiding the groups that he encountered, and finally entered the dwelling of a Christian woman, who sublet rooms to Jewish tenants. The information which awaited him here must have been important, for it was quite a while before he emerged into the street and retraced his steps towards the city. His path led directly past Mendel's synagogue. Through the window he heard the chant of the *hazan*, and he paused, reflectively.

"After all," he murmured, "what harm can it do if I go in. I am in search of facts and where shall I be better able to find them than in the Jews' stronghold, their synagogue?"

Crossing himself devoutly, he opened the door and entered.

The *shamas* (sexton), surprised to see a *gallach* (priest) in the synagogue, stood for some moments in doubt, but finally shuffled up to the stranger and showed him a seat in the last row of benches.

Mikail sat down passively. For a moment he seemed dazed and stupefied. Perhaps it was only the heat and the glare of the burning candles; but gradually a strange spell came over him, which he tried in vain to shake off.

He could not remember ever having been in a synagogue, and yet the praying-desks, the pulpit and the ark for the holy scrolls seemed singularly familiar. He looked up. Yes, there was the latticed gallery filled with women, just as he had expected to find it!

The *hazan* was intoning a prayer. Between the words he interjected a number of strange trills and turns. How weird it all sounded, and yet how familiar to the wondering priest. Mikail found himself almost instinctively supplying the following word before it was uttered by the reader. Then the congregation arose and responded to the prayer, and Mikail arose, too, and it seemed as though the words of the responses were laid upon his tongue.

It was strange, very strange, and yet it was fascinating.

Again the congregation arose. The Rabbi went to the ark at the back of the pulpit and took out one of the scrolls, covered with a red velvet cloth curiously embroidered with golden letters. Mikail followed his every movement with intense interest. He scarcely breathed.

"*Shema Israel,*" sang the Rabbi; "*Adonai Elohenu,*" and then he paused a moment to clear his throat of something he must have inhaled.

"Why don't he continue," thought Mikail, impatient at the momentary interruption, and then in a voice loud enough to be heard over the entire synagogue, he ended the sentence by crying:

"*Adonai Echod!*"

All turned to look at the speaker, and they whispered among themselves in surprise at hearing a monk recite the *shema* in a *schul*. The women looked down from the gallery in amazement.

Mikail's face flushed. His first impulse was to flee, to get out of the accursed place, to break the spell of enchantment that bound him. With a muttered prayer he strode to the door, only to find it locked from without. It was customary to bolt the door during certain portions of the service, to prevent noise and consequent disturbance.

The priest was therefore obliged to remain. Obeying a natural impulse, he made the sign of the cross, set his jaws firmly, and awaited further developments.

The *hazan* opened the Pentateuch and the *parnas* of the congregation was called to the *Torah*. Every movement was anticipated by the priest. The parnas reverently lifted the fringes of his *tallis*, and with them touched the sacred Scroll; then, kissing them, he recited the customary blessing. Mikail repeated it with him. It sounded almost as familiar as his own liturgy. Suddenly a reaction came over the stern and haughty priest as the services continued. A strange storm broke within his bosom; undefined recollections, visions of a once happy home, a tangled revery of fanciful memories chased each other through his excited brain. Without knowing why, he felt the hot tears coursing down his cheeks, tears which not even the harsh treatment he had endured during his early years at the monastery could force from their reservoirs. One after another, seven men were called to the *Torah*, and their actions and prayers were a repetition of those of the *parnas*. The monotonous reading at length came to an end, Mikail heard the bolts withdrawn, and with hasty strides he cleared the passage into the street. On he sped through the city, looking neither to the right nor the left, scarcely knowing whither he went, until he finally reached the Petcherskoi convent, where he had taken up his temporary quarters. Without returning the greetings of the monks, apparently unconscious of his surroundings, he went straight to his cell and there gave way to a flood of passion.

An hour afterwards a monk found him upon his knees before an icon, in fervent prayer.

"I have been bewitched, Sergeitch," he said, with his wonted calmness. "Pray for me that the evil spirit may leave me."

CHAPTER XXIX

LORIS FALLS IN LOVE

Kathinka, well wrapped in a heavy mantle, walked briskly along the darkening street. She had gone to the extreme end of the city to succor a sick and needy widow and was now hastening homeward with a light and happy heart. The world seemed bright and cheerful to the young girl whose every desire was gratified and every wish granted. As she neared her home, she became aware of the presence of a man some yards behind her, keeping pace with her own steps. Kathinka quickened her gait, but the man was evidently determined not to lose sight of her and hurried after her. The girl remembered that she had been followed by the same person some days before, and, while she attached no importance to the incident at that time, she now became frightened and glanced timidly about her. The street was deserted and there was no place of refuge in sight. With a little cry of alarm, she lifted her skirts and ran at full speed in the direction of her dwelling, but she had not proceeded far before the stranger caught up with her, and, grasping her by the arm, held her as in a vise. Kathinka stopped and, with flushed and angry look, faced the stranger.

"Lovely creature," said the man, insinuatingly, when he had recovered his breath, "why do you flee from me? Can you not see that I am anxious to speak with you?"

"Let me go!" cried the girl, indignantly. "You hurt me."

Loris, for the stranger was no other than the Governor's son, released the girl's arm, but he barred her escape by placing himself directly before her. Kathinka tried in vain to pass him; then, pausing, with heaving bosom, she cried:

"What do you mean, sir? Have you no manhood left, that you molest a defenceless woman?"

"Listen to me but a moment," answered Loris, passionately; "and then go your way if you will. I have been following your footsteps for the last two weeks, desiring, yet fearing, to speak to you. From the day I first beheld you, I have thought of nothing else. I have sighed for you and dreamed of you. I was happy when I caught a glimpse of you and sad when you were out of my sight, sad until I saw your features again. Do not now repulse me. Take pity upon me."

These sentences, expressed with all the passionate earnestness of which youth is capable, greatly terrified Kathinka.

"Sir, I do not know you," she exclaimed; "and if I did I could have nothing in common with you. Let me go, and if you are a gentleman, you will in future avoid troubling me."

"By God, you shall not leave me without giving me some encouragement. Kathinka, I love you! When you know who I am you will not treat me so cruelly."

"If you were the Governor himself I should have but one answer for you, and that is that you have outraged every sentiment of honor," cried the girl, with growing indignation.

Loris seized her hand.

"No, do not despise me; hear me to the end!" he cried, passionately. "I am Loris Drentell, the son of your Governor. I know what I am risking in loving a Jewess, but I cannot help it. Kathinka, you have bewitched me. I love you! Do you understand me? I love you! I only ask you to think kindly of me, to see me of your own free will, and to give me the blessed hope that you will in time return my affection. Do not consign me to misery!"

Kathinka struggled to free her hand from his grasp. Overcome by terror, it was some time before she could gain strength to reply.

"Count Drentell," she said, at length; "you have spoken the truth. I am a Jewess, and any contact with me would dishonor you. Moreover, I am betrothed to one of my own race, and while I feel the honor you would bestow upon me in offering me your love, I have but one reply to make: I do not wish to see you again."

"Don't drive me to despair, Kathinka; I cannot live without your friendship, without your love. Why should your betrothed stand in the way? I am rich and powerful. I can give you whatever your heart desires. You shall want for nothing, if you will only look upon me with favor." And he again seized her hand and covered it with kisses.

This flattering speech filled Kathinka with loathing. Well she knew that it meant not love, but the basest of passions, and that a Jewess could never become more than the passing fancy of Count Drentell. With a disdainful glance at him, she turned to go.

"Count Drentell," she answered, calmly; "this is disgraceful.

You seem to forget your position, your birth. You forget that I belong to a proscribed race."

"You are right," replied the young man, bitterly; "I forgot everything but my love for you."

"Then try and forget that. And now, sir, enough of this farce. Let me pass, or I shall call for help."

Loris bit his lips in vexation.

"Do not decide so hastily," he said. "A terrible danger threatens the Jews. My father, who detests your people, is even now plotting their destruction. I may, perhaps, avert the calamity, may dissuade him from his terrible projects. Will you allow me to serve you? One word of encouragement and I will be your willing slave."

Kathinka started. Was it true that a new danger menaced her people? She could not tell. Perhaps it was but an invention of the Count to further his own ends. In her opinion, he was base enough for anything.

"The God of Israel has been our support in the past," she answered, firmly; "He will not desert us in the future. Come what will, I shall not endeavor to avoid it by the loss of my self-respect. Now, make way, sir; let me go."

"And is this the end of all my dreams? Am I to abandon all hope of ever seeing you again?" asked Loris, gloomily.

"Count Drentell," replied the girl, with a proud glance. "Do not persecute me with your attentions, which are extremely distasteful to me. I trust we shall never meet again."

And with a haughty sweep of her beautiful head, she passed

the astonished Loris and walked rapidly down the street.

The young man looked after her for a moment in silence; then he stamped his foot in rage.

"She refuses my attentions, the proud Jewess! But I will conquer her in spite of her pride."

It was not until Kathinka reached home that her strong spirit gave way, and she threw herself into a chair and wept bitterly. Her mother and father, surprised at such an outburst of emotion, hastened to her side, but it was some time before the girl attempted an explanation. Then she told her parents of her encounter with the Governor's son.

The Rabbi walked up and down the room in great perturbation. The affair promised no pleasant conclusion.

"Alas, that your beauty should have attracted the young Count!" he said. "It is very unfortunate. Who knows to what extremes he may go to revenge himself upon you for having refused his advances."

"Was there any other course for me to take?" asked Kathinka.

"No, my child; you acted honorably. There was nothing else for you to do."

"But the calamity which the man predicted would befall Israel?" said Recha.

"It may have been an idle threat. There is no need of borrowing trouble. Misfortune has ever found the Jews steadfast and ready to bear the greatest hardships for their faith. If new troubles come, we will not be found wanting. In the meantime there is nothing to do but wait."

"If I should meet him again and he should again force his attentions upon me, what could I do?" sighed Kathinka, nervously.

"For the present do not venture out unless with me or Joseph. We must inform Kierson of this matter at once. He has doubtless frequent opportunities of seeing this young Count and can keep his eyes on him. Perhaps Drentell is honorable enough to desist if he sees that his advances are repelled."

Kathinka shook her head, despondently.

"I fear not, father. You should have seen his face and heard his words. Such passion is not subdued by neglect. I am afraid that he will become our implacable enemy and that we will eventually have more to fear from his hatred than from his love."

The Rabbi did not reply, but his heart echoed his daughter's forebodings.

CHAPTER XXX

AN UNFORTUNATE ENCOUNTER

Kathinka now rarely went out, and never alone. On her way to the synagogue and upon her little errands of mercy, she was invariably attended by her devoted Joseph. The very danger to which the girl had been exposed served to cement their hearts more closely.

For a time, nothing was seen of Loris. One day, however, Joseph and Kathinka had just left the Rabbi's house.

"Look," whispered Kathinka, pressing Joseph's arm, "he is following us."

Joseph turned rapidly and perceived the form of Loris at some distance behind them. The Count, seeing that he was observed, turned a corner and disappeared. For several months after, Kathinka saw nothing more of her persecutor, and the disagreeable episode gradually faded from her memory.

One bright afternoon the girl sat at her window, reading. Her father was engaged in his duties at the school, and her mother had gone from home to take a bottle of wine to a sick neighbor and would probably remain away until evening.

Milton Goldsmith

Kathinka was not alone, however, for she had the companionship of her books, more congenial entertainers than were the gossiping maidens of her intimate circle.

Suddenly there was a knock at the door; before she could rise it was thrown open, and Loris Drentell stood before her. He deliberately closed the door again and placed his hat and coat upon a chair.

Kathinka could not utter a word, so great was her consternation. Loris stood facing her for some moments in silence.

"Kathinka," he said, at length, "I have come at the risk of offending you, to repeat the declaration I made some time ago; to tell you that I love you. Do you still bear me the ill-will that you evinced towards me then?"

Kathinka rose from her chair and, drawing herself up to her full height, pointed to the door.

"Go!" she said, "or I shall summon help."

Loris smiled cynically.

"Do not excite yourself unnecessarily," he said, coolly. "You are alone in the house. I know it, for I have been watching for some time and saw both your parents leave. It will be useless for you to call for assistance. Sit down and hear me out."

Finding resistance useless, the girl fell back into her chair, and with a gesture of despair hid her face in her hands.

"Miss Winenki," said Loris, quietly at first, but gradually becoming more passionate in his appeal, "do not judge me harshly for taking this means of seeing you. I knew of no other way of gaining your ear. I love you sincerely, madly. For the last two months I have been vainly struggling with this feeling, have been trying to conquer my infatuation, but I am ever haunted by the vision of your beauty. Do not turn from me as though I were unworthy of you. Think not of me as a cold, selfish man who lives but to satisfy the desires of a moment. Never had maiden so devoted a lover as I will be to you. I will grant your every wish, I will bestow upon you wealth and luxury. You shall be the envied of all the ladies of the land and I will have no other aim than to make you happy. Can you still doubt me when I, who might win the proudest in the Empire, now kneel at your feet and ask you to smile upon me?"

Loris had fallen upon his knees and had seized the girl's hand, which he lifted passionately to his lips.

Alone with this singular man, who seemed swayed only by his passions, Kathinka was overcome by a terror which robbed her of the power of speech. She could only gaze into Loris' upturned face in mute despair.

Drentell interpreted her silence favorably, and with a joyful cry he arose and folded the astonished girl in his arms.

"You will be mine, you will not reject my love? Turn your eyes upon me and make me happy with your smile. Do not struggle in my embrace, but tell me that you love me."

By a violent effort Kathinka succeeded in freeing herself from his passionate clasp and now stood with her back to the wall. Her black eyes flashed with an angry fire, as she cried:

"Count Drentell, you have taken advantage of my helpless-ness to intrude upon my privacy and have acted, not as befits a gentleman, but in a manner that one would scarcely expect from the meanest of your father's serfs. Let us understand one another. In spite of my repulses you still continue to assert that you love me."

"To desperation," murmured the Count.

"Were I to yield to your entreaties and accept your love, would you make me your wife? Would you present me to the world as the Countess Drentell? Answer me, sir!"

Loris hesitated before replying.

"I would surround you with all the luxury and pomp that money could command. I would make you the happiest of women."

"I demand an unequivocal reply. Would you make me your wife?" insisted the girl.

"Before God we would be man and wife."

"Count Drentell, would you brave the anger of your father and the opinion of the entire court and present me, the Jewess, as your wife?"

Loris looked for a moment at the flashing eyes of the indignant girl, and then his glance sought the floor.

"I do not deny," he said, at length, "that there would be grave difficulties in the way of such a step. I fear the court would never recognize a Jewess as the Countess Drentell. But what of that? It is but an idle formality. Even though the world do not know of our relationship, we will be none the less man and wife."

"In other words, you would make of me your puppet, your

plaything, to be fondled to-day and cast aside to-morrow! You would have me renounce my family, my betrothed, my religion, my honor and my reputation, to become the creature of your pleasures until you weary of me! Vile wretch! you are a greater villain than I thought. Go, and never again darken my path with your presence."

Loris uttered a cry of fury. He had counted upon an easy victory over the poor Jewess, and he saw his wicked dreams rudely disturbed. With one bound he was by the side of Kathinka and wound his arms about her.

"So you think to brave me, poor fool!" he said, savagely. "You think to escape me! But I will have you yet; you shall be mine in spite of your petty scruples. If you will not come to my arms peaceably, I must use force; but come you shall!"

He clasped the frail girl in both his arms, and lifting her up from the ground, he bore her towards the door. Anger and despair lent Kathinka tenfold strength. With a cry for help, she struggled in his embrace and by a mighty effort freed herself.

Again, Loris, blinded by rage, seized her, and Kathinka, overcome by terror, uttered a piercing cry and fainted away.

At that moment the door opened and Joseph Kierson entered the room. He was on his way to Kathinka's house and her cry of terror had lent wings to his feet. He rushed upon the Count and threw him to the floor. In an instant the two men were locked in each other's grasp, the hand of each upon the other's throat.

The contest was almost equal. They were both of powerful physique and equally courageous and for some minutes the battle raged with varying success.

Joseph was aware that upon his victory depended the honor of his betrothed and his own happiness; he believed that if the Count obtained the mastery, he would not scruple to kill him outright. He exerted all his strength and freed himself from the powerful clasp of his foe. Then he struck the Count so violent a blow as to render him senseless.

Joseph paused for breath and for reflection. His first care was to restore Kathinka to consciousness, and he soon had the satisfaction of bringing her back to life. With a sigh she opened her eyes and turned them in gratitude upon her preserver. Then she gazed about her and, as her glance fell upon the prostrate form of the nobleman, she shuddered and stretched out her hands to Joseph. The young man helped her to her feet and led her to a sofa. In a few words she related all that had occurred previous to Joseph's arrival.

A great difficulty now presented itself; how to dispose of the Count. A glance showed Kierson that he was not dead, yet it was almost half an hour before Loris regained his senses and with difficulty rose to his feet. His face was badly bruised and scratched, one eye being entirely closed. Kierson humanely went to his assistance, but Loris, with an oath, declined the proffered aid and moved slowly to the door.

"You shall hear from me again," were his parting words; "my reckoning will come later on!"

Passing out into the street, he entered the *droshka* which was in waiting, and in which he had intended carrying off Kathinka, and was driven to his home.

The Rabbi on his return was at once informed of the occurrence. While his daughter related her story, he walked up and down with clenched fists and heaving breast. He now realized, for the first time, the terrible danger which threatened his beloved child, and his indignation against the villain who had molested her found vent in vigorous language. At the same time he did not close his eyes to the fact that the rage of the baffled man would spend itself not only upon Kathinka but upon the whole Jewish population.

"It is not likely," he said, after he had heard the end of the narrative, "that Drentell will allow the matter to rest. A man who is so unscrupulous as is this young tyrant, will go to extremes to carry out his purpose or to take vengeance upon those who have thwarted him. It is for your safety I fear most, Joseph, and I advise you to absent yourself from Kief for some time at least, until this affair has been forgotten."

"Never!" cried Joseph, bravely, "I have but done my duty and I will abide the consequences. To leave Kief would be to abandon the promising career I have mapped out for myself; besides, Kathinka may again require my assistance. I shall remain."

"You incur a great risk," admonished the Rabbi.

"I will not seek to escape it by flight, but will remain here and meet the danger."

Joseph returned to his parents' roof, but in spite of his courage he felt ill at ease. His parents heard him relate his adventures, and lifted their hearts in prayer to God to avert the catastrophe which they felt would in all probability follow the encounter between their boy and the Governor's son.

Their fears were not unfounded. At eight o'clock that evening there was a rap at the door of old Kierson's dwelling, and two uniformed officers confronted the terror-stricken family.

"We seek Joseph Kierson," said one of the soldiers.

"I am he," answered the young man, with as much firmness as he could command.

"I arrest you in the name of his majesty the Czar," continued the officer, placing a heavy hand upon the poor lad's shoulder.

"Of what am I accused?" asked Joseph.

"I do not know. Perhaps the warden of the prison can tell you."

Joseph was well aware that resistance would make the matter worse. Kissing his weeping parents and offering them all the consolation in his power, he accompanied the officers to the prison, there to await the action of the Governor.

Within an hour, the whole Jewish community knew the events of the day, and there were lamentations throughout the quarter, for the blow that had fallen upon the young man portended disaster to them all.

CHAPTER XXXI

KIERSON'S ESCAPE

For weeks Joseph languished in prison, in total ignorance of the fate that awaited him. At first the Governor was too busy to attend to the case and it afterward slipped his memory entirely. For reasons of his own, Loris did not interfere. Although he had instigated the arrest of the Jew, he was careful not to inform his father of the true cause of the trouble. His injured eye and general appearance required some explanation and a drinking bout with some of the University students was given as the cause. For the preservation of order, however, he advocated the arrest of the offender and Kierson was taken into custody. Loris' course was not dictated by caprice. If his august father knew that he had sought an alliance with a daughter of the despised Hebrew race, he would vent his wrath upon Loris' head for compromising the honor of the noble family of Drentell.

The punishment usually inflicted upon students for quarrelling among themselves was light and limited to a small fine. Kierson's was an aggravated offence, however. The dignity of the Governor's son had suffered, and as there was no precedent the case was allowed to drag on indefi-nitely. Loris used his influence with the authorities to keep Joseph in durance.

Meanwhile, the Israelites were not idle. Convinced that Kierson had done nothing but his duty, they drew up a petition to the Governor, pleading for mercy. Rabbi Mendel himself carried the document to the palace, trusting to supplement the petition with his own eloquence.

Alas! the time when Mendel Winenki was a power in the Governor's house had long since passed. There was a ruler now who knew not of the Rabbi and his deeds, and Mendel had not even the satisfaction of speaking to his excellency in person. He and his petition were referred to the Chief of Police, the official who was supposed to have the entire matter in charge.

Sick at heart, Mendel sought that worthy functionary. He carefully read the petition, put it in his pocket and promised to look up the case and report it to the Governor as soon as possible.

It was poor consolation that the Rabbi took to his people. Their petition had accomplished nothing. It was not even possible to discover where Joseph was concealed and whether he had already been sentenced or not. Kathinka was heart-broken. She knew not what to do. A praiseworthy impulse to go to the palace and throw herself at the Governor's feet was checked by the thought that Loris might be there to delight in her humiliation and to use his power to defeat her prayer.

After several weeks of suspense, the poor girl received a letter. It was in a strange handwriting and she opened it with trembling hands. She glanced hastily at the signature and with a cry allowed the missive to fall to the ground.

"What is it, Kathinka?" asked the Rabbi, who had been sitting near-by.

"Read it, father; it is from Drentell!" cried his daughter.

The Rabbi took the letter up anxiously and his eyes ran eagerly over its contents. Kathinka saw the deadly pallor that spread over his countenance, watched his quivering lip and darkening brow. He read to the end, and crumpling the letter in his hand, he threw himself upon the sofa in a paroxysm of grief. The girl who had never before seen her father so affected became seriously alarmed.

"What is it, father? What does he write?" she asked.

"Read it, my child; it is for you," sobbed the poor man. "Read it and decide," and he handed the letter to his daughter, while the tears ran down his cheeks.

Kathinka, with varied emotions, opened out the paper and read the contents. The note was as follows:

BELOVED KATHINKA:—You will justly reproach me for having remained silent so long, but do not attribute it to a waning of my affection. I love you more devotedly, more tenderly than ever. Your cruelty to me at our last interview has but served to fan the flame of my passion. I have since thought only of you. I know your heart is set against me on account of the arrest of your betrothed. Do not blame me for having a hand in his incarceration. The law of the land is severe, and although I exerted my influence, I was powerless to stay its hand in the matter. Your friend is condemned to a life-long exile in Siberia. It is a terrible fate, worse than death itself. You alone can save him from it. Consent to come to me, to share my heart, to make me the happiest of men, and I myself will plead with the Governor and obtain his pardon. The day that sees you at my side will restore your friend to liberty. Do not deem me cruel. I would serve you if you but gave me the right to do so. I await your reply. LORIS.

When Kathinka had ceased reading, she dropped the letter and hid her burning head in her hands, while her body rocked with grief and despair.

Her father gazed at her in silence, with a look of intense commiseration on his face.

"What can I do?" she moaned, at length. "What would Joseph have me do? He would rather die a thousand deaths than owe his liberty to my degradation. Father, my duty is clear! Joseph is innocent of any crime and the God of Israel will protect him."

"God bless you, my daughter," replied the Rabbi. "You have spoken well. Will you answer this letter?"

"No, father; I shall treat it with contempt. The writer can draw his own conclusions from my silence."

It was a sad day for both the Rabbi's and Kierson's families. The latter, much as they loved their only son, sincerely approved of Kathinka's decision.

"If he must go to Siberia," they sobbed; "he will go without a sin upon his soul. We are all in the hands of the Almighty."

Old Kierson thenceforth went daily to the police head-quarters, endeavoring in vain to obtain information about his son. He found no one that could enlighten him as to his present condition or future fate, and he trudged homeward, feeling daily more sick at heart, more depressed in spirit.

At the end of a week, Kathinka received a second letter from her persecutor. It was more offensive than the first. It stated that Joseph was still a prisoner; that owing to his (Loris') influence the sentence had not yet been carried out. There was still time to save him from ignominious exile. He hinted, moreover, at a movement to drive the Jews out of Kief and promised to avert the catastrophe if Kathinka yielded to his persuasions. There were passion and insult in every line.

The poor girl was almost distracted with grief and mortification, the more so as it became necessary to take the entire Jewish community into the secret.

Rabbi Mendel hastily summoned a meeting of the influential men of his congregation and laid the matter before them. There was great consternation when it was learned that a new danger threatened the race, but there was not one among them who would not have suffered the cruelest persecution rather than allow the Rabbi's daughter to sacrifice her honor for their salvation. It was impossible to form a plan of action, for as yet the peril that menaced them was too indefinite, but Mendel exhorted them to do nothing that might throw the slightest reproach upon Israel.

The Governor's animosity towards the Jews now became manifest. The acts of intolerance were in themselves insignificant, but they were like the distant rumblings of thunder that precede the storm and were not easily mistaken by the poor Hebrews.

Because of Kierson's thrashing the ruler's son, an edict was issued expelling Jewish students from the University of Kief. Some time after, a Jew who, through Mendel's influence during Pomeroff's palmy days had obtained the office of under-secretary to a police magistrate, was summarily dismissed "because he was a Hebrew." Then followed an edict restricting the attendance of Jewish children at the public schools, and expelling all children whose parents had not resided in the city for at least ten years, retaining the others only upon the payment of an exorbitant tax which none but the wealthy could afford. These and many other petty acts of intolerance caused the Jews no little uneasiness.

One day Rabbi Winenki was sitting in his study. It was raining in torrents without, and the landscape appeared deluged and desolate. The Rabbi gazed out at the dismal scene and sighed regretfully as he thought of those whose occupations compelled them to remain out of doors in such miserable weather.

Suddenly the door was thrown open and Joseph came, or rather rushed, into the room. His face was pale as death; his garments, torn and tattered, were soaked with rain. He had become thin through long confinement and every line of his features betokened abject misery.

The Rabbi started as though he beheld a spectre, but seeing that the young man was about to sink to the floor exhausted, he sprang to his feet and helped him to a chair.

"What, Joseph! God be praised! Kathinka, Recha, come quickly," he cried, running to the door leading to an adjoining apartment. "Bring some brandy."

Kathinka was not long in coming, and unmindful of his appearance, with a cry of joy, she fell upon Joseph's bosom and kissed him rapturously.

"Oh, Joseph, I am so happy!" murmured the girl. "Are you free, entirely free?"

Joseph gasped for breath. He could not speak. The Rabbi hastily poured some liquor into a glass which Recha had brought and held it to the young man's lips. The draught seemed to revive him.

"Hurry," he whispered, looking about him, anxiously; "hide me somewhere before the officers come after me."

A look of disappointment passed over the Rabbi's face.

"Then you are not acquitted?" he asked.

"No! I escaped. I'll tell you all about it, but not here. They might come and find me. Let us go upstairs, anywhere out of sight. Send for my parents! It would be dangerous for me to visit them, but I must see them before I leave."

"You are not going away again!" cried Kathinka.

"I must. It is death to remain here!"

The Rabbi supported the young man while he went to an upper floor, and leaving him to the ministrations of his wife and daughter, he despatched a messenger to the Kiersons to inform them of the arrival of the unexpected guest.

By the time they were all assembled, Joseph had, in a measure revived and recovered his cheerful spirits.

"But where have you been and what have you been doing?" asked the Rabbi, after the first loving greetings had been exchanged.

"I have been in a terrible place," sighed the student, shuddering at the mere recollection of his experience. "When I was taken from home I was led to the jail near the barracks, up in the Petcherskoi quarter, and without a trial, without a hearing of any kind, I was thrown into a cell about five feet square. After my eyes had become accustomed to the darkness, I looked about me. In one corner I found a bed of straw with a cover as thin as paper. A broken chair and a rough wooden basin completed the furniture. The place reeked with corruption and filth, and the stench was almost unbearable. Of the vile food they placed before me, I could eat nothing except the bread. It was *trefa*, but had it been prepared according to our rites, its nauseating appearance would have caused me to reject it.

"There I lay for weeks, perhaps months, for I lost all reckoning of time, without knowing what was to be done with me. I almost wished they would send me to Siberia, so that I might escape that foul atmosphere. If their jails are so terrible, what must be the condition of their Troubetzkoi prison?"

"Poor boy," sobbed his father, "what a terrible experience you have had. But tell us, how did you escape?"

"By the merest accident. They recently changed the warden of the prison, and the new incumbent, a kind-hearted man, at once visited the cells and inquired into the charges upon which each prisoner was detained. When he heard my story, he evinced the greatest surprise, and on investigating the matter, he came to the conclusion that I had been forgotten by the authorities, as it was not customary to detain a prisoner so long upon so slight an offence. The charge against me was simply participating in a student's quarrel, and the warden was inclined to be lenient with me. He at once made inquiries concerning my future fate, and learned that I was to be kept a prisoner until my punishment had been definitely decided upon. As there was no order to keep me in a cell, the warden allowed me to roam about the prison at will, and I made myself generally useful about the place. I tried to write to you, to inform you of my condition, but it was forbidden. To-day, the warden sent his assistant to town upon an errand, and he himself went down into one of the lower corridors to dispose of some new prisoners. He had left his keys upon his table. At last I saw liberty within reach! There was nobody about. I seized the keys, unlocked the outer gates and ran for my life. I feared I would be seen and recognized if I came directly through Kief, so I ran to the outskirts of the town and came here by a roundabout road. I have walked and run for the last two hours, through mud and rain, through swamps and ditches, until my feet would support me no longer. I thought I would never get here."

"And if you should be discovered?" asked the Rabbi.

"Then I will be taken back and treated more harshly than before. I would rather die than go back to that dreary cell. It is dangerous for you to harbor me. I must leave here at once, this very night."

"Where will you go?" asked Kathinka, who was seated at the sufferer's side, and wiped the perspiration from his fevered brow.

"I do not know. Anywhere! Wherever I can find friends to succor me, and where I can occasionally hear from you and see you."

Mendel reflected a moment.

"The Rabbi of Berditchef is my friend," he said, at length. "Go to him. I will give you a letter of introduction, and he will do all in his power to assist you. It is not far from here. If you start on foot to-night you can reach the place by morning."

"Oh, you surely are not going to-night, and in such weather," cried the girl. "Don't leave us yet, Joseph; stay with us. We will conceal you."

"Don't make my departure harder than I can bear, Kathinka. I must go—for your sake as well as for mine. I tremble even now, lest they should discover me. I will go to Berditchef for the present."

"And your aspirations for a physician's career—what will become of them?" asked his father.

Joseph sighed, and his eyes were dimmed with tears.

"It will be hard to give up my plans, but I see no alternative."

"Don't worry, my boy," said the Rabbi, consolingly. "There are more ways than one to make an honorable living. Honesty, thrift and energy will enable you to succeed in any undertaking. Whether you be a doctor or a cobbler, we will not think the less of you, and I am sure Kathinka will love you none the less."

Kathinka threw her arms about her lover's neck and clung to him affectionately. Joseph's face brightened.

"Get me something to eat," sighed the young man, "for I am famished and the way is long."

A meal was hastily brought, and a substantial lunch was prepared by Kathinka's hands, to cheer the wanderer upon his lonely path.

Night came. The storm had not abated, the wind still moaned and the rain fell in torrents. It was a wretched night for a foot-journey to Berditchef, and Joseph's mother and his affianced endeavored to persuade the young man to postpone his journey until morning.

Joseph shook his head, sorrowfully.

"I would be recaptured if I waited. No, I have no time to lose; every moment is precious. Think of me, my dear ones, and pray for me. When I can do so in safety, I shall return to Kief; until then, God bless you all."

Kissing his weeping friends farewell, he wrapped himself in a stout mantle which the Rabbi had procured for him, and stepped out into the inhospitable night.

For a time the sorrow-stricken families wept silently; then Mendel advised the Kiersons to return to their home at once.

"If the police follow him," he said, "they will naturally search your dwelling first. It will be unfortunate if they find you absent, and might lead to inquiries which would give them a clue to his whereabouts. As it is, you can truthfully say that he has not shown himself in your house."

The old people acted upon the suggestion and reached their house not a moment too soon. They had scarcely entered before a number of officers demanded admittance and began a thorough search of the premises. Satisfied by the replies of the lad's parents that he had not visited the house, they withdrew in no very amiable humor to continue their investigations at the house of the Rabbi, where they were equally unsuccessful. Failing to trace him in the Jewish quarter, the officers returned to the fortress and reported their lack of success to the warden. This worthy was at first inclined to lose his temper, but he finally shrugged his shoulders and muttered:

"Let him go, poor fellow! He has been here nearly two months, and that is punishment enough for having thrashed a man, were that man the Governor himself."

A few days later, Kathinka received two letters. The first she opened was from Joseph. It announced his safe arrival in Berditchef and his kind reception by the Rabbi's friend, who had at once found him congenial employment. It abounded in expressions of affection and undying love. Kathinka pressed it to her lips and, with an overflowing heart, thanked the Almighty that her lover was safe.

The second letter was from Loris. It, too, was full of passionate yearning, but its flowery phrases created a feeling of intense disgust. The Count, evidently ignorant of Joseph's escape, ended his missive with the assurance that unless Kathinka acceded to his demands, her friend would be sent to Siberia on the morrow.

Kathinka threw the paper into the fire.

CHAPTER XXXII

AN ATTEMPT UPON THE CZAR

Kathinka remained unmolested for some time, not because Loris had ceased to admire her, but because the young Count was condemned to a twelve-months' absence from Kief. This unsuspected stroke of good fortune for the girl happened in this wise:

Towards the end of the year 1879, it became very evident that Nihilism was spreading to an alarming extent in the army. Four officers of Loris' regiment were arrested on a charge of disseminating revolutionary pamphlets and were summarily exiled. Another officer had assisted eight political offenders to escape and was kept in close confinement. General Drentell, in consequence, declared Kief, Kharkov and other districts under martial law.

A stormy scene took place between the Governor and his son Loris, in which the former, mindful of the latter's past escapades, expressed his belief that his son was implicated in the plots of his comrades, while Loris indignantly denied all knowledge of the matter.

"Listen to me, Loris!" said the General, purple with rage. "I saved your life once, at the risk of losing my own. As true as

Milton Goldsmith

St. Nicholas hears us, if ever you repeat your plottings, I shall be as inexorable as though you were the meanest of the Czar's subjects."

Loris saw that his father was in earnest and recoiled before the wrath of the stern old soldier. He again asserted his ignorance of any conspiracy.

Not knowing how many more officers of the regiment were implicated, Drentell decided to transfer the entire division to another district, in the hope of severing any connection which might exist between the men and the Revolutionary Committee.

Loris had to obey the order and accompany his regiment to the steppes of Central Russia, where he remained until the active disorders in Kief a year later recalled him.

Nihilism was not to be rooted out by the removal of any particular set of men. It had spread its branches among all classes and conditions of society, and the number of its adherents was increasing with alarming rapidity.

The martyr who unflinchingly faces death for the sake of his faith, the Nihilist who exposes himself to imprisonment or death in the hope of attaining constitutional liberty, are examples of the heroic endurance of minds exalted by principle. The Jew's devotion to his religion has always been most intense when intolerance and persecution were at their height. In like manner the love of liberty is developed to its greatest extent when despotism seeks to stifle it.

"Brightest in dungeons, liberty thou art,
For there the habitation is the heart."

Twenty-one persons were arrested in Kief, and almost as

many in Kharkov, and still Nihilism was not stamped out. Phoenix-like it arose from the ashes of its martyrs.

On February the 17th, 1880, just as the imperial family were about to dine, a mine was exploded beneath the winter palace, the guard-room was demolished, ten soldiers were killed and forty-five wounded; but, the divinity which sometimes hedges a king preserved the royal family from harm.

Excitement was intense. A commission of public safety, with authority to preserve order at any cost, was at once appointed, with General Melikoff at the head.

On the second day of March, during the festival, General Melikoff was shot at as he alighted from his carriage. The would-be assassin was so close that the General struck him in the face, and the man was arrested.

At the trial it was discovered that the malefactor was a baptized Jew, by the name of Wadetsky Minsk. The trial excited universal interest. The culprit was asked by the judge why he had deserted his faith.

"Because I found it impossible to live as a Jew," he replied, bitterly. "You took from me my children to send them to the army; you deprived me of the lands I had cultivated and left me penniless; you despised and degraded me, and when I had suffered until the fibres of my heart were torn, you showed me a glowing picture of the happiness that awaited me here and in heaven if I became a Christian. I allowed myself to be baptized."

Minsk paused, and the expression of his face showed the mental anguish he was at that moment enduring. Suddenly, he continued, with great vehemence:

"Yes, I became a Christian, or rather a godless hypocrite, who had bartered away the sympathy of his co-religionists as well as his self-respect. How did you treat me after I had embraced your faith? Humiliations, worse than any I had experienced as a Jew, were showered upon me. I was regarded as something impure, shunned and execrated. It was too late to turn back, and in spite of your treatment, I remained a Christian, I adhered to the glorious faith which teaches 'Peace on earth and good-will to men.' In sheer desperation, I joined the band of unfortunates as reckless as myself, whose self-imposed mission it is to pave the way to liberty."

Minsk preserved a defiant demeanor throughout the trial. He made no defence, nor did he endeavor to have his punishment mitigated. His condemnation followed, as a matter of course.

The scaffold found him unsubdued.

"My attempt has failed," he cried, "but think not that General Melikoff is safe! After me will come a second, and after him a third. Melikoff must fall, and the Czar will not long survive him."

The fifth of March witnessed his death struggles upon the scaffold.

Darker and darker it grew in Israel. The sun of its brief prosperity was gradually becoming obscured by heavy clouds of intolerance and fanaticism, clouds which did not display the proverbial silver lining of hope and comfort. This was a period of great activity for Mikail; never before had he found such congenial employment. After making a series of one-sided investigations, in which he interrogated principally those who had real or imaginary cause for complaint against the Hebrews, the priest embodied his conclusions in a book, entitled "The Annihilation of the Jews." Unquenchable hatred breathed in every page. With a cunning hand, he subverted facts to suit his fancy. He drew a vivid picture of the great dissatisfaction existing because the Hebrews were achieving success in various branches of enterprise to the exclusion of the gentiles. With peculiar logic he argued that sooner or later quarrels must ensue between the races, that if there were no Jews there could be no trouble, and that they should therefore be driven out of the country. His work accused the Jews of thriving almost entirely upon usury and gross dishonesty, in spite of the fact that many of the chief industries of Russia were in the hands of thrifty and honorable Israelites. It purposed to forbid the Jews from keeping inns, on the ground that they fostered intemperance, in the face of statistics which showed drunkenness to be most prevalent in provinces where no Jews are allowed to reside. It finally advised the confiscation of all property belonging to the Jews and the summary expulsion of the despised race from the Empire.

Such a book, at a time when rulers and people were alike eager for sensation, acted like a firebrand. The newspapers, knowing that the author was a member of the commission appointed by the Czar to investigate the conduct of the Jews and that his work would receive the imperial sanction, published extracts from its pages and commented editorially upon its arguments. Mikail's conclusions were accepted, and the cry rang throughout Russia, "Down with the Jews!" In all the land there was not a man who dared raise his voice in defence of the unfortunate people.

That Minsk, the would-be slayer of Melikoff, had once been a Jew, served to increase the outcry against the race. Of the scores of Nihilists who had already been executed not one was alluded to as a Catholic, although that church claimed them as her own; but the newspapers added the word "Jew" every time they had occasion to mention his name.

There were as yet no open hostilities in Russia. The great majority of laborers and *moujiks* knew nothing of this agitation. They lived in peace with their Jewish neighbors, on whom many were dependent for work and wages. For the best of reasons, they did not read the newspapers and they cared little for the vague rumors of discontent that now and then assailed their ears. Occasionally there were quarrels, but these were unimportant and of rare occurrence.

A dispute arose one day in the shop of a man named Itikoff. A thief entered his place and having requested the proprietor to get him a certain article he rifled the money-box the moment the Jew's back was turned. Itikoff saw the act in a mirror, and turning suddenly he seized the man by the neck and beat him severely. The man's cries brought a crowd to the door who, seeing a fellow-gentile maltreated by a Jew, at once set upon the unfortunate shopkeeper and brutally assaulted him. They then sacked his shop and threw his merchandise into the street, whence it was quickly removed by the assembled mob. A number of policemen arrived and arrested Itikoff for instigating a riot. Despite his pleading he was carried to jail, and only released upon the payment of a fine of two hundred roubles.[19]

Such occasional incidents, while they were characteristic of Russian justice, were not of a nature to foster good feeling between the Jews and the gentiles.

Then came the event of March 3, 1881. Through the mighty Empire flashed the awful news, "The Czar has been assassinated!" For a time all other affairs were left in the background. Before that dire catastrophe the petty quarrels of the races faded into insignificance. Jew and gentile alike met to mourn over their ruler and looked forward with pleasant anticipation to the accession of the new Czar, Alexander III., to the throne. The Nihilists, satisfied with their work, rested upon their arms and waited to see if the new Emperor would yield to their demands. The agitators who had conceived the crusade against the Jews as a means of diverting public attention from St. Petersburg had been unsuccessful and for the time being found their occupation gone. The Jew-haters, Drentell, Mikail and others, were busy at the capital, currying favor with the new government, and the poor Jews breathed more freely and enjoyed a brief respite from danger.

FOOTNOTES:

[Footnote 19: See report of "Russian Outrages," in *London Times*.]

CHAPTER XXXIII

THE RIOTS AT ELIZABETHGRAD

Terrible is the havoc wrought by the elements, the devas-
ating flash, the furious wind; appalling is the destruction of
the roaring flames, the all-devouring flood; but what
elements can measure their forces with the fury of man, once
he has torn asunder the bonds of reason and rushes madly
and irresistibly onwards toward the accomplishment of his
passionate desires.

"Gefaehrlich ist's den Leu zu wecken,
Verderblich ist des Tigers Zahn;
Jedoch das schrecklichste der Schrecken,
Das ist der Mensch in seinem Wahn."

The animosity of the Russians towards the Jews had not
ceased, it had only been held in check for a final onslaught.
The unfortunate year 1881 dawned upon the Hebrews. Its
beginning found them hopeful, and confident that for the
future trouble would be averted; its close left them the
victims of a cruel and relentless persecution. We would
gladly spare the reader the harrowing details of this most
atrocious of outbreaks, but we must follow the fortunes of
our friends to the end.

The meagre statements which found their way into our

newspapers merely announced that riots against the Jews had occurred here and there, but were of so general a nature that they failed to impress the imagination. They never evoked pictures of the terrible scenes which actually occurred: men murdered, women outraged, infants butchered—arson, pillage, slaughter and lust combined.

The ceaseless workings and writings of Mikail and other members of his commission, had gradually aroused the fury of the masses. Their utterances were not only repeated in every *kretschma*, but were grossly exaggerated. Professional agitators, who had nothing to lose and everything to gain by promoting a race quarrel, were actively at work among the people, keeping alive the flame of hatred which they had taken such pains to kindle.

Elizabethgrad, a large city to the south of Kief, containing ten thousand Jews, was their first point of attack. Weeks before the event, proclamations were posted throughout the district, calling upon the inhabitants to throw off the yoke of the Jews and fixing Wednesday, April 27th, as the day for the general uprising. Copies of a fictitious *ukase*, commanding that the property of the Jews be confiscated and handed over to the Christians, were freely circulated and universally accepted as emanating from the Czar. Every lying accusation which had ever been employed against the Jews since the rise of Christianity was unearthed and used with telling effect. The atrocious calumny that the Jews required the blood of Christian children for their Passover rites was poured into eager ears. For a similar accusation the early Christians were tortured by the Romans, and in their days of prosperity they in their turn employed it against the Jews.

The Israelites were paralyzed with terror at the fate which hung over them. The most influential of their number waited upon the Governor, who after much deliberation received them. He listened with well-feigned attention, while the Jews proved that they were law-abiding and that the accusations against them were unjust. He smiled pityingly when they had finished, and, reminding them that they were in God's hands, dismissed them. No further notice was taken of their appeal.

On the twenty-seventh day of April came the crisis.

In a *cabaret*, kept by a Jew named Kirsanoff, a religious dispute arose. The matter was of small importance, but it led to a scuffle by which a large crowd of idlers was attracted. The mob grew in numbers and in lawlessness, and having ejected the proprietor of the shop, they proceeded to despoil the place of its liquors. Inflamed by their copious libations, the rioters were ripe for any excess. At this moment there arose a ringleader, a man whom no one knew, but who had been active for some weeks past in stirring up the neighborhood. He mounted a cask and addressed the maddened crowd:

"My friends," he cried, "your time has come! On to the Jewish quarter! Kill, destroy, take what you can! The Czar gives you their property."

With a rallying shout he left the inn, the crowd following close upon his heels.

"Down with the Jews!" arose the cry, and, as the mob increased, it was repeated by a thousand intoxicated wretches.

Then began a wild destruction of property. Shops and warehouses were attacked and their contents carried out into the street, to be destroyed or carried away. Costly linens and works of art, fine furniture and articles of apparel were served alike. What was too bulky to be stolen was carried into the street and burned. A dozen bonfires roared and blazed in the Jewish quarter.

The Jews could no longer look passively upon this wanton destruction. Hastily conferring, they placed themselves under the leadership of one of their merchants, one Zoletwenski, a powerful and courageous man. Armed with clubs and such rude weapons as were within their reach, they hurried to the scene and attempted to defend their own. Alas! the little group was soon routed by the infuriated mob. Their resistance served only to increase the anger of their assailants, who now left the shops and turned their attention to the dwellings of the Hebrews.

Zolotwenski's house was the first to be attacked. Down crashed the door and a hundred excited brutes forced their way through the house. They seized his wife, whom they found in bed sick and helpless, and choked her into insensibility. They followed his two daughters to a room in the upper story in which they had locked themselves, and with threats of vengeance worse than death they broke open the door. The poor girls threw themselves from the window to the ground below.

In the meantime, the Rabbi, accompanied by a number of his congregation, again hastened to the Governor's palace and besought him to protect the innocent women and children. This time the appeal bore fruit. The Governor promised to call out the military, and an hour afterwards a detachment of soldiers appeared upon the scene. At first they stood by, amused spectators, cheering the mob whenever it broke into a dwelling, taunting the poor women who ran hither and thither in frantic endeavors to escape the wretches who pursued them; but later in the day the temptation to join the plunderers proved irresistible, and the soldiers became active participants in the outrages which continually increased in brutality. Indeed, the leaders of the soldiers soon assumed command of the mob, and, with a refinement of cruelty, incited the people to lust rather than to pillage.

A number of rioters and soldiers broke into the dwelling of an old man named Pelikoff. The poor fellow had carried his sixteen-year-old daughter to the attic and barricaded the door. In vain his resistance. The rusty lock yielded to the onslaught from without; twenty men precipitated themselves into the apartment, and twenty men threw themselves upon the trembling child.

"Kill me," cried Pelikoff, "but spare my innocent daughter!"

"To the devil with them both!" laughed the leader.

Pelikoff fought with desperation. With his bare fists he felled two of the stalwart soldiers to the ground, but he was no match against the overpowering numbers. They seized him in their arms, carried him to the roof, and hurled him over into the street below, while a dozen of the ruffians attacked the unfortunate girl. When sympathizing friends visited the house next day, they found the child dead, and Pelikoff a hopeless maniac.

Night brought a cessation of hostilities, but not a glimmer of hope.

With early dawn, the outrages recommenced. The synagogue now became the point of attack. Thither many of the women and children had fled for refuge, and the mob, actuated rather by lust than by love of plunder, proceeded to demolish the building, which they set on fire. The poor women, as they fled from the burning pile, were set upon and cruelly assaulted by the rioters. All that day and the next, the Hebrew quarter was at the mercy of the savages. What the ax did not crush, fire destroyed. Five hundred houses and over one hundred stores and shops were ransacked; whole streets were demolished; property to the value of two million roubles was destroyed, and upwards of twenty people lost their lives while defending their possessions or their honor.

Thus ended the first anti-semitic riot. The plans for General Drentell's vengeance, through Mikail the priest, were in a fair way of being realized.[20]

CHAPTER XXXIV

RABBI AND PRIEST MEET

The enemies of the Jews persisted in their attacks. Ignorant greed, commercial rivalry, religious intolerance, all played their part in shaping coming events. The mobs soon had ringleaders; unscrupulous agitators who counted on the gain they could derive from a general pillage of the property of the wealthy Israelites.

The greatest terror reigned in Kief. But for the example of a few energetic men, prominent among whom was Rabbi Winenki, the Hebrew population would have been in despair.

Thousands of Jews, driven out of Elizabethgrad by the atrocities committed at that place, fled to Kief and implored shelter of their hospitable co-religionists. They were for the greater part destitute of the commonest necessities of life. Their appeal was not in vain. The charitable Jews opened their houses, and there was scarcely a home that did not entertain one or more refugees.

Rabbi Winenki hastily called a conference of his friends to devise means of assisting these unfortunates to emigrate. The project met with immediate approval, and an association was formed to aid all those who desired to find a home in distant America.

General Drentell heard of this benevolent undertaking, and while he was not unwilling to drive the Jews out of the Empire, he deemed it the duty of the Israelites to consult with him before engaging in any project which would deprive the Czar of his subjects. He therefore sent a communication to the Rabbi, stating that he had no objection to such a committee as had been formed, provided it was created under the auspices of the Government. It was customary, he said, for the ruling family to be identified with all movements of this sort, and as an evidence of good-will towards the Jews, his wife, Countess Louise, desired to be elected Honorary President of the newly-organized society.

The Israelites received this communication with undisguised contempt. The Rabbi denounced the inconsistency of the Governor, who had hitherto never denied his animosity towards the Jews, but who now desired to pose as their benefactor. A resolution was adopted declining to honor the Countess Drentell with the office she coveted.

The Governor seized upon this as a pretext for the wickedest measures against the unfortunate people. The following day, placards were issued from a secret printing-press in Kief, and distributed throughout the town and surrounding country, declaring that the Czar had confiscated the property of the Jews and had presented it to his loyal subjects. Wherever the commiserating face of a Madonna gazed down from her icon, there hung one of these placards, which was destined to let loose the worst passions of which man is capable. As if this were not potent enough, Mikail the priest travelled in person through the province, denouncing the Jews, and exhorting the orthodox Russians to wreak vengeance upon them for real or fictitious crimes.

On came the flood which, once started, threatened to engulf the entire Jewish population of Russia.

On May 6th, the mob attacked the Hebrew quarter at Smielo, and thirteen men were killed, twenty wounded and sixteen hundred left without homes.

It was authoritatively announced that a riot would begin in Kief on Sunday, the eighth of May. On weekdays the *moujiks* were for the greater part in the fields hard at work, while on Sunday they were free to take part in the plunder and destruction.

The seventh was a sad day for our friends. It was the Sabbath, the last that many of them would live to celebrate. The synagogues were filled to overflowing with weeping women and terror-stricken men. There was no hope, no consolation anywhere. Sadly and sorrowfully the services proceeded, each worshipper praying as though his end were close at hand. Not even the inspiring words of Rabbi Winenki could cheer them. In vain he recalled the many miraculous deliverances of their forefathers, and exhorted his hearers to place their faith in Jehovah. His sermon but increased the gloom which hung over the congregation.

During the afternoon a delegation, headed by Mendel, proceeded to the Governor's palace and begged for an interview. They were admitted into the cabinet, where Governor Drentell, his wife and the Catholic priest Mikail awaited them. Mikail was sitting at a table, writing.

"You wish to see me," said the Governor, curtly. "What is it you want?"

"Your excellency," began Mendel, with some hesitation, "we need scarcely remind you of the fact that we have always been loyal subjects; that we have never knowingly committed a wrong against the State, and that we have through our thrift and industry sought to add to the wealth of the country. We are now threatened with a serious calamity, one which will rob us of our hard-earned possessions and may possibly deprive us of our lives. Your excellency will surely not permit this outrage to be visited upon us. It lies in your power to prevent it and we beseech you, in the name of twenty thousand of the Czar's faithful subjects, who are now crowded in Kief, to vouchsafe us your gracious protection."

The Governor listened impatiently. When Mendel had finished speaking, he said:

"I do not see how I can help you. The Czar himself has declared your property forfeited, and I am afraid the people will insist upon their rights."

"But the pretended *ukase* confiscating our property is false!" cried Mendel, with great indignation. "Your excellency knows it is but an invention of a body of men who wish to enrich themselves at the cost of our people. Your excellency surely cannot allow such outrages to be perpetrated!"

"Moderate your language, man," cried the Governor, angrily, rising from his chair, "or you will find yourself outside the palace doors."

"I beg your excellency's pardon," answered Mendel, meekly, "if grief has made me disrespectful. In the name of my co-religionists, I desire to offer a proposition. If our property falls to the Czar's subjects, it is certainly better to preserve it intact than to expose it to the savage attacks of the rioters. If your excellency permits, we will bring you the keys of our houses and submit to any measures you may see fit to take. If the *ukase* is true, the property will revert to the State uninjured; if it is not true, your excellency will have the humanity to restore us to our rights."

The Governor, surprised at this unexpected and unique proposition, found himself without a reply. He glanced significantly at the priest.

"What do you say, Mikail?" he asked.

Mikail, who had been apparently absorbed in writing, but who had not lost a word of the discussion, now arose, and in his deep, sonorous voice, answered:

"The *ukase* is true, your excellency, and we have no right to render it nugatory. For twenty years the Jews have enjoyed equal rights with the Christians, and every endeavor has been made to assimilate them with the other inhabitants. In vain. The Jews constantly abused their new liberties, and by their acts brought upon themselves the ill-will of the entire nation. They form a state within the State, governing themselves by their own code of laws, which are often antagonistic to those of the land. I need not recapitulate the acts of cruelty they have perpetrated upon defenceless Christians, the wiles they have employed to defraud their creditors, or the usury for which they are notorious. I need not allude to the fact that they have driven the Catholic Russians from profitable fields of labor, and have appropriated to themselves every branch of trade. These acts and many others have now called forth the protests of the people, and the result is violence and robbery. It would be useless to control the mob, your excellency, for the wrongs under which they smart have driven them to desperation."

While Mikail was speaking, Mendel gazed at him as though fascinated. He could not take his eyes from the handsome features and commanding form of the monk. He must have seen him before, he thought—but where? Suddenly the priest's resemblance to his own father struck him as remarkable.

Ordinarily, the priest's unjust accusations would have called forth a vigorous protest from the Rabbi, but now he suddenly found himself bereft of reasoning power; he could but look upon his adversary in awe and wonder. The priest turned, and by the movement exposed his mutilated ear. The lobe had been torn completely off. Where could he have seen that ear before? Mendel stared as though in a dream. He struggled with his memory, but it failed him; all appeared a perfect blank. Then the priest, in the course of his denunciations, became more vehement than before, and made a movement with his left hand. The arm was stiff at the elbow, and the gesture appeared unnatural and restrained. Still Mendel looked and tried to reflect. That arm awoke a strange train of thoughts. His mind appeared sluggish to-day; he could remember nothing.

Suddenly the Rabbi uttered a piercing cry. Yes, it all came back to him now.

"Jacob!" he cried, advancing towards the priest. "My brother Jacob arrayed against his own people!"

The monk recoiled a step and looked at the Jew in surprise.

"Is the man mad?" he asked, addressing the Governor.

"No; I am not mad," cried Mendel, excitedly. "As true as there is a God above us, you are my brother Jacob!"

The priest, fully believing that the Rabbi had suddenly become insane, recoiled a step and drew his garments about him. The Governor glanced significantly at his wife, who had become as pale as death.

The Rabbi was unable to control his excitement.

"Jacob, my brother," he cried again; "do you not remember me, Mendel? Do you not remember our home in Togarog? Do you not recollect how we were both stolen away from home on the night of my *bar-mitzvah*; how we were taken to Kharkov by the soldiers, and how we escaped and fled into the country? Do you not remember how we travelled along, weary and foot-sore, until you could no longer walk, and I ran to a neighboring village for assistance? When I returned, you had disappeared. Jacob, do you remember nothing?"

Mikail stood with his head buried in his hands, drinking in every word of the gesticulating Rabbi.

Yes; he did remember something; indistinctly, of course, but as each event was recalled it evoked a corresponding picture in his brain. Many things suddenly became clear which had been hitherto shrouded in mystery. The secret of his birth, concerning which he had so often questioned Countess Drentell without receiving a satisfactory reply, the indistinct recollection of strange events, and, finally, the familiarity of the ritual in the synagogue. When Mendel had ceased speaking, he turned abruptly to the Countess, who, pale and agitated, was standing by the side of her husband. Surprise, anger, passion were portrayed in the priest's flashing eye and contracted features, and Louise shrank from him as he approached her.

"Madam," he said, hoarsely, "what can I say in reply to this charge? You have been my protectress from childhood. Tell this man that he lies, that I am not the brother of a Jew."

The Countess' lips parted, but neither she nor the Count

found a reply.

"See, their silence speaks for me!" cried Mendel, almost joyfully. "Jacob, it is true! I could not be mistaken. Your image has never left me since we parted on the highway, and I recognized you at once by your resemblance to our father, and by your torn ear and crippled arm."

"Marks which I received at the hands of the accursed Jews," cried the priest, fiercely.

"Not so, Jacob! Whoever told you that did not tell the truth. It was not the Jews, but a Christian, who tortured you because you were a Jew."

Again Mikail confronted the Countess.

"Madam, I demand to know whether this man speaks the truth or not?" he exclaimed, wildly.

"He does, Mikail," replied Louise, nervously. "For the sake of your own happiness, we endeavored to keep you in ignorance of the facts. You were a Jew when we found you insensible on the road near Poltava. I took you to my home, and to save you from the misery and degradation of being a Jew, and also to bring a new soul into our holy church, I had you brought up in a convent as a Catholic priest."

"And these injuries," asked Mikail, pale and trembling, "the marks of which I shall carry to the grave, were they not the work of the Jews?"

"Of that I know nothing," answered the Countess, carelessly. "This man," pointing to Mendel; "can tell you more about that than I."

The face of the priest became livid. "I am a Jew," he cried; "I, a Jew! Oh God," he moaned, convulsively, "why did you send me this agony? My life has been one living falsehood, my whole existence a lie. My tongue has been taught to execrate my religion, my mind to plan the destruction of my father's people. Ha! ha! ha! you are right; the Jews are an accursed race, and I am accursed with them!" The priest broke into a wild laugh which sent a chill through the blood of his hearers.

Mendel endeavored to speak to him, to grasp his hand; but Mikail looked at him with a meaningless stare, and turning, without another word, he fled like a maniac from the apartment.

General Drentell turned furiously upon the Israelites.

"Go!" he cried; "leave the palace! You have done mischief enough!"

Mendel's strong form shook with emotion; he was weeping. He collected himself for a final appeal.

"If your excellency would send us a regiment of soldiers," he said, preparing to leave; "our lives and our property might still be saved."

"What care I for your property or your wretched lives?" shouted the Governor, in a frenzy. "I shall not trouble my soldiers for a pack of miserable Jews."[21]

The Rabbi and his fellows found themselves outside of the palace walls, sad and disheartened.

"Friends," he said, in a broken voice, "you have been witnesses of this terrible scene. Oh, God! to think that my brother, whom we mourned as dead, should have become a Catholic priest and be plotting the destruction of his people." Here Mendel's grief overcame him and he remained silent for some moments. Recovering his composure with an effort, he continued, in a subdued voice: "I have a favor to ask of you, my friends. Speak to no one of this unfortunate meeting. If the news came to my father's ears it would kill him."

The men promised and the little band walked silently back to their homes.

FOOTNOTES:

[Footnote 20: In the description of the outrages and acts of lawlessness in this and succeeding chapters, the author has not drawn upon his imagination, but has followed as closely as possible the narration of the Russian refugees on their arrival in America, and the graphic account sent by a special correspondent to the *London Times*, and republished in pamphlet form in this country in 1883.]

[Footnote 21: Historical.]

CHAPTER XXXV

MAN'S INHUMANITY TO MAN

During that memorable Sabbath day, hundreds of refugees came in from the surrounding villages where the outrages had already begun. They fled to Kief as a place of refuge, vainly believing that a city with such important mercantile interests centred in the Jewish population would be exempt from serious danger. The poor Israelites feared to stir from their homes; they sat in prayer during the entire day and fasted as on the Day of Atonement.

Towards night, the door of Rabbi Winenki's house was suddenly thrown open, and Joseph Kierson, haggard and travel-stained, entered.

"What are you doing here?" ejaculated both the Rabbi and Kathinka, in a breath.

"Has there been a riot in Berditchef?" queried Mendel.

"No," answered Joseph, sinking into a chair; "not yet; but I heard that there would be danger here, and I hurried back to share it with you."

"Unhappy man," said Kathinka. "Think of the peril of

remaining here. If you are recognized they will take you back to prison."

"I do not care," answered the young man. "I could not remain in Berditchef, when I knew that you and my family were exposed to danger. My place is at your side; come what may, I will live or die with you."

"You are a noble boy," exclaimed the Rabbi, grasping his hand, affectionately. "Kathinka, get Joseph some supper; he must be hungry."

"You are right, Rabbi," returned Joseph. "I am hungry and tired, and yet since I have seen Kathinka I am supremely happy."

It was a sad and fearful night. Sleep was out of the question for the threatened Israelites. All night long the noise of hammering could be heard; the Christians were attaching little wooden crosses to their houses that they might be spared by the mob. The Jews gathered their portable treasures and trinkets and conveyed them to places of safety.

The morning of the eighth of May dawned; a quiet serene Sunday morning, the day on which is proclaimed throughout Christendom the golden rule: "Love your enemies."

At an early hour armed gangs appeared on the streets, wandering hither and thither, without any definite plan or object. Ringleaders, however, were not long in making their appearance.

As in Elizabethgrad, the first act of the mob was to storm the dram-shops; it needed the inspiration of *vodki*. Having broken in the doors and windows, they rolled the barrels out into the street. *Vodki* flowed in streams; the rioters waded, they bathed, they wallowed in whiskey. The women carried it away by the pailful. From shop to shop they went, becoming more hilarious, more boisterous as they proceeded. Through the uproar could be heard their shouts: "The Jews have lorded it over us long enough; it is our turn now! Down with the Jews!"

They came to the inn of a man named Rykelmann and here they met their first resistance. Rykelmann refused to admit them. He had barricaded himself and his family behind stout doors and stood guard over his premises with a pistol. The mob besieged the place from all sides and finally succeeded in forcing an entrance in the rear. The poor proprietor was forced to accompany the rioters to his wine cellar, where they amused themselves staving in the barrels and breaking the bottles, while some of the drunken ruffians in the rooms above cut the throats of his wife and six children. It was the first blood shed in Kief and it served to stimulate the appetites of the vampires.

Onward sped the rioters. They divided into groups, each, under a self-appointed leader, attacking a different quarter. Here and there houses were burning fiercely, and to the crackling of the flames was added the piteous cries of women and children consigned to a fiery death.

At this stage several companies of soldiers, headed by Loris Drentell, appeared upon the scene. The Governor fearing that Christians might suffer in the general massacre, had at length yielded to the importunities of his counsellors and sent his son with a detachment of men as a protection, not to the Jews, but to the Christians. Loris had returned to Kief shortly after the assassination of the Czar.

For an hour the soldiers allowed the work of destruction to go on unhindered, and then, no longer able to control their appetites, they joined the mob.

The rioters came to the house of Hirsch Bensef.

"He is the richest of them all," shouted a Russian, who had once been employed by him. "His house is a regular mine of wealth. I've been in it."

"Down with the house!" shouted the mob. "His wealth belongs to us. Show him no mercy!"

They battered down the door, and regardless of the piteous pleadings of the aged man and his wife they pillaged and plundered from cellar to attic. Nothing was left intact. What could not be carried away was destroyed. Loris himself, stimulated by reports of the fabulous wealth which Bensef was said to possess, led the charge and took an active part in the attack. When he left the house it was because he could conceal no more of the booty about his person. Valuable property was scattered upon the ground by the rioters and lay in mud-bespattered heaps, to be picked up by the crowds of women and children that followed in their wake. Bensef and his wife escaped assault at the hands of the ruffians by fleeing precipitately through a rear door and taking refuge in the house of a Christian friend.

Haim Goldheim's dwelling, not far from that of Bensef, was next attacked. Father, mother and children had fled at the approach of the rioters, but the rich furniture and works of art which the well-to-do banker had accumulated fell into the destroying hands of the mob. An hour afterwards, hungry flames devoured all that remained of the once luxurious home.

At the further end of the street was the house of one David Wienarski.

"He, too, is rich!" shouted a Russian, and the rabble attacked the place without delay. A search failed to discover the wealth they expected to find, for the poor man had buried his meagre possessions in the garden, the night before. Disappointed in their search for plunder, they caught up his three-year-old child and threw it out of the window. It fell dead upon the pavement at the feet of Loris and his soldiers, and the poor corpse was mercilessly thrust into the gutter, to be out of the way.

Still on they went! When their ardor slackened, the ringleaders harangued them and stimulated their flagging energies.

"Leave nothing untouched!" they shouted. "The Czar has given it all to you! Take what belongs to you! Let not a Jew escape!"

There were many among the ferocious gathering who really liked the Jews, who had for years lived side by side with them in peace and amity. They arose against their former friends, because the Czar, in a *ukase*, desired it; and his imperial will must be fulfilled. In the heat of the turmoil, the example set them by their leaders spurred them on; and on they went, thoroughly regardless of consequences.

It would be impossible to describe all the outrages of that bloody day; the pen refuses to depict the appalling scenes, the dire calamities, the nameless atrocities that were visited upon the helpless Israelites.

The Jews performed prodigies of valor. Though unarmed, many made a heroic resistance to the onslaught of the rioters.

Down near the Dnieper stood the house of David Kierson. It was one of the earliest attacked during the day, and the rioters were crazed with drink and passion. David and his son Joseph, without any other weapons than their hands, kept the horde from entering their home. Joseph engaged three of the rabble at one time, while his father disabled man after man, until the drunken wretches desisted and turned their attention to houses where they would find less resistance.

Suddenly there was a shout of terror, and the attention of the attacking party was directed towards the river.

"A man overboard!" was the cry.

"Let him drown," answered the mob, derisively; "it is only a Jew!"

Joseph, who was still guarding the door of his father's house, saw the struggling creature in the waves of the muddy river. In an instant he had divested himself of his coat and shoes, and, edging his way through the crowd that lined the banks, he sprang into the water. A few powerful strokes brought him to the drowning man, whom he seized by the collar of his coat and held above the surface of the water. Then he swam slowly and laboriously to the shore, and, amid the silence of the spectators, he landed the man upon the banks. It was a Russian he had saved; one of the ringleaders of the men who had so recently besieged his home.

For a moment the crowd was hushed in admiration of the heroic deed, but it was only for a moment.

"Forwards, we are losing time!" shouted one of the principals, and the rioters rushed down the streets to continue their work of destruction.

Suddenly a priest, laboring under powerful excitement, appeared before them. His features were deadly pale and a strange fire gleamed in his eyes.

"Stop!" he cried; "in the name of the Madonna, I command you to stop!"

The mob, overawed by his aspect as well as by his words, paused in their mad career. The ringleaders fell back for a moment in surprise.

"Hush!" said one; "it is Mikail the priest who appointed us to our posts and gave us our instructions. Let us hear what he has to say."

"You have been deceived," cried the priest, wildly. "Stop your mad slaughter. The Jews are innocent of the wrongs that have been imputed to them. Do you hear me? The Jews must not be persecuted! The *ukase* giving you their property does not exist; it was but an invention!"

"Nonsense," answered one of the leaders; "I saw it with my own eyes. On, friends! We want the wealth of the Jews; we want their blood! Down with them!"

Mikail endeavored to bar the way.

"You shall not do further harm, I tell you! Hear me! In the name of the Czar, I command you to halt!"

The monk's incoherent sentences fell upon deaf ears. Like an avalanche, the mighty mob swept down upon him, carrying him along upon the resistless tide.

When Joseph found his street deserted, he uttered a fervent prayer of gratitude.

"We are safe for the moment, father," he said; "it will be

some time before the rabble returns this way. I shall change my wet clothing, and while you guard the house, I will go to Rabbi Winenki's. Perhaps he needs my assistance."

"Go, my boy," answered the old man; "and God be with you."

A frightful scene had in the meantime been enacted at the Rabbi's dwelling, whither many an unprotected woman and child had hastened in the belief that it would be safe from the mob. The detachment of rioters under the leadership of Loris had already attacked it and the crying and pleading of the inmates could be heard above the confusion of the mob. But they pleaded in vain. Had anyone but Loris been in command, the house of the beloved and honored Rabbi might have been spared, for his many acts of kindness had endeared him to the *moujiks* as well as to his own people. When Loris arrived before the humble dwelling, however, there was but one sentiment in his heart—revenge. Too well he remembered the ignominious defeat he had experienced within those walls, and at the recollection of Kathinka, the base passion which absence had not subdued broke forth again and transformed the man into a savage. There was no pity, no mercy to be expected from him.

At the windows of Winenki's house stood the women, their faces blanched with fear as they looked upon the blood-thirsty army without.

"Down with the door!" shouted Loris, and a dozen ready hands shook the door upon its fastenings.

Suddenly the men stopped in their mad work. Mikail the monk had rushed into their midst. His priestly robes were torn and covered with mud, his eyes were bloodshot, his face the picture of wild despair; his bosom heaved and his clenched hands gyrated madly in an effort to command silence.

"Men of Kief!" he cried, hoarsely, "this bloody work must cease. In the name of the Czar I command you to go to your homes and molest the Jews no further! They are innocent of the charges brought against them."

"Ha! ha! ha!" laughed Loris. "Since when has Mikail turned protector of the Jews?"

"They are innocent, I tell you!" cried the priest. "Leave them in peace!"

"Down with the Jews!" cried one of the band. "The Czar has given us their property and we will have it!"

"It is false!" shouted Mikail. "The *ukase* is a forgery. I myself wrote it and had it circulated. It never had the Czar's sanction."

"The priest is mad!" cried Loris. "For three years he has incited us to enmity against the Jews and now he pleads their cause. On with the work! We have much to do before night."

"In the name of his majesty, I command you to cease!" yelled the priest, in a hoarse voice.

"In the name of the Governor of Kief, I command you to go on!" shouted Loris. "Down with Rabbi Winenki and his family! Down with the miserable race that killed our Saviour!"

The battering at the door was resumed with renewed vigor. A cry of triumph announced to the crowd that the barrier was down, and a portion of the infuriated mob rushed into the house.

In vain did Mikail circulate among the men, by turns commanding and pleading, to induce them to desist from their work of destruction.

They looked at him askance and then at each other, significantly. But yesterday this same priest spurred them on to vengeance, filling them with passion against the people whose cause he now espoused.

"He is mad," they whispered, and turning their backs upon him, they continued their excesses.

Loris had in the meantime entered the room in which he had kneeled to the beautiful Kathinka.

The Rabbi with his aged father and a number of beardless youths, pupils of his school, guarded the door leading to the inner room, in which the women and girls had taken refuge. They had armed themselves with chairs and whatever happened to be within reach, and with these primitive weapons they expected to hold the enemy in check. As well endeavor to stay the flood of the mighty Dnieper with a net drawn across its stream! The mob charged upon them with an impetus that could not be resisted. The Rabbi, single-handed, felled two powerful *moujiks*; then he himself fell bleeding to the floor. His gray-bearded father was dealt a blow on the head from a stout cudgel, and he lay upon the ground in the agonies of death. The young men seeing that resistance but increased their peril, threw down their weapons and fled, leaving the inner room with its helpless inmates in the hands of the rioters.

Loris was the first to enter, and his companions were not slow in following his example. A number of maidens, crazed with horror, sprang from the windows, only to fall into the arms of the rabble without. Three of the women were killed in the heroic struggle for their honor and not less than twenty suffered indignities worse than death.

The Rabbi's wife, Recha, succeeding in escaping the vigilance of the invading party and hurried into the outer room. Suddenly her eyes encountered the form of her husband lying upon the floor, bathed in blood and apparently dead. With a shriek she threw herself upon his prostrate body. When her friends attempted to move her after the danger had passed, they found that terror and grief had done their work. Recha had lost her reason.

On his entrance into the room, Loris gazed about him, and soon singled out Kathinka, standing among her friends, silently praying. With a cry of mingled joy and rage, he threw himself upon her and put his arms firmly around her.

"Ha! beautiful Kathinka!" he said, ironically; "so we meet again. How happy you must be to see me! Yes, I love you still, and you shall be mine, all mine! Don't struggle, sweet one; I shall remove you to my dwelling, far from all this noise and tumult. Ho, there! make room there for me and my prize!"

Lifting the struggling maiden in his arms, he pressed through the crowd, out into the street. There he set down his precious burden and paused to regain his breath.

Kathinka looked hastily about her. There were many in the crowd who had known her since her childhood, many whom her father had befriended, but they stood passively by and abstained from offering her either assistance or sympathy. Then, as Loris again wound his arms about her; she cried loudly for help:

"Come to my aid," she cried, imploringly. "Do none of you know me; will none lend me a helping hand? I am Kathinka, the daughter of Rabbi Winenki! Will no one raise his arm in my defence?"

There was no reply to her appeal; the rioters had no mercy for the despised Jewess.

Of a sudden the crowd parted. Thank God, there was a champion for Kathinka. Mikail the priest elbowed his way through the dense mass of maddened humanity and with eyes wilder and face more haggard than before, he approached the shrieking girl. With a cry of fury, he fell upon Loris and endeavored to tear him from his victim. Loris was for a moment too astonished to offer any resistance.

"What do you want with me, priest?" he cried, angrily, when he recognized his assailant.

"I am here to remind you of your honor, of your manhood; to plead with you in behalf of that poor maiden. You shall not harm a hair of her head while I have strength to defend her."

"This is, indeed, wonderful!" laughed Loris, mockingly. "The arch Jew-hater has become the champion of innocence! Go to your monastery, priest, and leave the battle-field to soldiers!" and pushing Mikail contemptuously aside, he renewed his hold upon the girl, who, overpowered by her terror and despair, had become insensible.

At that moment another form pushed its way through the crowd. It was Joseph, who after great difficulties, had at length succeeded in reaching the spot. He, too, had heard Kathinka's despairing cry, and had hastened to protect her. A rapid glance made the situation clear to him and he at once prepared to attack the Governor's son. But the priest had forestalled him. With a yell of rage, Mikail threw himself upon the young ruffian and the two were instantly engaged in a desperate combat. Loris was inspired by passion and revenge; the priest was moved by a feeling which he could not himself analyze. The hatred which he bore Loris broke out in unreasoning fury; he had heard Kathinka's cry of distress, had heard her assert that she was the daughter of his own brother, and in the strange revulsion of feeling which had overcome him since yesterday, he determined to effect her release at all hazards.

The men twined and twisted about each other, swayed to and fro in their endeavor to gain the mastery, while the crowd, forgetting its own passions, formed a circle about them, applauding now the one, now the other.

Meanwhile Joseph had raised the helpless form of his betrothed from the ground and endeavored to carry her through the mob. A score of brawny arms barred the way.

Fear for his beloved gave the young man almost superhuman strength. Seizing in his right hand a cudgel which was lying on the ground, while his left arm still supported Kathinka, he hewed a passage through the ranks. Eight men lay sprawling upon the ground and their companions retreated before the telling blows of Joseph's club. When he found himself unembarrassed by the rioters, he lifted Kathinka in both his arms and ran as fast as his feet would bear him to his father's house, which, having already been attacked, he hoped would escape a second visit.

The combat between Loris and Mikail was short. The priest labored under a manifest disadvantage in being crippled in one arm, while Loris, driven to desperation by seeing Kathinka carried off, gathered all his strength and with a mighty blow hurled the monk to the ground. There was a dull crash. The priest's head had struck the pavement with such force that his skull was crushed and a crimson stream of blood gushed from his lips and nostrils, his body quivered, his maimed arm fell heavily at his side. Mikail, the Jew-hater, had ceased to exist.

For a moment Loris was dazed and conscience-stricken. To kill a priest was a serious crime. Moreover, that priest had been his father's friend and favorite adviser, and Loris had much to fear from parental wrath. The mischief was done, however, and bestowing upon the dead body a parting glance of ineffable hatred, he set to work to reunite his scattered band.

The outrages in the Jewish quarter had been duly reported to the Governor, who shrugged his shoulders, rubbed his palms and smiled with secret satisfaction.

"Revenge is sweet," he muttered, and he placed himself at the window, where he could witness the burning of the houses.

About noon the body of Mikail was carried past the palace to the Petcherskoi convent, and at the same time exaggerated accounts reached Drentell's ears of the dangers to which his beloved son had been exposed.

"It is time to put an end to the attack," thought the Governor, and another detachment of soldiers was sent out to assist the first in quelling the riot and to arrest all disorderly persons found upon the streets. This order was vigorously enforced. About two thousand people were made prisoners, nearly half of them Jews, arrested for protecting their lives and property.

The scenes in the Jewish quarter at the close of the riot, beggar description. Dust and feathers filled the air, for one of the mob's chief amusements consisted in tearing open feather-beds and pillows and scattering their contents. Broken furniture, dishes and stoves strewed the pavements. Not a pane of glass or door was left entire. It was as though an army had invaded the place. Nearly three thousand Israelites were without shelter, their houses having been burned or otherwise demolished. Many hundreds more were reduced to poverty, having been despoiled of everything. The destruction of human life was appalling, many corpses being recovered from the river, days after the occurrence; and the number of people who were driven to insanity by the atrocities committed will probably never be known.[22]

Rabbi Winenki, who had received a dangerous wound, recovered slowly. His grief at the apparently hopeless insanity of his wife and the death of his father were indescribable; they were in a slight measure mitigated by the knowledge that his daughter had been spared the barbarous fate that had befallen so many of Israel's women.

CHAPTER XXXVI

WHAT THE PRIEST HAD ACCOMPLISHED

The horrible crimes which have been described in preceding chapters were insignificant compared with those to be committed. Mikail the priest, the Jew-hater, was dead, but the evil of which he had been the author, lived after him. His ghost stalked through the Empire, converting it into one vast charnel-house.

Simultaneously with the riots in Kief, there were outbreaks in every town and village throughout the province. At Browary, the synagogue in which the terrified people had congregated was attacked and destroyed. The mob attacked the Jewesses, and assaulted many of them. Three of the poor victims died and a number of others found their only escape in the river.

Scenes like these occurred daily throughout Southern Russia. Whole towns and districts were ablaze with riot and violence. The story that the Czar had handed Jewish property over to his Catholic subjects spread upon the breath of the wind, and the populace was not slow to appropriate its new possessions. The Governors of the various provinces looked on with folded arms at the barbarities enacted under their eyes. Occasionally the pleadings of the poor Jews appeared

Milton Goldsmith

to prevail and the military was called out; but it was not to protect the Hebrews, but to prevent them from defending themselves.

The riots were invariably announced for days, often weeks, beforehand, the police frequently stimulating the people to hatred and violence.

The municipalities, with the consent of the provincial government, had taken every means to add to the misery of the situation. Mikail's book, "The Annihilation of the Jews," became the bible of the fanatical masses. Its sentences were distorted and exaggerated and then read to the intoxicated wretches at the village *kretschmas*. Petitions were circulated in the provinces to devise means to drive the Jews out of the towns in which they had no legal right to live. In other places where no such restrictions existed, petitions were sent to the authorities requesting the adoption of measures to prevent the increase of Jewish residents.

At Kief, the day after the riot, Governor Drentell called an assembly of his counsellors to form a plan for expelling the Jews. Old documents were unearthed and a rigid scrutiny instituted to discover what were the restrictions upon the Jewish population of the city. The laws enacted under the tyrannical reign of Nicholas were examined and the discovery was made that nine thousand of the Jews in Kief had no legal right to live there. For twenty years these laws had slumbered unenforced. With a cruelty without parallel in the history of the world, Drentell determined to enforce these ancient edicts and to expel all Jews in excess of the legal number.

The Jews were accordingly notified that before August the number in excess of the lawful population would be expected to seek another domicile.

Wailing and lamentations broke out afresh in Israel. Many families did not possess the means of departing, having lost everything in the recent attacks. Others did not know in what direction to turn their weary steps, for persecutions were reported all through Russia and in Germany as well. Others again mourned at the thought of leaving behind them aged relatives, beloved friends, the graves of their cherished dead and the thousand memories that hallowed their old homes.

In their extremity, the Jews again petitioned the Governor to temper his authority with mercy, and one of Drentell's counsellors, moved by the piteous appeal, recommended leniency in dealing with the stricken race.

"Gentlemen," replied Drentell, rising in anger; "either I or the Jews must go! Russia is not large enough for both. I insist upon a strict enforcement of these regulations."

The Governor's word prevailed. By the beginning of July, over eight thousand Jews had been expelled from Kief alone.

It was a sultry day towards the end of June. The air was unusually oppressive, the reapers in the fields moved list-lessly under the scorching sun, the leaves on the trees were motionless and the birds had ceased their warbling.

The Jewish quarter was quiet, almost deserted. A pall hung over the dismal homes; there were no children in the streets to stir the air with their merry voices. As men passed each other their greetings were short and formal; they scarcely stopped to bid each other good-day. The entire Jewish population was in mourning. Hearts were bleeding for some departed soul cut off in the midst of life by the lawless mob, or throbbing with suppressed sorrow at the enforced departure of relatives or friends for the distant shores of America.

One by one a number of our old acquaintances and some of their friends entered the dwelling of Rabbi Winenki, glancing furtively behind them as though in fear of being watched. In the Rabbi's house there was some show of festivity, although the attempt was half-hearted and conveyed an impression far from joyous.

It was the long anticipated wedding day of Kathinka and Joseph. All their bright prospects and pleasant anticipations of a professional life at home were at an end. Their one desire was to be married before seeking a new existence in America. The guests spoke in subdued voices, as though fearful of exciting the animosity of their gentile neighbors.

Rabbi Mendel, who had but recently risen from a bed of pain, was wan and pale; his tall and stately form had shrunk, his massive head was bowed, his raven locks had become gray.

Quietly and without ostentation, the good man performed the ceremony according to the Jewish rites. The ring was given, the glass broken, the blessings pronounced, and the couple stood hand in hand to receive the congratulations of their assembled friends. Smiles and merry laughter gave way to tears and sobs. It was a touching spectacle! The young couple were to remain in Kief until the following Sunday, and then, with two thousand other unfortunates, to leave the place in which they had lived and loved, prospered and suffered.

On the Sabbath, the synagogue was crowded; for many of the worshippers it would be the last service they would attend in their native land. Tearful and heartfelt were the prayers that ascended to Jehovah's throne. The service for the dead was as impressive as scalding tears and broken hearts could make it. Mendel ascended the pulpit, that place from which he had so often instructed his people in wisdom and godliness, and with streaming eyes bid the wanderers farewell.

He spoke briefly but impressively, concluding by giving them much good advice as to their conduct in their new homes in America.

"Lead irreproachable lives," he said. "And remember one thing more: stoop not to deceit or to crime. In America, as in Russia, every evil act of the individual Jew will rebound upon the entire race. If the gentile sins, he alone bears the brunt of the punishment. If a Jew transgresses the law of the land, his religion is heralded to the world and the wrong he has committed brings odium upon the entire household of Israel. It has been so in the past, it will continue so for generations to come. Does not this admonish you to avoid evil, to make your conduct exemplary, and to be models of virtue and righteousness?"

While the Rabbi was speaking, it seemed as though an angel of comfort and hope had entered the holy place. Tears were dried and the unfortunates whose destiny was hurrying them far from all that earth held dear, no longer dreaded the approaching journey.

The rest of that memorable Sabbath was spent in bidding farewell to friends and relatives. There was grief in every household.

We have seen how Mordecai Winenki perished, a victim of the infuriated mob. His wife, Leah, died a short time afterward, broken-hearted at the separation from her life-long companion. Hirsch Bensef and his wife declared they were too old to brave the rigors of a journey to America, and, though broken in spirit as well as in fortune, they preferred to remain in Kief. The Rabbi would have gladly accompanied his daughter to the New World, but devotion to duty bound him to his old home. The Kiersons accompanied their son and his bride upon their long voyage. The refugees who left Kief consisted chiefly of the poorer classes, who, being without means, were assisted by their more fortunate co-religionists to emigrate. There were many sturdy young people among the group, who, like Joseph Kierson and his wife, hoped for better opportunities than were possible in their own intolerant land. The wealthier classes, those who still had important mercantile interests in Russia, as a rule, remained at home, in expectation of a speedy end of the persecutions.

On the next day a sad and sorrowful procession moved slowly out of Kief. They were accompanied part of the way by grieving friends, and trudged bravely along on foot to Brody, on the Austrian frontier, where they arrived after many days, foot-sore and weary. A pitiful state of affairs confronted them here. Nearly six thousand refugees from Russian villages had assembled in Brody and were in a completely helpless state. Huddled in cellars, stowed away in sheds, in boxes, under lumber, lay the unfortunate people, many of whom but a few weeks before had been rich and prosperous. The travellers from Kief did what they could to mitigate the horrible condition of these wretches, but the trouble was of such magnitude that they could do little to relieve it.

On to Hamburg went our friends, on foot, in wagons, or by rail, as their means warranted; on to Hamburg, there to take ship for the haven of their hopes, the free and hospitable shores of America.

FOOTNOTES:

[Footnote 22: For the corroboration of these facts, see the account of the *London Times* special correspondent; also, Mr. Evarts' speech delivered in Chickering Hall, New York, in March, 1882.]

CHAPTER XXXVII

THE LAND OF THE FREE

A letter from Kathinka Kierson to her father:

JULY 1, 1887.

DEAR FATHER:—We grieved and rejoiced on the receipt of your last letter: grieved that the Jews of Russia are still smarting under the lash of persecution, that outbreaks of intolerance still continue; and we rejoice to learn that dear mother has almost entirely recovered her reason. We trust that her cure will be permanent, and that the evening of your life will be as happy as you so richly deserve. It is truly as you so often said: "Sorrow is essential in bringing out the best there is in man." As a severe storm in nature purifies the elements and the earth, reviving the plants, clarifying the air, causing the sun to shine more gloriously, so, too, do the storms which beset the soul and wring from it its groans and sighs, purify the spiritual man and place him nearer to the throne of his Maker. I cannot but thank the Lord, when I contrast our present position with what would have been our lot had we remained in Kief. I know we have been favored by a kind Providence above many of our fellow-refugees, and we do not forget to thank God for his blessings.

After the trials we experienced on coming to America, the desperate struggle with poverty, the difficulties Joseph experienced in securing work, the drifting from city to city in hopes of bettering our condition, and the reverses which almost drove us to despair, the sun of prosperity is at length beginning to shine for us. Our experience is but another illustration of the adage, that "opportunities come to him who seeks them."

It is now nearly a year since a combination of circumstances brought us to Chicago. I have already written how Joseph obtained employment in a large furniture factory, and by indomitable energy and close attention to business, worked his way up from a simple laborer to be the overseer of the entire works. I now have more good news for you, news which your kind heart will be glad to hear.

About six months ago we met an old gentleman, named Pesach Harretzki, or, as he calls himself, Philip Harris. He is a large manufacturer of cloth, and had business transactions with the factory in which Joseph was employed. When he heard that my husband was from Kief, he evinced the liveliest interest and eagerly inquired after the welfare of a man whom he remembered as a boy of fourteen, one Mendel Winenki. When Joseph told him that he had married the daughter of Rabbi Winenki, Mr. Harris could scarcely restrain his impatience until he saw me. He called at our home that same evening and whiled away the time with anecdotes of you, dear father. He told us how ambitious you were to study, and that he gave you the first German books you ever possessed. He said that his conscience frequently smote him when he thought of the terrible risk to which he had exposed you in giving you those books. Altogether, he is a most agreeable man, and, having known you as a boy, he naturally took a paternal interest in me. One day he made Joseph a tempting offer to take a position in his factory. He was getting old, he said, and needed a young assistant upon whom he could rely. Joseph at once accepted and entered Mr. Harris' employ. My husband has a wonderful mind. I would not tell him so to his face, for fear of making him vain, but he is undoubtedly a genius. He had been in his new position scarcely a month before he had so revolutionized and improved upon the hitherto neglected establishment that the business of the house increased materially. Yesterday, Mr. Harris offered to take him into partnership with him, and, as he is getting old and is very wealthy, the probabilities are that he will eventually retire and leave the business entirely in Joseph's hands. We are, therefore, on the high road to prosperity.

And now, dear father, we have but one desire, namely, to have you with us. Leave your onerous duties in Kief, take passage in a good vessel for mother and yourself, and spend the remainder of your life with us in contentment and peace. You need not pass your time in idleness. There are many of our countrymen here and your talents will be appreciated in America as well as in Kief. Joseph unites with me in hoping that you will not decline our invitation.

It will interest you to learn that David Kierson and his wife are prominent members of the Hebrew colony at Vineland, New Jersey, founded by a number of benevolent Jews of Philadelphia. They are prospering and happy. Both the children are well and send their kisses to you and mother. Little Mordecai (we call him Morris, as it sounds more American) is a very bright little fellow, with more questions in an hour than I can answer in a day. Will he ever resemble his grandfather?

CHAPTER XXXVIII

LETTER FROM RABBI MENDEL WINENKI
TO HIS DAUGHTER:

KIEF, August 16, 1887.

I cannot attempt, my dear children, to describe the feelings of joy and gratitude with which I read your letter. God be praised for his love and goodness. I will write to Pesach Harretzki at once. Whatever I am or have been I owe to the inspiration of those two books he gave me.

I am sorry to disappoint you, my dear ones, by not accepting your invitation to come to America.

I have a great and holy duty to perform in my native land. The misery here is acute, active persecution still continues, the poverty of our people increases every day, and with such misfortunes they would fast fall into mental and moral stupor were there not some one constantly with them to cheer and instruct them. My mission, while difficult, is a glorious one. I have not an idle moment. I must visit the sick, console the bereaved, assist the poor, instruct the ignorant and sym-pathize with the unfortu-nate. By my own example I must seek to inculcate such moral lessons as will tend to elevate them above the condition into which their misfortunes might degrade them. To desert my post at such a time would be cowardly.

Moreover, your mother, while sufficiently well to resume her household duties, is still suffering, is often melancholy and requires constant attention. In the company of her old friends and associates she may entirely recover, but removed to a strange land, among a strange people, she might suffer a relapse. No, believe me, my children, I am happier here than I could be in America.

Over a thousand of our towns-people will emigrate this week. Under the new laws, which deprive us of every right and liberty, these unfortunates find it impossible to live at home and are bound for the promising land of America. Should any of them find their way to your city, receive them cordially, for "all Israel is one family." In your prosperity forget not those who are less fortunate than you, and give praise to the Lord for the blessings he has bestowed upon you.

Choose from Thousands of 1stWorldLibrary Classics By

A. M. Barnard
Ada Leverson
Adolphus William Ward
Aesop
Agatha Christie
Alexander Aaronsohn
Alexander Kielland
Alexandre Dumas
Alfred Gatty
Alfred Ollivant
Alice Duer Miller
Alice Turner Curtis
Alice Dunbar
Allen Chapman
Alleyne Ireland
Ambrose Bierce
Amelia E. Barr
Amory H. Bradford
Andrew Lang
Andrew McFarland Davis
Andy Adams
Angela Brazil
Anna Alice Chapin
Anna Sewell
Annie Besant
Annie Hamilton Donnell
Annie Payson Call
Annie Roe Carr
Annonaymous
Anton Chekhov
Archibald Lee Fletcher
Arnold Bennett
Arthur C. Benson
Arthur Conan Doyle
Arthur M. Winfield
Arthur Ransome
Arthur Schnitzler
Arthur Train
Atticus
B.H. Baden-Powell
B. M. Bower
B. C. Chatterjee
Baroness Emmuska Orczy
Baroness Orczy
Basil King
Bayard Taylor
Ben Macomber
Bertha Muzzy Bower
Bjornstjerne Bjornson

Booth Tarkington
Boyd Cable
Bram Stoker
C. Collodi
C. E. Orr
C. M. Ingleby
Carolyn Wells
Catherine Parr Traill
Charles A. Eastman
Charles Amory Beach
Charles Dickens
Charles Dudley Warner
Charles Farrar Browne
Charles Ives
Charles Kingsley
Charles Klein
Charles Hanson Towne
Charles Lathrop Pack
Charles Romyn Dake
Charles Whibley
Charles Willing Beale
Charlotte M. Braeme
Charlotte M. Yonge
Charlotte Perkins Stetson
Clair W. Hayes
Clarence Day Jr.
Clarence E. Mulford
Clemence Housman
Confucius
Coningsby Dawson
Cornelis DeWitt Wilcox
Cyril Burleigh
D. H. Lawrence
Daniel Defoe
David Garnett
Dinah Craik
Don Carlos Janes
Donald Keyhoe
Dorothy Kilner
Dougan Clark
Douglas Fairbanks
E. Nesbit
E. P. Roe
E. Phillips Oppenheim
E. S. Brooks
Earl Barnes
Edgar Rice Burroughs
Edith Van Dyne
Edith Wharton

Edward Everett Hale
Edward J. O'Biren
Edward S. Ellis
Edwin L. Arnold
Eleanor Atkins
Eleanor Hallowell Abbott
Eliot Gregory
Elizabeth Gaskell
Elizabeth McCracken
Elizabeth Von Arnim
Ellem Key
Emerson Hough
Emilie F. Carlen
Emily Bronte
Emily Dickinson
Enid Bagnold
Enilor Macartney Lane
Erasmus W. Jones
Ernie Howard Pie
Ethel May Dell
Ethel Turner
Ethel Watts Mumford
Eugene Sue
Eugenie Foa
Eugene Wood
Eustace Hale Ball
Evelyn Everett-green
Everard Cotes
F. H. Cheley
F. J. Cross
F. Marion Crawford
Fannie E. Newberry
Federick Austin Ogg
Ferdinand Ossendowski
Fergus Hume
Florence A. Kilpatrick
Fremont B. Deering
Francis Bacon
Francis Darwin
Frances Hodgson Burnett
Frances Parkinson Keyes
Frank Gee Patchin
Frank Harris
Frank Jewett Mather
Frank L. Packard
Frank V. Webster
Frederic Stewart Isham
Frederick Trevor Hill
Frederick Winslow Taylor

Friedrich Kerst
Friedrich Nietzsche
Fyodor Dostoyevsky
G.A. Henty
G.K. Chesterton
Gabrielle E. Jackson
Garrett P. Serviss
Gaston Leroux
George A. Warren
George Ade
Geroge Bernard Shaw
George Cary Eggleston
George Durston
George Ebers
George Eliot
George Gissing
George MacDonald
George Meredith
George Orwell
George Sylvester Viereck
George Tucker
George W. Cable
George Wharton James
Gertrude Atherton
Gordon Casserly
Grace E. King
Grace Gallatin
Grace Greenwood
Grant Allen
Guillermo A. Sherwell
Gulielma Zollinger
Gustav Flaubert
H. A. Cody
H. B. Irving
H.C. Bailey
H. G. Wells
H. H. Munro
H. Irving Hancock
H. R. Naylor
H. Rider Haggard
H. W. C. Davis
Haldeman Julius
Hall Caine
Hamilton Wright Mabie
Hans Christian Andersen
Harold Avery
Harold McGrath
Harriet Beecher Stowe
Harry Castlemon
Harry Coghill
Harry Houidini

Hayden Carruth
Helent Hunt Jackson
Helen Nicolay
Hendrik Conscience
Hendy David Thoreau
Henri Barbusse
Henrik Ibsen
Henry Adams
Henry Ford
Henry Frost
Henry James
Henry Jones Ford
Henry Seton Merriman
Henry W Longfellow
Herbert A. Giles
Herbert Carter
Herbert N. Casson
Herman Hesse
Hildegard G. Frey
Homer
Honore De Balzac
Horace B. Day
Horace Walpole
Horatio Alger Jr.
Howard Pyle
Howard R. Garis
Hugh Lofting
Hugh Walpole
Humphry Ward
Ian Maclaren
Inez Haynes Gillmore
Irving Bacheller
Isabel Cecilia Williams
Isabel Hornibrook
Israel Abrahams
Ivan Turgenev
J.G.Austin
J. Henri Fabre
J. M. Barrie
J. M. Walsh
J. Macdonald Oxley
J. R. Miller
J. S. Fletcher
J. S. Knowles
J. Storer Clouston
J. W. Duffield
Jack London
Jacob Abbott
James Allen
James Andrews
James Baldwin

James Branch Cabell
James DeMille
James Joyce
James Lane Allen
James Lane Allen
James Oliver Curwood
James Oppenheim
James Otis
James R. Driscoll
Jane Abbott
Jane Austen
Jane L. Stewart
Janet Aldridge
Jens Peter Jacobsen
Jerome K. Jerome
Jessie Graham Flower
John Buchan
John Burroughs
John Cournos
John F. Kennedy
John Gay
John Glasworthy
John Habberton
John Joy Bell
John Kendrick Bangs
John Milton
John Philip Sousa
John Taintor Foote
Jonas Lauritz Idemil Lie
Jonathan Swift
Joseph A. Altsheler
Joseph Carey
Joseph Conrad
Joseph E. Badger Jr
Joseph Hergesheimer
Joseph Jacobs
Jules Vernes
Julian Hawthrone
Julie A Lippmann
Justin Huntly McCarthy
Kakuzo Okakura
Karle Wilson Baker
Kate Chopin
Kenneth Grahame
Kenneth McGaffey
Kate Langley Bosher
Kate Langley Bosher
Katherine Cecil Thurston
Katherine Stokes
L. A. Abbot
L. T. Meade

L. Frank Baum
Latta Griswold
Laura Dent Crane
Laura Lee Hope
Laurence Housman
Lawrence Beasley
Leo Tolstoy
Leonid Andreyev
Lewis Carroll
Lewis Sperry Chafer
Lilian Bell
Lloyd Osbourne
Louis Hughes
Louis Joseph Vance
Louis Tracy
Louisa May Alcott
Lucy Fitch Perkins
Lucy Maud Montgomery
Luther Benson
Lydia Miller Middleton
Lyndon Orr
M. Corvus
M. H. Adams
Margaret E. Sangster
Margret Howth
Margaret Vandercook
Margaret W. Hungerford
Margret Penrose
Maria Edgeworth
Maria Thompson Daviess
Mariano Azuela
Marion Polk Angellotti
Mark Overton
Mark Twain
Mary Austin
Mary Catherine Crowley
Mary Cole
Mary Hastings Bradley
Mary Roberts Rinehart
Mary Rowlandson
M. Wollstonecraft Shelley
Maud Lindsay
Max Beerbohm
Myra Kelly
Nathaniel Hawthrone
Nicolo Machiavelli
O. F. Walton
Oscar Wilde

Owen Johnson
P.G. Wodehouse
Paul and Mabel Thorne
Paul G. Tomlinson
Paul Severing
Percy Brebner
Percy Keese Fitzhugh
Peter B. Kyne
Plato
Quincy Allen
R. Derby Holmes
R. L. Stevenson
R. S. Ball
Rabindranath Tagore
Rahul Alvares
Ralph Bonehill
Ralph Henry Barbour
Ralph Victor
Ralph Waldo Emmerson
Rene Descartes
Ray Cummings
Rex Beach
Rex E. Beach
Richard Harding Davis
Richard Jefferies
Richard Le Gallienne
Robert Barr
Robert Frost
Robert Gordon Anderson
Robert L. Drake
Robert Lansing
Robert Lynd
Robert Michael Ballantyne
Robert W. Chambers
Rosa Nouchette Carey
Rudyard Kipling
Saint Augustine
Samuel B. Allison
Samuel Hopkins Adams
Sarah Bernhardt
Sarah C. Hallowell
Selma Lagerlof
Sherwood Anderson
Sigmund Freud
Standish O'Grady
Stanley Weyman
Stella Benson
Stella M. Francis

Stephen Crane
Stewart Edward White
Stijn Streuvels
Swami Abhedananda
Swami Parmananda
T. S. Ackland
T. S. Arthur
The Princess Der Ling
Thomas A. Janvier
Thomas A Kempis
Thomas Anderton
Thomas Bailey Aldrich
Thomas Bulfinch
Thomas De Quincey
Thomas Dixon
Thomas H. Huxley
Thomas Hardy
Thomas More
Thornton W. Burgess
U. S. Grant
Upton Sinclair
Valentine Williams
Various Authors
Vaughan Kester
Victor Appleton
Victor G. Durham
Victoria Cross
Virginia Woolf
Wadsworth Camp
Walter Camp
Walter Scott
Washington Irving
Wilbur Lawton
Wilkie Collins
Willa Cather
Willard F. Baker
William Dean Howells
William le Queux
W. Makepeace Thackeray
William W. Walter
William Shakespeare
Winston Churchill
Yei Theodora Ozaki
Yogi Ramacharaka
Young E. Allison
Zane Grey